BLACKSTOKE

Rob Parker

**RED DOG
UK**

www.reddogpress.co.uk

EARLY PRAISE FOR BLACKSTOKE

"It's been a while since I read any horror but this was such a great way to rediscover of the genre. There's an unmistakeable sense of tangible terror building right from the start, and when it spills over into action, it literally grabs you by the scruff of the neck for the duration." —ROBERT SCRAGG

"Rob Parker has created a world that pulls you in from the very first page—the Blackstoke estate becoming your home for the duration. The tension starts high and only ratchets up from there. The band of characters are well drawn, threat is a constant companion and the all-out action of the final half of the book is so brilliantly written that you feel like you are the middle of it, deflecting blows and scrabbling in the darkness. It's visceral, adrenaline packed and an absolute vital addition to your shelf." —CHRIS MCDONALD

"Rob Parker has tremendous fun preying on our primal fears in this deeply unsettling and dark slice of suburban gothic. An exciting and taut horror novel for the ages. It'll put you off moving into a new build for life!" —CHRISTOPHER GOLDIE, THE TAPES PODCAST

"Bloody hell! Blackstoke is a truly terrifying trip into the dark unknown. Arterial sprays of Death Line, The Descent, The Hills Have Eyes, and The X-Files, all crammed into a creepy half-built housing estate, where bloody hell lurks under the middle class suburban veneer. One to read with the lights on." —DL MARSHALL

To all the things that kept me awake in the night as a kid.
This one's for you.

And Becky, always.

Prologue

HE WAS SMALL. So small.

As if some higher being had agreed to grant him life—but begrudgingly, using only the scantest of table scraps.

Months early, he was fully formed yet scaled down almost to the quick, and had spent each of the three days he'd been alive in a Perspex box.

Alone.

But suddenly, that changed. The lights around the box took on a far more intrusive hue, flickering wildly, and screaming erupted all around him. He was crying.

Alone.

A shadow cast over the box, and it was ripped open with a loud bellow. Hands plunged in to grab him, and he was lifted out urgently. He knew the touch immediately—the speed of movement couldn't mask the softness and smell he knew innately.

Not alone anymore.

He was carried away from the noise, away from the heat, and away from the churning, rasping thickness that suddenly choked the air.

Down.

Then down again.

'It's okay,' a gentle voice repeated to him as they moved. 'It's fine. It's going to be just fine. You and me,' she said, and she echoed those words until there was only darkness for them both.

1

THEY HAD OFFICIALLY moved in the day before, although the process was, somewhat inevitably, ongoing. The possessions and obsessions, the things that make up a family, were all airborne, unsure of where to land. How his family would carry on, now that their lives had been upended and rearranged, was still to be determined.

It was 7.24 a.m. Peter West stood downstairs in his new house holding a clipboard, like a regiment leader whose squad comprised rows and rows of cardboard cubes. Yesterday had been for the boxes. Today was furniture. Seemed a stupid way round to do it to Peter. But Pam had said they needed the *little things* first, and there was so much of that that the whole event had to be spread over two days... so they had camped in a cardboard prison overnight—with no furniture. That stuff, on which all this bric-a-brac would sit, was due at half past. Six minutes.

Peter was forty-two, broad-shouldered but with a softening gut, and he didn't know, in the harsh precision of the deep-dark-truth, why the hell they'd done this. The real reasons, he meant. He had no trouble recalling what led to it, but now it all seemed so stupid, petty and, worse, *clichéd*.

The wife was driving him nuts. The kids were driving him up the wall. He was driving *himself* round the bend. Too much driving with no end in sight. No destination. Peter had felt, as a family, they were going nowhere. A rut, that's what they were in.

And it had taken him a long time to admit it.

He walked across the rows of boxes, looking at the mountain of sorting that lay ahead of them. That burden, and fitting it in with his actual nine-to-five workload, had kept him awake all night. That and the slow, steady deflation of their airbed. What kind of family moved house and took a burst airbed with them? *His.*

It had all changed with his promotion—well, it was *supposed* to have changed. His wage had doubled in an instant, a reward for his loyalty to Wilson PR, plucking him from middle-management in a move offering that thing all nine-to-fivers crave: upward mobility.

He didn't know that would bring its own problems and expectations. Every day after his new wage had been revealed, he felt like his wife, Pam, looked at him funny, as if to say 'I know what you're earning and you expect us to keep on living *here?*.' He got sick of it very quickly, and made an offer on a house in the slick new housing development a few miles away. The Blackstoke Estate, from development titans Community Developments, or COMUDEV as they were otherwise known, which promised erstwhile unattainable luxury at accessible prices. Swanky and pretentious, but on a budget—they would be entry-level arseholes.

When he'd been promoted, the estate wasn't even built. The land was mired in construction, the diggers from COMUDEV only just breaking ground. That was two years ago. Meanwhile, there had been plenty of slaps on the back and suggestions that Peter was destined for 'big things'. He went with it. The house, at that time, was out of their price range, but he could sort the deposit out immediately, so he decided not to wait. That distant date of completion, tentatively marked for a couple of years into the future, was when Peter had expected his financial status to have leapt forward again. He'd believed his own hype.

It didn't pan out that way. His career, while still better paid, was in stasis again. And suddenly the house was ready, and he felt he couldn't let his family down. Too much talk of their new life had been aired and taken root. He had to take an eye-watering mortgage and go with it.

He poked open the corner of one of the top boxes with his pen to see what was inside, help him get a flavour for the work to come. It was chock full of Beanie Babies. Over a hundred of them. Why, in all hell, had they needed to bring this garbage with them? They were already dusty through years of neglect, and would only gather more here.

He turned away, and took in his new home.

The house itself was nice. Three stories high, with six bedrooms. They'd need all that space, because standing here looking at the mass of stuff they'd brought with them, at least three of those bedrooms would end up as junk rooms.

The bottom floor was a large open wraparound space, encircling the central column of the house in which the stairs stood guard. It was, aside from the ordered boxes in the living room, tastefully bare, with white walls and polished wood floors. Despite Peter's concerns, he thought it all looked rather good.

He kept finding himself doing exactly this. Standing there, taking in their new surroundings, musing interminably on the weight, practicality, and sanity of the decision they'd made. He was scared. Yes, it was grand, but, with the giant mortgage looming over them like a jittery nightclub bouncer, they were one false move away from it all going to hell in a handbasket.

He was sure people would look at the house with envy. He thought Pam still did, even though they now lived in it.

Pam.

He'd already seen her once this morning, and that's how he'd ended up downstairs. They'd had a frank and fraught discussion about toothbrush placement in their plush private bathroom, just off the master suite. Peter couldn't give a perfect shit about where he kept his sodding toothbrush, but to his wife, it had proven an apparent dealbreaker. She said they should start as they meant to go on, putting things in their rightful place until the act became habit as opposed to chore.

And so it turned out, given there were now two sinks in their bathroom, that he was to use one and she the other. His sink had been decreed, without his consent, to be the one furthest from the door, deepest into the bathroom.

Peter knew it was a small thing, and that he should just forget about it. It was a tiny thing, a pinprick, but a pinprick that belied so much more. That solitary foot of extra bathroom tiles he had to walk each morning and night, well, that represented her selfishness—her innate value of her convenience above his—and in his acknowledged pettiness at assuming this, he had become aware their relationship had stagnated.

Peter was already finding it hard not to see that overpriced foot of hideously on-trend Azteca bathroom tile as a metaphor for not just the move, but their marriage as a whole. Such was their nit-picking and bickering, he knew that it would take considerable effort not to let that pinprick rip into a huge gushing wound. And that it would be the first of many as they settled into their new lives. He didn't want it to be like this.

He checked his watch. Seven thirty. He wondered if they'd called for directions, and checked his phone but alas, as expected, there was no reception. COMUDEV had indeed been great at getting them in here so quick, but they hadn't been so great at making sure the mobile phone mast was up.

He walked a circle around the central column of stairs, taking in every area, from kitchen to living room, to dining space, to reception, right back around to the entrance hall where he'd started, and as he arrived back to the faux marble tiles, his foot caught the corner of one of the boxes stacked by the stairs.

'*Jesus*,' he winced, hopping on his undamaged foot, and crunching down on the bottom step. 'Damn boxes.'

'It's so pathetic, the way you blame other things for your ineptitude. *You* walked into the box,' said a female voice he recognised immediately. He had kind of hoped the tone it was laced with wasn't going to move house with them.

'That doesn't stop it from hurting,' said Peter, stretching out his toes. Nothing broken, he'd be fine in a minute. He caught Alice walk straight past him down the stairs without pausing to say *hello* or see if he was alright.

'It's called resistentialism,' she said, and all he could see were those jogging pants she'd begged for—Superdry emblazoned up the leg in vivid pink on navy—as she strutted around the corner to the kitchen, her voice carrying as she went. 'The belief that inanimate objects are hostile to humans.'

'What about the belief that teenage daughters are hostile to their fathers? You have a fancy name for that?' he replied.

And with that, the removal van arrived outside with a loud sigh of exhaust. That would be all the new furniture he'd been forced to buy. They just couldn't take their exhausted old furniture to their smart new home. Pam had made that clear. But he didn't actually know what kind of furniture it was. He hadn't picked it.

He opened the front door to the glimmering early November morning, as the removal van started reversing up their four-car drive, only half of which was occupied by the West's measly two vehicles.

Their corner of the estate was the first finished, and therefore the first deemed habitable. There were five houses here on the northeast corner of a development that would eventually boast two hundred properties in total, each house with its own grandstanding name on its own regal-sounding street. Peter West and his family lived in Iron Rise on Broadoak Avenue, a phrase that he would no doubt eventually take much delight in recounting to future visitors.

Broadoak ended with a cul-de-sac in which Iron Rise sat, with another even grander home opposite across a circle of tarmac, after intersecting with Lance Drive, which was a very bold name for a tiny, twenty-yard street that had a single much smaller house on it. Two other houses occupied the same side of the street as Iron Rise, and all five in this little pocket were occupied.

Peter just hoped that the people living in those other houses were as normal and functional as his family pretended to be.

2

PAM HEARD THE van from the master bedroom as she stood working out whether to hang her dresses in order of colour, or occasion. What frustrated her was that it would organise itself in the end, the least worn pushed further back on the rail to the far end in a little squad of flat, dusty relics, while the near end would be where she put the favourites, flustered, fresh from the drier.

No, she thought. This would be a fresh start, in more ways than one. She brushed a lock of deep, brown hair from her forehead, and tucked it behind her ear like a builder would a pencil.

'Your furniture's here!' shouted Peter from downstairs. She rolled her eyes, unable to stop herself from doing it, just like he had been unable to resist having a little dig about the furniture. That damn furniture. If only he had given the slightest shit about it, they could be excited *together*. No, instead, Peter had just given her some budgets, relating to finance deals she wasn't sure he could afford, and had told her to choose. So, like the good little wife, she had done exactly that, and tried to pick the ones that wouldn't offend him too much, and stuck to the financial rules rigorously.

Whatever happened, she was sure to have got it wrong. Just like the chat about sinks earlier that morning. She had weighed up the pros and cons of the two sinks for both parties, and noticed that the second sink was right next to the electric shaver point. She suggested Peter had that one, simply because he actually had an electric shaver. He didn't see it that way, and another petty argument had broiled out of nothing. At least she knew she'd tried.

Determined to smile, she started for the stairs, and dropped down with ease. She was forty-one, in better shape than most of her peers, and looked five years younger than she actually was, with flowing dark curls and the easy poise of natural beauty. She could easily have passed for one of the younger yummy mummies at the primary school gates she no longer had to go to. Not that Peter put much stock in things like that. She was convinced he just looked at her as a ball and chain forged from the shinier qualities of their earlier years together.

Arriving in the hall, she saw Peter opening the front door to the street, and could hear the sigh as he fortified himself for what was to come. They had only been there twenty-four hours and already he seemed stressed out of his mind, and Pam was even more concerned that him dragging them here, to this faceless estate in the middle of nowhere, had the makings of a supremely bad idea.

3

'CHRIST, HE LOOKS even more stressed than you did on moving day,' said David Lyon, looking out along the street from his kitchen window—the perfect spot from which to monitor all the comings and goings on Broadoak Avenue and have a coffee and a read of the paper. If he actually had a paper, that is—the paper delivery services, if there were any round here, hadn't gotten out to them yet to offer their wares, and with the nearest shop over in the next village, he wasn't about to make a seven-mile round trip before breakfast just so he could get the news. So his spot in the kitchen window in their house, Longpike, at the breakfast bar he was growing quite fond of, was part of a new coffee and iPad routine. At least the internet guy had made it out.

He was joined by Christian, who merely hovered by the breakfast bar without taking a seat, and looked out the window gesturing with a coffee of his own. 'You'd have thought they'd be finished with the vans after yesterday,' he said. 'They had so much stuff I was sure they were one of those tabloid families with surprise octuplets.'

David laughed, remembering he had seen two kids. Two teens, awkward and trailing. A girl buzzing, a boy trepidatious. He then remembered his own child, which was something he was trying his hardest to get used to, but somehow kept forgetting—not that he would ever admit that to Christian.

'How's Olivia?' he asked, trying to sound like he hadn't just remembered. Happy as he was, he was still getting used to the idea—something he was forced to admit.

Christian moved over to the fridge, and began rooting in the juices. 'She's just on her morning nap,' he replied. 'You know how it is when she's had an early start.'

'What time was it?'

'About five.'

David checked his watch. Bugger, it had just gone nine. 'I'm sorry, I—'

'Forget it,' Christian interrupted, 'I was happy to do it. Do you mind calling the maintenance company today?'

'The smell still bothering you?' Christian had been mumbling about a funny odour in the air, that David himself couldn't detect, but didn't want to cause any friction over small details.

'Yeah, it's not so much me, but it can't be nice for poor Olivia.'

'Yeah, course I will.'

Christian gave David a squeeze on the shoulder, which David appreciated, before heading off to the door, when they both turned back to the windows again. A car was heading up the street, going a little quicker than it should, and they heard its tyres screech as it rounded the bend onto Broadoak.

'Bloody hell, is he just getting in?' gasped David. A black Mercedes shot down the road, swerving around the removal van and pulling up outside the vast property opposite the one the new neighbours had moved into. It was the biggest house on Broadoak, by some margin.

'Dirty stopout,' said Christian, resuming his exit. 'We've only been here two weeks and you can already tell he gets away with everything.'

David couldn't work out whether that was a muted plea for Christian himself to get away with everything, but he let it slide.

Times were turbulent enough for the new adopters—new house, new baby, a new life they had fought tooth and nail to get their hands on, but truthfully hadn't got a clue what to do with now they were in it.

4

'BEFORE YOU ASK,' said Fletcher Adams, the front door not yet shut after his whirlwind entrance, which sprayed the hall with cheap aftershave and fag smoke, 'it was work'. The door thunked behind him, and he stood still for a moment, wiping sweat from his brow and steadying himself. He looked like roadkill fried in grease and packed in a rumpled suit.

'I never ask,' replied Joyce, who sat at the bottom of the ornate walnut stairwell opposite the front door, swaddled in a dressing gown with fluffy slippers stretched out in front of her. She too was struggling to compose herself—she wanted Fletcher to believe she had been waiting there for hours—as opposed to the truth, which was that she had simply flung herself out of bed on hearing the car approach. For whatever reason, she always slept better when he wasn't home. She knew it shouldn't be like that, yet it was—but she certainly didn't want him to know it.

'It was work,' Fletcher pointed out again, probably too quickly, wiping his hands together in such a way he flicked the sheen he just swabbed from his head onto the floor. Joyce felt like gagging just looking at him. She knew *work* could mean anything when it came to Fletcher, so when she said she never asked, she really meant it. And when some wives say they don't want to know, Joyce genuinely, *vehemently*, didn't want to know.

'I hope you got a lot done,' she said, unsure whether it came out as sarcastic, but not that bothered if it did.

'Loads actually, darling,' Fletcher replied, his shoulder

loosening a touch now he realised that the storm he'd been fearing had whipped straight on out over the horizon without even a cursory grumble. 'Could do with a shower though.'

Joyce didn't want to holler in agreement but she certainly could have. She got up, and pottered into the kitchen, trying not to run but desperate to avoid a rushed kiss from Fletcher as he headed upstairs to the showers.

'The twins are in the front room,' she said. 'They are playing that computer game you were upset about. They won't listen to me, I can't get them to stop.'

She got to the sink and looked out through the slatted windows onto the street, waiting for a sign of combustion. That game was Grand Theft Auto 5, the game that Fletcher made such a song and dance about on the local radio stations and in the local rag years prior. Politicians needed a cause, needed something between their teeth. Fletcher decided that something as obviously poisonous as that *antisocial* game—which looked to Joyce as a cathartic riot, on the odd occasion she had watched the twins running people over, giggling in glee—would be exactly the right thing to show his constituents how morally upstanding he was, how the core values of society were soldered to his own conscience, and how the developing fibre of the region's youth was a cornerstone of his everyday thinking.

Fletcher didn't answer.

Being the wife of a moderately young MP was all about the sacrifice and scrutiny, as well as learning to stand fast, while your erstwhile-wonderful husband was dragged increasingly out of shape by expectation, pressure and, worse, in Fletcher's case, his own unspoken, maniacal lust for power and influence.

All Joyce could do was hang on for dear life. She had invested so much in this family to see it slip from her now. Stripped of her own professional livelihood with the birth of the twins, she adjusted focus and sought the silver linings associated with her decision. She had made her family, and its prosperity, her job. And she poured herself all over it, far too thinly at times, to make it work. And that's precisely what she was doing now.

The kitchen window overlooked the side street, Lance Drive that ran directly alongside the edge of their vast property, off the monstrous sounding Broadoak Avenue. And as she looked left, she saw the house on the corner of Broadoak and Lance, the smallest the estate had to offer, but nonetheless well-appointed and perfectly in-keeping with the design of the whole estate. And out into the sunshine stepped Grace Milligan, carrying a briefcase and a silver thermos.

Working on a Sunday. Good for her. Joyce knew she'd be at her own brand of work all weekend in any event, but she couldn't help but feel a pang of envy at the attractive young woman who was heading to her parked car opposite. She must have been doing well to afford a place like that on her own, and at that age, which had to be early- to mid-twenties. She must feel like she had the world at her feet.

Long-buried feelings threatened to burrow their way to the surface, like a bitter, resent-fuelled tapeworm. Grace looked up and waved, the sun catching her right in the eye as she did so, causing her to wave awkwardly in the general direction of the house with eyes squeezed shut. Joyce waved back politely, knowing the poor girl couldn't see a damn thing.

Like all her gestures. Made, but never noticed or acknowledged.

5

AND NOW I feel like a proper dick, thought Grace. *It's okay, keep going, it's important.*

Make the effort, keep the neighbours on side. She felt self-conscious as it was—at her age, in this fancy neighbourhood—without the neighbours turning on her when she'd barely been here any time at all.

As she finally stopped waving, she turned back to her own house, to look for Dewey in the front window. He should have been there by now, he always was. She felt bad abandoning him on a Sunday, after she had been out hard at it all week, but what can you do? Mortgage payments on a house like this dictated all the stops had to be pulled out. *It'd be an investment*, her dad had said. *Bricks and mortar is better than any bank, especially in this climate.* She had heard this so many times over tea at home, usually when her dad had just started his third glass of Tempranillo, so much so that putting an offer on this place was almost just to shut him up.

There was Dewey now, his nose pressed up to the glass, fogging the window with his panting breaths. He was a big dog, an Irish wolfhound. Grace's mum and dad insisted that he came with her when she said she was going to live on her own, and she didn't mind too much. He'd been the family dog for a good number of years, didn't need any training, and she could always do with the company. But after only three weeks here, she was already worrying about Dewey, and the effect her near constant absences were having on him. Needs must. Can't be helped.

She waved back to Dewey, who barked twice. She consoled herself with the notion that that was his acceptance of her duty. Good dog.

She got in the car, but sloshed hot tea from the thermos onto her thumb. She cursed and sucked her thumb, wondering how any tea got out of the tiny opening on the thermos lid. Her briefcase started to get heavy as she heaved it across to the footwell, fingers slipping on the worn handle, and it dropped to the carpet.

She took a deep breath, long in, strong out. She'd faced many more challenges than a belligerent cuppa and some luggage. Like in court, for example, and the near-daily occurrence of her client throwing a curveball, making her look like a dipshit in front of the judge. She composed herself in an instant—pick up, forget and press forth.

She settled behind the wheel of her tasty BMW M2 as it purred to life. No matter how confused, uncomfortable or constricted she felt in that godawful house, her car was always a source of comfort. It was the first thing she really spent money on, as a freshly qualified lawyer with the first cheques coming through. It was the first thing of note that had been truly hers. A monument to her hard work and early successes. She'd live in it if she could. A bit small for Dewey, mind. When she took him out, she had to flatten the front passenger side and he sprawled across the whole car interior on each of the other three seats.

She pushed off her own short driveway, entering Lance Drive just to turn straight off it onto Broadoak, and accelerated a touch. She adjusted her mirror, to check her make up one last time, when she noticed the Fenchurches up ahead. Both of them, in their garden, looking at her approaching car. Out of a mix of self-consciousness and eagerness to please, she waved animatedly. The Fenchurches waved back, with broad smiles, causing Grace to smile herself. Whatever the others were up to, she seemed to be able to rely on these two. The friendly grandparents of their little community, never short of a smile or wave. Maybe moving here wasn't such a bad move after all, Grace thought, as she headed off down the estate.

6

'HOW DOES SHE afford a place like that?' said Quint Fenchurch through a broad smile, while waving with as much enthusiasm as he could muster. He didn't want to, but Wendy would surely crawl right up his arse if he didn't. He watched the Beemer disappear off through the estate. 'It's taken us all our lives to get to this point, and this girl who doesn't even know she's bloody born, just swans in here with her ridiculous car and massive bloody dog like she owns the place.'

He turned back to the house, his own, and couldn't help but compare it to Grace Milligan's home. *Yes*, he thought immediately. *Whatever happens, mine is still bigger.* 'What has she done to earn it?' he said in a mutter. 'I mean really?'

'Maybe she just works hard and saves her pennies, like you always moan about people *not* doing,' said Wendy from the porch. A cardigan covered her shoulders, a chair pulled up tight to the stone of their entrance arch way (which nobody else had, Quint noted when he put the offer in), so she could sit and muse. That's what they wanted in retirement. A quiet spot to pontificate and potter, in a nice area.

'She's been saving her pennies since she was a twinkle in her daddy's crotch, then,' said Quint, marching slowly back to the house. 'In fact, that's probably it. It's daddy's money, not hers. She's just a rich kid, a brat who stamped her feet. It won't be long before she stamps her feet for a pony and she'll be building a stable in that little garden of hers. That hound is big enough for a stable and all.'

'Come on, Quint, it's Sunday, aren't there more important things to be doing than moaning?'

Quint literally harrumphed, his shoulders selling the gesture, and marched off around the side of the house.

WENDY SMIRKED. She found it sweet that after all these years, he still had that fire she found so attractive in the first place, like he constantly had a piece of steak stuck between his molars and his righteous tongue couldn't rest until it had been dug out. It had been the part of his job, as a full time beat policeman, that had fuelled his purpose and focussed his energies. Retirement, when it came almost exactly ten years ago, brought about a shift in priority. No longer could he direct his passion at meaningful pursuits like law and order, so he now took that same 'search and destroy' attitude to everyday mundanities. Shopping was now a military excursion. Every gesture was borne out of a measured adherence to protocol. And for Quint, that protocol suggested he should be making all the right noises for their new neighbours.

He often told her how important community was, and that a community strong enough could repel all challenges, and remain strong through testing times. He'd doled out that speech a hundred times throughout his forty-year police career, indiscriminately, both for her and the people he encountered through work in equal measure.

Wendy knew she would follow him to the ends of the earth. Their love was as concrete as an emotional attachment could get. She knew what she'd get from him, and vice versa. Although she had adapted to retirement a lot better than he had. It took her all of ten minutes to forget her job as head nurse at Warrington

Hospital gastro-intestinal unit. She was ready. Quint, however, still felt he had something to prove. Wendy thought Quint still didn't know that, by the end, she had been earning more than he. She had hidden it from him, so as not to wound the pride she knew gripped him so fiercely.

Quint reappeared around the corner now, heralded fractionally by the trundle of plastic tyres on gravel.

Mowing. Again, Wendy thought. *Well, if it keeps him happy.*

7

HE HAD TO concede it. The living room looked pretty good. Peter even cracked a smile. *Maybe this could work after all.*

'Okay gang, let's be having you,' he shouted up the stairs.

Jacob bounded down immediately, his arms windmilling either side of him, getting used to the extra space around him. Peter's smile broadened. He looked happy, his son—his cheeks high in a grin, sending his round, boy-wizard spectacles high up his brow.

'You like it here?' he asked, as Jacob sailed down the stairs on blurred tip toes.

'Yep,' he said in a gleeful exhalation. 'The smell's a bit weird though'.

'Smell?'

Jacob landed at the bottom, planting both feet. 'Yeah, can't you smell it?'

Peter hadn't smelled anything, but there was so much new to take in that maybe his otherwise-occupied senses had overlooked it. 'Is it just a new housey smell? New carpets and stuff?'

'Nah, it smells rotten. A bit like when we go to the tip.'

'Really? I hadn't noticed.'

'Just the air around here I suppose,' said Jacob, who skid-slid joyously in his socks over to the front door for his shoes, but misjudged it slightly and knocked a box by the door, which clanked angrily in reply.

'Hey, careful, careful,' said Peter. 'I'd hoped they would make it to the neighbours with the wine *inside* the bottle.'

'Schmoozing tactics to defcon 5?' asked Pam, as she came down the stairs.

'Something like that,' replied Peter. 'You look nice.'

Pam smiled as she joined him, in a dark, tasteful dress and her hair pinned up with just as much care. 'Want to make a good impression before they see me in all my first-thing-in-the-morning, lost-cast-member-of-The-Walking-Dead glory when I creep out to grab the post.'

Peter returned the smile, enjoying the moment. Was that a bit of easy banter between them? He thought it just might have been. 'And Alice?'

With that Alice herself appeared from the kitchen, dark eye make-up raccooning her eyes. She too had dolled herself up a bit too much for the occasion, resembling a teenage floozy on the lookout for an older man. It turned Peter's stomach. He could ask her to change, but he couldn't be bothered with the instant friction it would cause. Fifteen-year-old daughters would always be fifteen-year-old daughters.

'Are we ready?' Pam asked, fiddling with an earring in the hallway mirror by the front door.

'Best foot forward,' answered Peter, before grabbing a bottle of red from the previously clinking box. 'I'll pop back for another one between visits—save lugging it about.' He checked that the bottle wasn't damaged—a Les Porte des Prince Grenache. He had no idea what to go with, and his knowledge of wines was Peter Pan-like—locked in a long-term infancy, not that he'd like to admit it. Rather than looking at grape or region he tended to look at price band, and saw Tesco as the perfect place to scour for a new drop. Tonight, instead of going for a zero-to-five-quid bottle, he really pushed the boat out, going even past the five-to-ten-quid range he would usually go for on a special occasion. He had neighbours to impress in a neighbourhood that screamed faux-snobbery. The bottle needed to set the tone of the move, show their new life-colleagues what they were all about. Ten-to-fifteen-quid it was.

They lined up by the door, and headed out into the cooling spring evening—and for the first time, Peter noticed it. A slight, sickly sweet odour, partially hidden by a waft of fresh-cut grass—the kind you taste more than smell.

8

'WELL, THAT IS extremely kind of you!' said Wendy Fenchurch, taking the bottle and passing it over to Quint for his examination. He took his glasses out, which caused Peter's breath to catch halfway up his gullet. He stood with Pam and the kids on the doorstop, half in and half out of the doorway, having presented themselves there like carol singers.

Quint nodded, but didn't offer a hand. Peter found it a little strange, but not everyone was a born-and-bred handshaker. This was a man of stiff movements, and an even stiffer moustache. Wendy, on the other hand, offered him a frail squeeze that smelled of cabbage soup and Chanel No. 5, before furnishing Pam with the same. Peter thought, despite the limp handshake, that she was in fantastic shape for whatever age she was, with her hair neatly pushed back by an alice-band, blue eyes alive and undimmed.

'Have you settled in well so far?' asked Wendy, as she pinched Jacob's cheeks before he could dodge her, causing Alice to keep a mortified distance.

'Yes, it's been a dream,' said Pam.

'Well, if you need anything, do let us know,' Wendy said, and to Peter's amazement, Quint started walking off back down the hallway into the house, waving over his shoulder with one hand and carrying the bottle with the other.

Before they knew it, the West's were back on the pavement outside the Fenchurch property, staring at each other as if to ask what just happened?

'I hope they all go as easily as that,' said Peter. 'We'll be home in half an hour.'

Even Alice cracked a smile, and they moved to the next house.

'Let me just grab the next bottle,' said Peter, as he jogged back to Iron Rise. The evening was settling lower now, lilac blues carrying the soft hiss of the motorway off the back of the estate. Still something felt amiss.

Newness. The fug of the unfamiliar. It had to be that.

9

AS SOON AS Jacob pressed the doorbell, and the ding-dong chime echoed somewhere within, the house erupted into a hellish cacophony of canine excitement. The rampant, urgent barking got closer, and louder, until the front door started rattling on its hinges. Jacob took a step back, and joined the rest of his family. He had taken a sneaky step ahead of his family, to be at the front when the door was answered. He had seen *her* yesterday—but he hadn't seen her *dog*.

The door opened, and the barking spilled out onto the street. Jacob saw a sight that would probably live with him forever—the first tangible strut of a crush he could see lasting for years. Grace Milligan, with her fantasy-girl platinum hair in her cute, figure-hugging pyjamas, wrestling a dog almost as big as her. He could barely move, while the rest of his family had taken a step back, watching the massive, shaggy hound with trepidation.

'Sorry,' she said, finally squeezing herself in the doorframe, spreading her legs wide to block the dog from the outside. 'He means no harm, he's just a bit excited.'

Jacob was transfixed, but his dad stepped forward to make the intros.

'We're so sorry to disturb you,' said Peter. 'We just wanted to say hello, and to give you this.' He stepped forward to hand over the wine, which the dog lunged for as if it were a missing chew toy.

'Dewey, down,' hissed Grace. Jacob noticed her flush.

Another pillar to the temple of his infatuation.

'What make is he?' Jacob asked, his voice thick and slow.

'Make?' Grace asked, and laughed. Jacob felt very warm suddenly, and a little light between the ears.

'Umm... Breed?' Jacob replied, amazed his brain would let him find the right word, but seriously grateful it did.

'He's an Irish wolfhound,' she replied. 'And a big one too.'

'Wow...' murmured Jacob, not sure whether he was directing his adulation at the dog or Grace's jiggling anatomy as she tried to keep both from escaping into the night air.

'Well, you seem to have your hands full. We are the Wests, and we just moved in over there,' his father said, while pointing back to the house on the diagonal opposite side of the junction. 'We'll see you around.'

'It's nice to meet you,' Grace replied, waving to each in turn. 'And thanks so much for the wine. Goodnight!' She turned and manhandled the ragged grey dog back into the house.

The family turned back to the street, a little more shell-shocked. This was going much quicker than they anticipated.

10

DAVID LYONS GAVE Alice a blonde-haired infant, and she seemed willing to give it a try, while Olivia smiled, more than happy to be handed to this stranger. David and Christian had invited them in immediately, and suggested they open up the wine pronto. In fairness, that was how Pam had thought these visits would go. She just hadn't thought it would take until the third introduction to get invited in. Christian gave her a glass, and fixed juices for the kids, and they stood in the kitchen, staring each other down.

'To new neighbours,' ventured Christian, offering a toast.

'New neighbours,' everyone else echoed, with an unintentional sombreness more reminiscent of a Viking feast honouring their recently departed. *We're in this together, chaps.*

Pam watched Peter closely. Pam knew before they arrived tonight that the couple next door were gay, but she didn't think Peter had realised until they got there. Both athletic, fairly toned and mid-thirties, one blond (David), one dark (Christian). As she watched her husband, seeing his nostrils flare a little as he rehearsed everything he wanted to say in his head before saying it, she couldn't help feeling a slight thrill at his discomfort. Served him right for ogling that girl earlier. And then there was Jacob, who looked like he'd gone from one extreme to the other—about to detonate his loins one moment to fathoming a sexual Rubik's Cube the next.

Pam looked at the baby and her admiration surprisingly

sparked envy. The two parents seemed to rotate around the child, as if they were vast planets and the young one was the centre of their orbit. It looked effortless and natural. The way they looked at each other, easy glances of affection, no judgement in sight, made her flat out jealous. Had she and Peter been like this? She couldn't remember.

The conversation soon slid easily into the one thing that they had in common—the estate.

'Have you met everyone yet?' asked David. 'They seem to be a decent bunch.'

'I think we've met most on this little corner,' answered Peter. 'We just have one stop after this one—the big house.'

'The Adams,' said Christian. 'Can't seem to miss Fletcher jetting about this way and that.'

Peter's face pulsed realisation. 'Not Fletcher Adams, the gobby MP?! Here?' David laughed heartily at that.

'Watch your mouth, Peter,' she said in mock horror.

'Oh, you don't have to watch it round here,' said Christian. 'Obviously we don't want the air blue around the little one, but please, where he is concerned, tell it like it is.'

'You've met him?' asked Peter.

'Once or twice,' replied Christian. 'Enough to wave to him, and smile. He's always been very charming where we are concerned, and very engaging. But I know for a fact that he voted against the legalisation of gay marriage.'

Now it was David's turn to berate his other half. 'Chris, come on…'

'Well, it is what it is. I'm just calling a spade a spade here. Plus his personal life seems an utter cluster-you-know-what.'

Pam smiled. She liked these guys.

'They are married?' she asked

'Yes, and I might add that Joyce is lovely. An utter saint. You two should get on very well,' responded David. 'Oh dear, here we are. First meeting with our new neighbours and we come across like a proper pair of gossiping queens.'

'Don't be silly,' Peter rushed in as though it were a compliment: 'You're not even camp!'

Pam cringed, inwardly horrified, and a second of silence seemed to last forever. Peter looked like he wished the ground would not just swallow him up, but chop his tongue out on the way down. Mercifully, Christian burst out laughing.

'No, that's right!' he said. *Thank Christ*, thought Pam. 'It's too much of an effort keeping up that charade for too long!'

'I didn't mean to say anything out of turn…' scrambled Peter.

'Oh you didn't, don't be daft,' replied David. 'We are self-aware enough to know that our relationship might irk some people, and I know it confuses them when they see us out and about with Olivia and we aren't mincing about all over the place.'

'If anything, it really winds *us* up when we see that,' says Christian.

Pam caught sight of Jacob, who hadn't a clue what to do or where to look. This was as far from his comfort zone as he'd ever been, she imagined, but she also appreciated that this was good for him. She'd always wanted broad-minded children, and this would go a long way to help—but even then she caught herself, and, worried that, in thinking such a thing, she was leaking a deep-seated prejudice all her own.

'Well, I don't know about you, hun, but I'm actually quite excited about meeting them now,' said Peter, conspiratorially. He had noticeably mellowed now, and seemed chuffed to have a couple of decent blokes about.

The baby started crying, suddenly rowdy of voice and wriggling against Alice.

'Oh, I think she's bored of me,' said Alice, holding Olivia out like a prized salmon to be photographed. Pam handed Peter her wine, and took the crying baby, eager for a hold for herself, to remind herself what this part of the parental journey was like— while Peter just stood there with a glass in hand, just as he always had.

11

'ARE YOU A football man, Peter?' asked Fletcher, thrusting a glass of wine at him. Peter was grateful the question was so broad and mundane, since he had managed to get himself rather worked up about Fletcher asking him his political allegiance. Peter couldn't even remember the party Fletcher represented, making catering an answer to his political leanings all the more difficult. And the last thing he wanted to blunder into was a lecture, which still could have been on the table, should he play his cards the wrong way.

'I was brought up an Everton fan,' said Peter. 'But I'm largely happy to see any North West side doing well. You?'

Fletcher, a tall, angular man of salt and pepper hair and unfair facial definition, settled back into the luxurious armchair, stationed in prime viewing position for the inordinately large flatscreen TV. The way he sat in it let you know it was his domain, and his domain alone. Peter doubted even the curious-looking twins sitting over there on the floor would dare sit in it. He thought Joyce might. She seemed to have a bit about her. She looked every inch the whip smart, rock-solid, loyal-to-the-last politician's wife, but with a poise and voice that showed she was much more than mere window-dressing or a voter-friendly check box tick.

Pam and Joyce sat on a sofa in the window, looking more than a little like sisters with their matching dark hair, wine glasses perched on knees—and more than that, they seemed to be getting on like the proverbial burning dwelling. The same couldn't really be said for Jacob, Alice and the identical weirdos. They looked all about the same age, sort of anywhere between twelve and fourteen, with Peter's kids bookending the twins. It looked uncomfortable, with the twins watching TV under apparent hypnosis, with Jacob and Alice waiting for someone to say something, anything.

'Good, good. We should be proud of our heritage in the footballing hierarchy,' said Fletcher, in a voice that didn't plead acquiescence so much as bludgeon you with it. 'How has the move gone? Settling in okay?' Fletcher took a long swig of wine—the wine Peter just bought in—and swilled it south with a slight grimace. Peter couldn't help but notice it and tried his damnedest not to blush.

'Good, I think. Painless so far, as these things go,' he replied, then chugged a bit of wine himself to see if it was alright. Tasted just like it did at the Lyons' place, but they hadn't made any funny faces.

'Touch wood,' said Fletcher with a broad smile, and knocked on the wood frame of the chair arm with a rude fist. The twins echoed with a 'touch wood' of their own, and rapped the tops of their own heads with their knuckles. If looks could kill, Alice would have already killed them both, buried their bodies and built a hasty patio over their graves.

'Anything I need to know about the estate?' Peter asked, hoping Fletcher hasn't noticed his daughter's petulance. He'd have to have a word with her later.

'Not really, aside from what I'm sure you already know,' Fletcher responded. 'It's a nice neighbourhood, no trouble. It's a respectable quiet, *appropriate* neighbourhood. It's why we are all here after all, I assume. There comes a point in life when you want to live comfortably, and extend those same comforts to your family. Not that I'd particularly share that information with my constituents, you understand.'

'It's West Lancashire, isn't it? Your constituency?'

'Yes that's right.'

'But you live here in… um, where is this?'

'Warrington North.'

'Warrington North, right.'

'I learned pretty early in this ongoing campaign of a life that it's best to live somewhere where the people can't vote you in or out. It lets us, as a family, be ourselves a little bit more.'

Peter found the frankness of the admission fascinating. This wasn't the scripted bureaucrat he had seen numerous times on television, stoking the fires of… whatever it was, he couldn't remember. *Best get into my current affairs*, Peter thought. 'I can understand that,' he said. 'Makes sense.'

'More sense than you can imagine. I wouldn't be able to go for a pint in my local boozer, or even stop for petrol without it being a gamble as to whether the people in there gave you their votes. It brought out the worst in me, and brought out the worst in them, I'm sure. Never again. Lesson learned.'

It might have been the wine, but Peter felt full of brio and candour of his own. 'There's an adage for it, isn't there? Don't shit where you eat?' he whispered, for the sake of the children.

Fletcher guffawed animatedly, and sounded just like one of those hecklers in the background at Prime Minister's Question Time. 'Very good. Nail on the head.'

'So, how about your family. Do your political commitments leave much time for them?'

'Not the most. The twins are somewhat self-sufficient,' said Fletcher, looking almost wistfully at the identikit teens stationed on the floor. 'They're in their own world half the time. It's Joyce I feel for.'

'Behind every good man is an even better woman, that sort of thing?'

'You're an educated man, Peter. Funny too. We'll get on famously,' Fletcher said. Peter found that a bit strange. A summary of why they would get along, delivered so soon after meeting. *I can't be that funny*, he thought, given that he was struggling with a comeback. In fact, he felt a little fuzzy. A little liberated maybe. *Loose lips sink ships, but if you can't trust your friendly neighbourhood politician, who can you trust?*

Peter almost laughed out loud at the thought, then realised he might just be funny after all.

12

IT WAS THE third time the doorbell had rung, once after the other, filling the house with that infernal 'Ode to Joy' mono-serenade that had been pre-installed when Grace moved in. She caught sight of the digital bedside clock, saw it was 7.45am, and groaned. It was her morning off, with only afternoon cases scheduled for the day, plus she'd polished off that bottle of red she was gifted the night before, all in a solitary sitting. The doorbell thrusting angrily through her hangover was about the last thing she needed.

She closed the door as she exited the bedroom, shutting Dewey in, who was asleep across two thirds of the bed, before heading downstairs to the front door. She threw it open immediately, and was greeted by an extremely angry, extremely flustered Quint Fenchurch. The kindly retiree façade was nowhere to be seen.

'Hello Mr Fenchurch,' said Grace. 'Is everything okay?'

'No, it bloody well isn't,' said Quint, clearly struggling to keep his ire in check. His patchy white hair was all over the place, and he looked like he'd got dressed in a heartbeat. Behind him, loitering at the end of the drive, hovered Wendy in a dressing gown of her own.

'What's happened?' asked Grace, confused.

'That bloody dog of yours.'

'What about him?'

'He's relieved himself on my front lawn overnight, that's

what.'

'I don't follow.'

'A shit. A big dirty *shit*. Right on the grass.'

'No, I mean *I don't understand*. Dewey was in with me all night, and when he needs to do his business, he goes in my back garden and my back garden alone, then I immediately dispose of it. And he hasn't been out of my sight since yesterday evening.'

'Oh, give over. You expect me to believe that?'

'Yes, I do, considering that's precisely what I've just told you, and it's the truth. Mr Fenchurch, if there is a problem with your lawn, it isn't because of my dog.'

Quint wasn't finished, and threw his hands to his hips and jutted his paunch out at her. 'Well, what do you suppose happened then? An owl did it, passing overhead? Perhaps that little baby next door? No, this was a big fat shit. And what do I know that is big enough to do something like that, and who we already know likes to do his business in gardens, by your own admission?'

Grace went into full lawyer mode, as if ready to defend her client, in this case Dewey the wolfhound, to the hilt.

'Mr Fenchurch, you have absolutely no evidence aside from your own assertions that my dog is responsible for what happened. I don't even need to ask whether you saw Dewey do it because you've already betrayed the fact that you didn't. You are acting out of wild assumption, and I urge you not to. I have tried to be as considerate as possible with the requirements of my dog, who I know to be of considerable size. I know that having such an animal in their midst might not be everyone's cup of tea. But I have been as respectful and cordial as I can. I would not allow such a thing as you're suggesting to happen, and I know that on this occasion it didn't.'

Quint squinted at her. 'Are you calling me a liar, missy?'

'No, I am suggesting you are mistaken. And there is never any necessity for sexist patronisation. Now please, if you don't mind.'

'Who's going to clean it up?'

'I haven't a clue, Mr Fenchurch. Goodbye,' she said, closing the door, chalking the win up in her head, but simultaneously sad that the erstwhile kindly neighbours had turned on her without a moment's notice. Maybe moving here hadn't been such a good idea, she thought, before heading back to bed and the poor, oblivious accused.

13

'COME IN, BOYS,' said Peter, stifling the surprise and confusion in his voice, mangling it back down with the sickly aftertaste of too much wine some twelve hours ago. The twins walked into the house without a word, and dropped immediately to undo their shoelaces.

'Don't worry about that,' he said. The boys didn't listen, and continued detangling the laces on their identical school shoes. They were in full school regalia—shirts, ties tied far too short, trousers slightly too baggy, blazers with sticky sleeves, and identical record bags slung over their shoulders. Their reddish hair was identically parted into a lopsided McDonald's M.

Peter couldn't tell them apart if his life depended on it.

'The boys are here,' he shouted upstairs, and in immediate answer, Jacob appeared around the corner to the kitchen holding a piece of part-inhaled toast, a swipe of butter on his cheek.

'Umm, hi,' he said, still chewing. Alice's head appeared over the bannister, her hair half-straightened. The twins looked straight up the stairs at her, framed in light from the skylight high over the stairs.

She ducked her head back immediately, and Peter caught her mutter 'Oh, Christ...'. He should have really been shocked at her attitude, and how grown up she'd just sounded, but he couldn't avoid finding her horror funny. They were indeed weird boys, he thought, and noted that he wouldn't like to be caught half-dressed by them either.

'Go on in lads, fix yourself some toast if you'd like,' Peter said, ushering the besocked boys towards Jacob and the kitchen, but they were still transfixed by the spot on the bannister where Alice had disappeared.

Their sudden fixation unnerved Peter, tickling something high in the back of his head. Protection, anger, discomfort, all on a small scale. These urchins were eyeing up his little girl after all, but then he remembered that Alice wasn't so little anymore, and, given the way she'd looked at them last night, he didn't really have anything to fear from these two misfits, save for a little schoolboy infatuation. It could even be regarded as sweet, so he cast his fears aside.

'Chop chop,' he said jovially, and the boys did just that.

'Do you want to come and meet LeBron?' Jacob asked. 'I have to feed him.'

The boys followed Jacob back through the house, as Peter watched with curiosity. The twins seemed to ghost through as if they were on autopilot, content to be guided by decisions made in advance for them. Apart from the shoes, which they were adamant about.

Peter gravitated towards the living room window, and peered through the wooden Venetian blinds, out at the rear patio. The twins dropped to their knees in front of the hutch, watching Jacob open the small side door and put three handfuls of flaky-looking feed in the bowl on the outside of the mesh. LeBron, a black and white guinea pig, watched, shuffling his nose and whiskers. He was named after LeBron James during Jacob's long-forgotten basketball phase a couple of years ago. The guinea pig's hair was so straight and long, he could be an elegant wig with eyes, only in a bizarre cow-hide pattern.

The twins watched with a fervour, an intensity that seemed unbefitting of lowly LeBron. It was as if they had never seen a guinea pig before, and regarded his sitting in his own shit and occasionally nibbling on it a sight worthy of deification.

'They are extremely weird, Dad,' said Alice quietly into Peter's ear, having suddenly appeared next to him. 'They freak me out.'

'Me too,' said Peter, turning to note that her hair was now finished. 'I take it you guys agreed to go to the school bus stop together this morning?'

'We absolutely did not,' she replied, adjusting her own uniform. 'I want to make an impression on my first day, but going with those two isn't exactly the impression I was hoping for.'

Peter had forgotten that it was the kids' first day at a new school, and felt more than a little guilty. The move was big news for all of them, not just him.

'How do you feel about it?' he asked, while watching Jacob try to hand LeBron to the twins to be petted, but they refused to take him, preferring to ogle the rodent instead.

'Alright, I suppose. In all the films the mysterious girl always joins the class midway through the school year. It feels as close as my life will ever get to a movie.'

'I don't know whether that's a good or a bad thing,' he replied.

She buttoned her blazer, and flicked her hair out from behind the lapels. 'I'm not sure either. I'm sure I'll know soon enough. Do you mind if I slip out early? I think Jake's got this.'

Peter looked out at the boys again, as Jacob seemed to be giving the twins an in-depth lesson into what goes into making the perfect sawdust-based bedding. Then he remembered the way those boys looked up at his daughter moments earlier, and felt a swell of protection again. This morning was the first time he had properly sensed it, and it scared him a bit.

'Sure, sweetheart. Your secret's safe with me.'

'Thanks Dad,' she said, before pecking him on the cheek and marching to the front door, leaving him to watch the peculiar scene through the glass beyond. Peter couldn't help but flush with pride.

The move was working.

14

THE HOUSE WAS empty for the first time since they'd moved in. Pam stood at the top of the stairs, embracing the glacial quiet, letting the fervour of the weekend dissolve. The kids were at school. Peter had taken the morning off and built some flatpack metal shelves for the garage—his self-proclaimed domain—before going to the office for the afternoon. So Pam had the brand new house all to herself.

It felt strange to be the first ever occupants of a property. Everywhere she had ever lived had already carried someone else's history before her arrival. It gave places a comforting feel, like the houses possessed more experience, were older and could mother them. Now, it was completely different.

There was no history here. At all. It was neutral, unblemished in neither a positive or negative light. Everything the house would witness was forward from this point, never backwards. Pam found it quite daunting.

She floated down the stairs, her ankle-socked feet silent. At the bottom she glanced into the living room, seeing the new furniture arranged in a formation yet to be confirmed. It looked okay, good for both viewing the big screen TV and facilitating conversation when hosting.

A shadow crossed the far window, nothing more than a waft of darkness, right to left, causing her to start. She took a step closer, emboldened by the daylight and the fact she knew the back door was locked (she'd checked it after Peter had left), and saw LeBron in his cage, running in tight circles around his hutch as he always did. He was only exercising, her unease dissipating with a smile. It had to be quite the change for him too.

She passed into the kitchen, and surveyed her new domestic domain. It was a walnut-clad, culinary behemoth, black metal appliances tastefully ordaining the warm wood. A centre island stood monumental in the middle, with a near-ornate chopping board at one end. She hadn't cooked a feast there yet, but she would, in time—although at the moment it still looked sparse, unwelcoming. Sparkling, but with little sub-surface quality to write home about, as if lifted straight from the showroom and dropped by a crane into the hub of the house. It would take some getting used to as well—yet another thing to add to the growing list of assimilatory tasks.

She strode to the smart looking espresso machine, which Peter had ordered despite never having had an espresso. She had always seen espresso as the pep of the well-to-do, reasoning you didn't often catch the homeless bumming change for a 'cup of espresso'. She herself liked the taste of coffee, and was game to give it a try. There were still a hundred and one things to do in the house, but there was nothing like the new and partially exciting, so she decided to have one. The complicated looking machine—all tubes, filters, spouts, buttons and beepers—stood by the sink and, as she got there, she glanced out of the window.

A curious sight, further down the street, caught her eye. It was Quint Fenchurch, the fellow who had behaved so strangely the night before. He was in the final touches of unravelling a wire fence around the perimeter of his front lawn, pacing out yards with long strides, then tying it to narrow green fence poles he must have already erected. The fence was a couple of feet high, with dark green zigzags top to bottom along its length.

It looked a bit over the top, and more than a bit unsightly. It was on his property, she remembered, so he could do whatever the hell he liked—but that didn't necessarily make it the most considerate of things to do. He put the last post in, firmly surrounding his front lawn in what now looked like chicken wire.

Pam wondered what prompted this, and why he was going to such measures. Quint seemed to fix something to the last fence post, and walked back to his house, following some coil from the fence to the porch, where he picked up a black box.

No way, Pam thought.

Quint fiddled with the box, and walked back to the fence. He bent over, as if to listen to it. He stood again, before surveying it. Pam was transfixed as he repeated the ritual, returning to the house to mess with the box, before coming back to listen to the fence again. He seemed dissatisfied, and Pam watched in horror as he reached out to the fence with his hand.

Quint's body pitched backwards into the air, his back spasming arrow straight, his head thrown skyward, and he landed in a heap on his lawn. Pam was shocked herself, but suddenly realised that tears were streaming down her cheeks, and she was convulsing with laughter. Quint shook his hands furiously, rubbing them together, before crawling to his feet.

Pam composed herself, and reminded herself to tell the children when they got home, under no circumstances to go near the Fenchurch house. As funny as that was, she didn't want to see that happen to one of her own—apart from Peter maybe if he was in a particularly dour mood. *That would be hilarious*, she thought.

15

AS SOON AS five o'clock hit, the West house was overrun by visitors. Overrun was perhaps an overstatement, but that was certainly how Peter felt, as he waded through the still-packed shopping bags in the new pantry trying to find a bottle of wine comparable to or better than last night's gifts. He worried that he'd set the bar too high, because now all he could find were a few bottles of four quid sparkling pink and a couple of dusty bottles of red which could have been nice once, had they not been left to rack and ruin.

Peter brought the pink fizz back into the kitchen, hoping to holy hell that it didn't offend his guests, David and Christian, who had appeared with a gift of their own, to welcome the West family to the neighbourhood—a cellophane wrapped cheeseboard, complete with sample cheeses and little twirly knife thingies to slice them with. Peter thought it was nice but fiddly. Bells, whistles and little else, but he appreciated the gesture.

'I'm afraid we are still so disorganised that all we have in are some cheap bottles of rose,' Peter said, holding the bottles of his embarrassment aloft. 'And please don't mistake the bottles of pink as a cheap pop or anything.'

'Oh dear, Peter,' Pam said with an exaggerated sigh, 'cheap pop is *exactly* what they are.'

David and Christian laughed and Peter cracked a smile, relaxing. 'I can see we are going to have a bit of fun us lot,' Christian said, chuckling Olivia back and to.

'Yes, if you can discount the fact that I'm turning into a present-day Basil Fawlty,' replied Peter, as he shoved two of the bottles in the freezer, and fetched glasses for the contents of the third.

'What is it you do Peter?' asked David.

'PR, I'm afraid. I've got two weeks off for the move—took some holiday time early, but I've still ended up going in. Pam was a teacher.'

'Now I'm the dutiful, house-bound cave-wife,' she interjected, to Peter's chagrin.

'You miss it?' asked David.

'Yes, but two kids of my own is full time enough. And you guys are…?'

'Sales and advertising,' David said, thumbing towards himself then Christian respectively. 'Hum drum. Buy this, wear that, eat this, do that.'

'Yeah, aside from you Pam, the rest of us are proper drones for the corporate capitalist machine,' says Christian.

That irked Peter a little, who had never seen himself that way, but he couldn't shake the truth in it, even though David and Christian seemed to have begrudgingly made their bed with it.

Alice appeared, changed from her uniform back into what was fast becoming her other one—those Superdry pants and a jumper. 'Hello,' she said as she walked into the kitchen. 'What's for tea, mum?'

Pam looked stumped, and glanced at David. 'Ah, you see what I mean about this being full time?' Peter placed a glass of rose in front of David, who raised it instantly in acknowledgement of Pam's comment. 'I hadn't really thought. The last few days have been such a whirlwind, we've barely done any shopping at all.'

'Haven't we?' asked Peter, his voice unmistakably barbed. He wondered what on earth he'd paid for in those bags back there.

'Well, you've got cheese,' said Christian, taking the lead.

'For tea?' replied Alice with a grimace.

'Alice,' admonished Pam.

'She has a point,' said Peter, sliding a glass of wine in front of Pam. Pam's mouth hung slightly open, flabbergasted that he would have such a sly dig at her in front of the children, let alone their guests.

The doorbell sprang to life, a shard of music that popped the cloying atmosphere in the kitchen.

'Can you get it Alice?' Peter asked, leaning against the counter. In truth, he felt bad—he should have kept his mouth shut, but... he couldn't help it. He felt so railroaded, cajoled and forced into this move, and lavished so much money on kitting the house out, that the bubble of resentment in his throat kept growing ever stronger—and it prompted little barbs like the one he just made.

Alice sighed, and marched to the door in a stompy motion so forced, clichéd and over the top it could be a stage-school improviser's incarnation of teenage angst.

'Sorry folks,' said Peter. 'It's been a hell of a few days. We are all a bit tired and cranky.'

'Hello, there,' boomed a voice from the hall, with a grand imposing primness. *Oh no*, thought Peter.

With a dramatic flourish, Fletcher Adams swanned into the kitchen. He looked charged and febrile, and very self-important. 'You're all here, it seems,' he said. 'Wonderful.'

'Hi Fletcher,' Pam said, while Peter reached for another wine glass. David and Christian got up to shake hands.

'Yes, so good to see you both,' says Fletcher, as if he was suddenly the host. Peter poured wine and handed it over, which Fletcher accepted without a word of gratitude. 'Now, neighbourhood watch,' he said.

'What about it?' said Peter, looking at Pam for support. He wanted to catch her eye, to give her a look to say he was sorry, but she pointedly made no eye contact. Peter knew she was hurt, and he cursed himself.

'I'll lead it obviously,' said Fletcher.

'Is there one?' asked Christian.

'Not yet, but there should be.'

'And I assume you want us involved?' said Peter.

'Yes, of course. We should share responsibility over it. This is a lovely little corner, we need to take good care of it.'

Peter tried very hard not to sigh. Last thing he wanted at this stage was more responsibility.

'Isn't this a gated community?' asked David. Peter pointed at him, as if to say 'good one'.

'And?' replied Fletcher, taking a healthy slug of wine. *He's either thirsty or he's already got the taste today*, thought Peter.

'Well, don't we already pay a fee to a security and maintenance firm to keep an eye on that sort of thing? We have a gate security guard, I'd hate to see him put out of a job.'

Fletcher fixed David with a vibrant stare, one that seemed honed by hours of eyeing down the opposition in the House of Commons. 'That changes nothing.'

David laughed nervously. 'Well what I'm asking is, do we really need a neighbourhood watch?'

'Well our new postcode does have an absurdly high crime rate. Over three hundred and fifty reported incidents of crime in the past year. I think that's ample justification, don't you?'

'This place wasn't even built for most of this past year,' said Christian, shifting in his seat as if uncomfortable with the words coming out of his own mouth. 'Are you saying that the building site was somehow a crime hotbed?' He looked at Pam and Peter for support.

'It does seem strange,' said Pam.

'The stats don't lie,' hurried Fletcher, pulling a folded piece of paper from his inner jacket pocket. 'See for yourself.'

The document was laid flat on the kitchen island, in front of David and Christian, like a corpse on a mortuary slab ready for examination.

'There,' said Fletcher, jabbing at a map on the paper. 'Surely that is cause for concern.' He pulled back with an air of triumph, and sipped his champagne while examining the kitchen fittings, as if his work here was done.

Peter peered over reluctantly, as did Pam. The map showed about ten square miles of the vicinity, and sure enough, the stats were grossly higher in their postcode than in the surrounding area, depicted by a jagged red square set against green, like an unpolished ruby lying on grass.

'Why is that?' asked David. 'There must be a reason.'

'Who knows?' replied Fletcher, reclaiming the paper. 'But one can never be too careful.'

'It seems not,' added Christian, a note of indecision obvious in his voice.

'Wouldn't chasing up the mobile mast installation be more important at this point?' said David. 'We're still in the stone age here.'

'Very true,' added Peter.

'I can't make that hurry along,' replied Fletcher. 'No strings I can pull there. But I can with *this*. Priorities folks, priorities. So if I make myself the main signatory, would one of you chaps co-sign? Formalise this arrangement? It needs two signatories to be recognised by the national Neighbourhood Watch organisation. Plus there's a bursary to get you up and running, it won't cost a thing.'

Peter felt a familiar flush at the back of his neck, one that he occasionally felt at work and felt far more at high school. The inexorable reverse tractor beam of peer pressure. His desire for fewer responsibilities clawed him some backbone. 'Is this really necessary? It seems a bit... keen.'

'Crime is statistically lower in areas that have a formally recognised neighbourhood watch scheme,' puffed Fletcher. 'It acts as a deterrent in itself, since criminals can see it on the online interactive maps.'

Peter caught David narrow his eyes in mocking doubt, but his mouth had opened before he could stop himself—his resistance proving extremely short-lived. 'I'll do it.'

'Good man, Peter,' said Fletcher, slapping him on the arm. 'I knew there'd be at least one real man here.'

The words left his mouth like an alligator of verbal offence, floating into the middle of the room predatorily, waiting for someone to bite. Whether he meant it to come out like that or not, Peter recognised the not-so-subtle dig at the Lyons and steeled himself. David's eyes clouded gloomily, and Christian merely stared at Fletcher with pity. They must have heard this so many times before, and each had their own reaction to it.

Pam suddenly filled the room with words, trying to pause the brimming ire. 'Peter are you sure you need to take on something else at the minute? We've got so much going on, you'll end up spreading yourself too thin...'

'Says the woman who forgot to buy dinner for her family!' Peter replied too quickly, so eager to move the conversation on that he blurted out something he certainly shouldn't. The atmosphere, already fragile, crystallised in an instant. Pam's face flushed hurt, then bitterness.

'You can't speak to your wife like that Peter,' said Fletcher, admonishing him pompously.

Peter stared at a spot on the table, knowing he couldn't undo this latest *faux pas*. He felt the eyes of their guests on him. He waited for it—that first shuffle of someone edging to the door. He hoped it wouldn't come, because when the house emptied he'd be alone with an angry Pam. And he knew he deserved as good as she'd give.

He searched desperately for a joke to smooth over what he said—a carefully judged remark that was part apology, part self-deprecation. But he couldn't think of anything. Moreover, the only thought that really gained any foothold in his frantic mindscape was bitterness and indignant anger. Pam was causing trouble for him again. How could she lead him to make such a complete repugnant *twat* out of himself in front of these savvy and sophisticated new neighbours? *Fuck you Pam*, he thought coldly—but guilt came back again quickly.

'It's been a stressful few weeks for all of us,' he eventually said, but it was an excuse nobody seemed ready to take on. He felt the heat on his neck, just a little prickle at first, down by his Adam's apple. He knew a full-flush beet-red blush was on the way, and he couldn't bear the thought of it. 'I'll just take the bin out,' he says. 'Excuse me.'

He motioned for the broad kitchen exit, but stopped and turned. He grabbed the carrier bag that Christian and David brought the cheese gift in, and stuffed the cork and the cork wire from the rose into it, all the while knowing full well that what he was doing was extremely awkward and only digging his social hole deeper.

Without further ado, he headed to the door. 'Goodnight,' he said and exited into the cool evening air, which came to his burning cheeks like a cold face mask after a sauna.

16

SHE HAD ONLY just finished looping the thick rope lead around Dewey's collar when Grace heard a door slam somewhere. Dewey's ears pricked immediately at the sound, and she glanced in its direction. She had felt exposed and shy since the confrontation with Quint Fenchurch, feelings she was burying hard and fast, but that didn't stop her from hoping she didn't bump into anybody, especially not him.

The noise had come from the big house on the corner with the fancy Iron Rise plaque—not the biggest one the MP lived in. The man who owned Iron Rise was walking down the drive holding a white rag in his hand. She realised quickly it wasn't a rag at all, but an empty carrier bag, and his march, twinned with the urgent clatter of the door shutting, seemed to suggest not all was right in his world. She couldn't for the life of her work out the importance of the carrier bag, and found it funny, the way he was gripping it like a wounded pheasant.

She lowered her gaze, and pretended to fuss with Dewey's lead. She was wearing wellies, scuffed combats and a raincoat, her usual evening walking wear. It wasn't really all that cold tonight, but when the winter sun went down it certainly dropped a number of degrees—the kind of thing only evening dog walkers noticed.

She planned to head into the cul-de-sac between the two bigger houses to see what was down there, but tonight she felt like going the other way, strictly to avoid any conversation with

the man opposite, who had thrown his carrier bag into the black
wheelie bin and was staring up at the sky. Trouble at mill,
evidently. But a change in route to avoid him would mean
walking past the Fenchurch house and risking Quint's
scrutinising gaze.

Grace weighed the two up, but before she could make her
mind up, Dewey made it up for her by running towards the
middle of the cul-de-sac, his huge body and lithe frame dragging
her bodily (and embarrassingly) along behind him. The scrape of
her shoes as she tried to regain her balance echoed in the night,
causing the man opposite to turn. She tried to remember his
name but couldn't, remembering only that he had a decent taste
in red wine.

Dewey moved with purposeful strong strides. The man at the
house stared, and Grace found herself straightening her back
into a runner's stance, and tried to feign that she was jogging
alongside Dewey in some deranged evening fitness activity.
Dewey interpreted her acceleration as nothing more than
encouragement, so he pushed harder away.

Grace wanted the ground to swallow her up, and had to
throw any pretence of control out of the window. 'Dewey!' she
whispered harshly, with no reaction. The man on the corner
seemed to break out of his own reverie, and moved out into the
cul-de-sac with his arms wide.

'Hey boy, stop!' he shouted, spreading himself. Dewey side-
stepped him easily, but the change in direction wrenched the
rope from Grace's wrist. She yelled as the cord burned her skin,
and clattered into the man, who caught her. She smelt wine and
office sweat as she landed against him. It was a smell she was
familiar with. He righted her, holding her shoulders, his face
flushed at the sudden intimacy.

'Dewey!' she shouted, before saying to the man 'Thanks...'

'Peter,' he said. 'The dog's Dewey?' They both started to run after the dog.

'Yeah. I don't know what's got into him. Dewey!'

Dewey was charging ahead out of the cul-de-sac and down a footpath at the bottom, between the hedgerows separating Peter's house from the politician's. The streetlights no longer reached him as he disappeared into the foliage. He barked twice, and Grace recognised the urgency of the bark. It was the sound Dewey made when someone was at the door and he wanted to take a gander at them. It always comforted Grace, because it meant Dewey was watching out for her—but this time it did no such thing. It scared her, hearing her dog's bellows in a different context.

She chased after him, and her neighbour, Peter, appeared at her side, matching her. She was fitter than he was, not through anything other than dog walking and youth, and his strides were more ragged.

'It's okay, I'll get him,' she said to him, as the hedges narrowed around her at the mouth of the footpath.

'No, let me help, it's bloody dark this way,' he said between pants.

Dewey hollered again, as if to let them know they were on the right track—a little reminder of his genetic roots as a hunting dog in previous generations, with the hound running on ahead to chase down their quarry. What Dewey was after right now was anyone's guess, and it unnerved Grace that her gentle giant was so animated.

The hedgerows opened into a flattened muddy field, with piles of earth in a row to their left and the blackness of woodland to their right. In the distance the lights of the main road into the estate blinked, over a long field of shallow tree stumps standing like an army of squat, flat-capped gnomes. This was the nonglamorous side of their new home—the shineless banality of the sacrifices needed to create the new. It made Grace feel quite hollow, that her new comfort had come at the expense of so much greenery.

'Where is he?' said Peter, arriving just behind her.

'Dewey!' Grace shouted, only to be answered by the silent flicker of breeze.

They stood listening, waiting, when under that same whisper of breeze came the sound of a low growl. Peter tapped her forearm, and pointed to the woods to their right, and sure enough, Grace could just make out Dewey's pale grey coat against the darker forest.

Taking a few steps towards him, the growl getting louder, she saw his head was high, his ears pricked, his legs bent in readiness. He was fixed on the woods. Grace looked at the trees, but because of the pitch darkness, could see nothing at all. No lights within, no visible movement, just black nothing. But Dewey was mesmerised.

She reached him, and patted his fur. 'Dewey, calm down boy,' she whispered.

'Can you smell that?' Peter said, appearing next to them.

'Ummm… yeah,' Grace replied. Come to think of it, she could. There was something in the air.

'My kids have noticed it, but something really does stink out here.'

Dewey shifted, and his growl went up a pitch. It sounded less aggressive, even though his stance was the same. Grace thought he sounded… scared. He had moved in front of the two people, still fixed on the trees, as if shielding them. 'Come on Dew,' she said, patting his behind.

But Dewey's head began to sag, his shoulders withered, his growl became more pleading. He made sounds Grace hadn't heard him make since he was a puppy. His head bobbed up and down.

'What on earth has he seen?' Peter asked.

'Not a clue,' replied Grace. 'Dewey, come on.'

Grace had built her adult life around control and hard work, in the way that her own hard work had brought her control. She took no stock in messing about or dilly dallying. She was a woman of action and decision. So this, seeing her dog this way, in such a strange place, chiselled away some of that control to reveal coiled unease beneath. To feel this powerless over something was new to her, and she hated it.

'Now Dewey, come on,' she said firmly. She tugged his lead back to make the point.

Then deep in the trees, so quiet it could have been imagined, something cracked. A branch maybe.

Dewey turned to look at her with wet, wide eyes and then looked back to the woods. He fell quiet. They all stood there in silence, Grace wondering if she'd actually heard it, a deep, disconcerting unrest growing.

She didn't feel, somehow, that they were alone.

Then… Dewey briefly nuzzled Peter's hand, and began trotting back to the footpath, the hedges and the estate. Grace and Peter followed just behind. Grace was completely dumbfounded, and even the bloke running with her was quiet.

Dewey didn't run ahead, or panic—he merely kept pace a couple of yards ahead of them, and almost guided them out of the enclosed footpath. As they emerged into the sodium wash of the cul-de-sac street lamps, Dewey didn't stop. Peter slowed in front of his house, and shouted, 'See you, I suppose.'

'Yeah thanks for the help,' Grace replied, not even beginning to slow with him, mainly because Dewey simply showed no signs of stopping at all, even if she tried to make him. This was a side to her dog that she had simply never come across before. The affable hound was now a picture of agitation and peculiarity. And she couldn't shake the sound she'd heard, and the disquiet it prompted.

As Grace passed Iron Rise, the house Peter lived in, she noticed someone on the front step, haloed by the porch light.

No, she thought. Herself, and a married man, emerging from the darkness of the bushes—all seen by that man's wife.

Pam. She remembered *her* name. And even though she couldn't make out her expression thanks to the casting shadows, Grace could see that her body language had tensed, her arms frozen and her shoulders suddenly bunched.

Oh shit.

Dewey kept her pressing on, for which she was grateful. Any excuse to get away from the burgeoning domestic. He loped over the road to Grace's front door, but instead of waiting patiently, he head butted the side gate open, causing it to swing ajar with a clang. Grace's concern and confusion grew. Once in the side passage of the house, she let go of his lead and latched the side gate behind them, while a veil of acute sadness settled around her.

She knew this was coming. It had to be coming sooner or later. She had seen it in her only other pet when she was younger, a rabbit called Onesie. She was a beautiful, friendly, fluffy thing—a Cheshire lop with big ears and bigger feet—that suddenly, over the course of a weekend, lost half its body weight, became confused, sprayed an almost neon-yellow urine everywhere (which was odd since she had even managed to toilet train the damn thing).

Grace had slept by the cage on the Sunday night, and was awoken by the urgent flopping of furry limbs against the metal bars. Onesie was having some kind of huge seizure, and after a couple of seconds of critical indecision on Grace's part (*what do I do?!*), Onesie stopped moving and her chest puffed out one last time with an audible wheeze.

It was odd, and something Grace wasn't very proud of, but for the next couple of years at least, that look in Onesie's eyes, with the backdrop of that high-pitched whistling death rattle, was the only thing she could see when she shut her eyes at night. It was like she was cursing herself over and over again, torturing herself, with the idea that she could have done something as soon as she'd noticed Onesie's erratic behaviour.

And now, she was seeing history start to repeat itself, with dear old Dewey showing similar signs. Her heart felt slowly crushed as she came around the corner of the house into the garden, to see Dewey darting about animatedly, and relieving himself in random spots. She sat on the step and watched him, tears stinging her cheeks, until he nudged her to take them both inside.

17

THAT DAMN ESPRESSO machine was still a mystery. Pam would have given anything for a cup of any kind of coffee—a genuine, synapse-blasting, honest-to-god hit of deep, black caffeine. She checked the cupboard for instant mix, but couldn't find any. She knew she hadn't bought any—the failings of yesterday's shopping trip had been made abundantly clear to her—but that didn't stop her wondering if Peter had stashed any.

Peter. Upstairs, getting ready for work. The kids already gone, Alice off first to avoid being near those twins from *The Shining* sequel, leaving Jacob to that particular duty.

Peter. He forced his way into her mind again, as he had many times last night, through no desire of his own. After he had stormed out like an obstinate child, she had been left alone with the other men. Fletcher had been condescending and crass, and despite what he had said when Peter had been there, he made considerable allusion to a woman's place being at home, working wonders with the bread provided by the bread winner. Pam had been too dumbstruck to say anything, his duplicity so fickle and obvious. Christian and David made swift excuses and left, leaving Pam to clear up.

Having cooled a touch, she had gone to the front door to see where Peter had got to, and she saw him emerge breathless from the bushes with *her.* The fucking *bimbo.*

Why, of all the neighbours they could have had, did they have to have some ode to youthful Scandinavian beauty just over the road? She'd already noticed Jacob peeking at her house through the blinds, but now her own husband...

This was not helping her feelings about the move at all. Not one bit.

Click.

Pam paused, and looked in the direction of the sound. The hallway. This couldn't be what their marriage had descended to, could it? Surely not. She ran to the front windows, and separated the blinds with her fingers.

Yes, yes it was. Peter was getting in his car, dressed for work. With no glance back to the house, he slammed his car door shut and started the engine. Pam let the blinds fall shut again, in the hope of remaining unseen while she worked out her feelings on this turn of events as well.

When Peter had seen her last night, confused and hurt, she turned back into the house and went straight upstairs. Peter had run after her, saying *it wasn't what it looked like*, and Pam thought there couldn't be a more guilty sounding phrase in the whole world. She had shut the bedroom door, and told him she didn't want to see him. Peter had given her the space and never actually made it to bed, and when she emerged this morning, she heard him showering in the main family bathroom off the middle floor landing.

Pam had then come down and sent the kids off to school, waiting for Peter to emerge so they could dissect what had happened and how they were to go forward.

But Peter had walked out without saying goodbye.

And Pam now felt bad that she hadn't listened to him when she had the chance, instead of giving him the cold shoulder.

No. Her feeling bad was Peter's plan. He wanted her to see his hurt, wanted her to sweat on it.

Wanted her to want him.

She started trying to unpack and fathom the utensils for the espresso machine, all still in their individual plastic packets. If there was one thing she would get right today, it would be this bloody contraption.

Pam didn't think for one minute her husband had been in the bushes having sex with that girl, not at all. But there was no denying that he had humiliated her in front of their new neighbours and when he'd got pulled up on it, he'd run straight off to her. They looked like they'd had a chat, walked the dog, and had a laugh. Maybe even a bit of a flirt. And there's no denying how bad it looked when they both emerged flustered from the bushes. And the look on her face. She looked... rumbled. Embarrassed. And Peter did just the same when he noticed his wife on the doorstep, calling the tom cat back in.

The machine, nor its instructions made any sense, so she bunged it all back in the box and went to get ready for the day, applying make-up direct from a removal box, which was filled with foam packaging peanuts. It reminded her of an earlier move, when Alice was just a baby. She had sat her in such a box stuffed with those soft peanut-shaped blobs of foam, and Alice had sat there happily chucking them all out in greedy handfuls, while never catching on that Pam herself was replacing them. It seemed to keep her happy for hours.

That was during their first move.

That move was when they had been happy.

At about eleven in the morning, the doorbell chimed again, a sound that was becoming as regular in their new house as a cuckoo clock. It was Joyce, Fletcher's wife. She was dressed in sweats and appeared from her pink cheeks to have just got back from a jog. She was holding a bottle in her hand. Pam was thrown a little off kilter by the fact that it was a wine bottle and not a water bottle.

'I'm sorry to disturb you,' she said, sweeping her damp hair over her shoulder. Pam felt a pang of jealousy, seeing Joyce look fit and toned in her workout gear while she was indoors mooning about. She also felt a small unwanted spike of competition.

'It's no trouble at all!' Pam said, opening the door wide. The gesture was a subconscious invitation, on the back of having truthfully enjoyed her company the other night.

'Oh I won't come in, I must stink!'

The honesty caught Pam off guard and made her laugh. 'Get in here, the air round here is shocking, you'll be like pot pourri.'

Joyce crossed the threshold and shimmied out of her trainers on the mat. They headed for the kitchen.

'Good run?' asked Pam.

'Not bad. I can't find a route that fits to be honest. Everything is either too short or too long. I enjoy it, and it passes the time, but I don't want to be doing it all day. Oh God, sorry this is for you. Return the favour and all that.' Joyce put the wine on the centre island.

'You shouldn't have, thank you.'

'I wanted to!' said Joyce with obvious warmth. 'I have to say it's such a relief to see a kindred spirit here.'

Pam was genuinely touched by the gesture, and after the fight with Peter, felt a lot less lonely in an instant. She looked at the wine.

'I'll drink to that,' Pam said, off the cuff, and caught Joyce's eyebrows flick upwards. 'Oh, I didn't mean…'

'No, I wasn't…' Joyce said. 'I meant to say…'

They both looked at the wine, and Pam felt a desire, after their horrible night, to take the edge off, just a bit. The longer the silence went on, the louder it seemed to get. The corner of

Joyce's mouth broke cover and spread into a smile. That was all Pam needed.

'Oh sod it, it's midday somewhere, right?' she said, as she reached for the bottle.

18

THE FIRST THING Peter could smell when he opened the front door was the booze, and that stale sweaty sweetness of people enjoying it. It wafted in from the kitchen like the musk of old garbage, given how unexpected it was. It reminded him of university halls at 4pm, returning from the day's last lectures to find your cohabitants have started early.

He kicked his brogues off and dumped his work bag, following the sounds of female laughter, riffling his pencil tie from his shirt collar. He'd been ready to come back to apologies and explanations, not… a piss up. As he rounded to the corner, it was plainly obvious.

Two empty bottles of wine stood on the centre island like sentinels guarding a third that bore little but dregs. He couldn't see anybody, but he could hear them, and as he rounded the island he spotted two lycra clad calves topped by feet in hot pink sports socks. He had somehow worked out they weren't his wife's, when his wife herself suddenly popped her head over the other side of the countertop. Her eyes were wide and lazily bandit-masked by smudged mascara, and her hair was messy. There were wet-looking chunks of dark *something* on her cheeks, which were altogether pinker than usual.

'You're home?' Pam said, a bit too loud.

'It seems you weren't expecting that?' Peter replied with surprise.

'It's five o'clock?' she asked, as if this was the most normal thing in the world.

'Five forty-five,' he replied. With a grunt and a sigh, the pink socked visitor got up and stood beside Pam. She too looked worse for wear, with those funny blobs smeared on her cheeks.

'Oh my god—is that the time?!' said Joyce, suddenly jolted into life.

'Yeah it is,' Peter said, trying to hold his reaction—and anger. He never really gave a damn what Pam got up to while he was at work, as long as she was responsibly looking after the kids. He wasn't sure that this little get-together fulfilled that remit. And he felt he'd already made a tit of himself by speaking out of turn in front of the neighbours last night, so he wasn't about to do it again so soon after.

'I need to go, the boys will be back,' said Joyce, before a minor fit of giggles seemed to come for her. 'They'll be staring at the empty kitchen wondering where tea magically comes from.'

'Are our kids in?' Peter asked, while Joyce shimmied out to the hall.

'Yeah, they're all upstairs. Jacob's playing on his PS4 and Alice is having a shower,' answered Pam, through a lazy grin. 'Speaking of a shower, you two look like you need cleaning up yourselves.'

That paused Joyce, who stopped at the hall mirror and suddenly burst out laughing.

'How long have we been like this?!' she asked.

'I was hoping you wouldn't notice,' said Pam, herself now creasing with laughter. She chucked a tea towel at Joyce from the counter, which she caught and cleaned herself off.

'Oh, dear me, Peter, you must think I'm a proper nutter,' said Joyce.

'No, it's nice to see Pam making friends and having a good

time,' he replied, only partially meaning it.

'Even if it is with the village idiot. I gotta go—see you later!' And with that Joyce was gone, leaving nothing but a mucky tea towel on the hall side table.

Peter and Pam stared at each other, neither knowing which way to take the ensuing conversation. They both knew this immediate moment of potential frisson so well that they seemed almost jaded at the thought of falling out again.

'It's coffee grounds,' Pam blurted suddenly. 'I was trying to get that stupid machine working and...' Her hand flashed to her face to check it was all still there, which it sure was.

Peter's anger was punctured slightly at the thought of the coffee machine spitting at them belligerently. He exhaled in mock chastisement and his eyebrows raised.

'Look, I know,' Pam said, the straight blade of her shoulders melting into relaxation. 'I know it's not perfect, it was just a one off. I felt bad about last night, I felt bad about fighting, I felt... just bad, you know? It's been a hell of a few days and I just switched off. I'm sorry.'

Peter smiled fully and put his arm around her, a feeling that felt quite foreign to him, such was the lack of times he found himself doing it. 'It's okay. I'm sorry too. I'm sorry I was such an arse in front of everyone last night, and I'm sorry if you got the wrong idea about that girl. Honestly when I went down to the bin last night, her dog scarpered off down that passageway, and I was just trying to help. You know, make a good impression and all that?'

'I know, I should have trusted you...'

'It's an emotional time, moving house. It's weird for us all.' He hugged her properly, which seemed to catch her by surprise and she dropped away from him.

He looked a little taken aback. 'What?'

'Nothing, just the coffee. You look so nice in your work clothes, I wouldn't want to mess you up.'

'I'm taking them off any minute, what's the matter?'

Peter was genuinely confused, lamenting his inability to ever be able to read his wife properly. Before another standoff could ensue, Jacob's voice broke in from the living room. 'Mum! Dad! Come here quick!'

Pam and Peter swapped confused glances, before she ran out of the kitchen, with Peter following at a more sedate pace. As he rounded the corner to the living room, Jacob was already leaving through the passage towards the back door, which he threw open with a bang. Pam followed in a panic, and satisfied that Pam was covering the drama from a parental aspect, Peter drifted to the large rear window overlooking the back garden.

Through the glass he could see Jacob on his knees, opening LeBron's hutch, throwing his hands into the wadded bedding and all Peter could think about was all that piss-soaked sawdust and rodent droppings on his son's hands.

'He's not here, he's not here,' he could hear Jacob repeating in a muffled voice. Pam had been reduced to simply rubbing Jacob's back while he searched, and she sneaked a glance to Peter through the pane. She shrugged as if to say *I've no idea*, but Peter saw something else in her attentiveness to Jacob.

Bare guilt.

19

THE SUN WAS drifting lower over the Blackstoke estate, dropping a quilt of dull blue over all within it, forcing the streetlamps to fight back mutedly—while the West family stood around the kitchen island at Iron Rise.

'He's not there,' said Peter. 'I looked everywhere outside and in. I'm sorry to say it, but I do think he's gone.'

'But how did he get out?!' sobbed Jacob, having spent the last hour trying to hold his emotions in before abandoning all pretence and snivelling heartily. Peter put a hand on his son's shoulder—a hand that was still dirty from rummaging in the front garden's flower beds.

Pam watched from the other side of the table, the way her husband exuded a sort of calm under pressure. It was at odds with his lack of coolness in other social situations, although she did remember the old adage of *when the chips are down*, etc. She admired him for it, then remembered how she had flinched at his attempted hug earlier.

Pam didn't really know what the matter was, but that level of affection from her husband was so unprecedented in recent weeks that she didn't know how to take it—and at the time she really *was* covered in mashed coffee grounds. It wasn't that her husband repulsed her, not at all. It was more that she simply wasn't used to the affection. It had jarred. Had the love actually gone? Like an unseen vapour, had it vanished without her even realising?

'I know this will probably sound really heartless, but he's just a guinea pig and we'd had him a while,' said Alice, hoisting herself up to sit on the countertop. She popped open a can of Pringles when she got there, which made Pam realise that she was famished too. She grabbed a handful for herself.

'Alice, that's not entirely helpful, sweetheart,' said Peter.

'Better than finding him dead,' replied Alice through a mouthful of crisp shards. Peter shot her an altogether more serious look, to which she added: 'You think we still might?'

'That's enough Alice,' interjected Pam. 'We need calm heads here, that's all. He can't have gone far.'

'Come on mum,' quivered Jacob. 'I looked out the window and saw he wasn't there. So I shouted for you, and you were with me when I got to the hutch, so you know it was locked. It's not got any holes in it, so how did he get out? He just unlocked it and locked it again before he went? I don't understand.'

'I know it seems strange son, but there'll be a logical explanation. There always is,' said Peter.

'Someone must have let him out!'

'Nonsense, who would do such a thing—we haven't even had any visitors yet, nobody knows where LeBron lives now.'

'Yeah they do. Those twins—they know.'

Pam and Peter locked eyes again. It was true, and they both knew it. Aside from those in the room, the only people who knew about LeBron were the twins. 'But why would they…?' Pam asked, thinking out loud.

Peter raised his eyebrows to Pam, highlighting that that was a real possibility. Pam herself remembered how unnerving and downright weird they were, not to mention how Peter had described, albeit jokingly at the time, their quiet fascination with LeBron when Jacob had shown the animal to them.

Peter's eyes had taken a stubborn steel to them and he gave

71

Pam one grave nod. 'Who's up for a takeaway?' he asked, snapping into joviality with a theatrical flourish. 'Chinese? Thai?'

'Have we worked out what our local is yet?' Pam asked.

'We'll just use an online order thing like we did at the old place—they'll find us.'

'Okay, but use my card, my treat.'

Peter looked at her in silent query, as so much of their interactions around their children were.

Pam nodded, and gave a pensive little smile. It was a small thing, but something she hoped Peter would recognise. She knew what he was thinking, and hoped to God the kids didn't feel it too—the horrible nag that if she had just been a good little housewife today, doing the washing, not getting on the wine with Joyce (who she thought was a bundle of fun, but felt too guilty to admit it just yet), she would probably know just what had happened to LeBron. In other words, if she'd done exactly what MP Fletcher Adams had suggested.

Or more likely, nothing would have happened to him at all, if she'd been *compos mentis*.

As if by magic, the washing machine chimed in the utility room near the back door, which caught Pam a little unawares as she couldn't remember putting anything on. She excused herself briefly and went through to the back, her mind retracing the hazy map of the day in her head.

The lights on the machine were blinking, the signal she had only yesterday learned meant that the cycle was over. The window on the front was filled with something that looked a bit like a wig, long strands of some mystery garment tangled and pressed against the glass. Before she could really work out what was going on, she had opened the door, and the mystery of poor LeBron's whereabouts was suddenly solved.

20

WHEN FLETCHER ADAMS entered the West's house that night, he was not expecting a wake for some pointless fucking pet. Seeing the snot-covered face of their lone son was enough for him, and he resolved to make his visit brief. He held his irritation back, and set his mode to full politician.

'All of God's creatures have to go to a better place eventually,' he announced in his best Sunday School tones.

'But the washing machine?! Why the washing machine!' the boy cried. Fletcher really had to try hard not to snort at that. His mother was babying him, both their names utterly lost to Fletcher—but then, when you press as much flesh as he did every day, names just went in one ear and out the other.

He'd remembered the father's though. Peter. His ally. He always remembered the names of the useful ones, it made them feel important.

'What can we do for you Mr Adams?' asked Peter, while he pulled crockery and cutlery from the kitchen cabinets.

'Fletcher, please. I'm so sorry. This is clearly an unfortunate and sensitive time. I'm very happy to come back later… but it's these forms for you to sign.'

'What forms?' Peter said, but his memory caught up before the last syllable left his throat. 'The Neighbourhood Watch?'

'Yes. I've filled everything in, I just need your John Hancock then we are all set.'

'Okay, if you really think it's necessary…' Peter was teetering again, Fletcher could see it. He was on the edge, and like any good politician, Fletcher knew just where to give him a nudge.

'Peter, perhaps we could discuss this in private?' said Fletcher, gesturing to the hall behind him. Peter nodded and they both huddled by the front door for a moment.

'This pet of yours, the guinea pig,' Fletcher whispered. 'Bit of a weird one, isn't it? The animal somehow finds its way into the washing machine and… dies. You think it somehow found its own way in there? Because I don't buy that for a minute.'

'Come on, he got out of the cage somehow, and when she was putting a load on my wife just scooped him up and shoved the lot in, clothes and all.'

'You really think so?' Fletcher looked at him pointedly.

'She'd been on the piss all day with your wife, so yeah I think so.'

'Joyce? Don't be absurd!' Fletcher was not going to be swayed from his objective with the focus being pushed anywhere unhelpful. He knew full well that Joyce imbibed while he was out and about—it was no surprise to him whatsoever—and he was well acquainted with hearty denial. 'The point I'm making is that anyone could have done this. Quiet neighbourhood like this? We need to look after each other, and show that we are capable of looking after ourselves. Remember statistics show that areas with an active neighbourhood watch—'

'Have statistically much lower crime rates. I remember.'

'Then your question of necessity has been answered, particularly in light of the day's events.'

Peter sighed and signed the papers on the hall side-table. Inside, Fletcher's smugness took a healthy swelling. This would look excellent for his campaigns, himself the leader of a thriving Neighbourhood Watch group in an area with zero crime. And that little bonus would come in very handy. Two grand, straight in his pocket—to manage crime in an area that saw none. It was ingenious, even if he did think so himself. And enlarging that map's borders, just enough so that the bottom corner of the area selected nudged into a nearby postcode that *did* have a high crime rate... masterful.

After he'd finished signing, Peter turned to him and lowered his voice even further. 'I say this with the greatest of respect as neighbours, but...' he stalled, the words jammed like a car engine that simply wouldn't start up again.

'Yes, Peter, anything,' Fletcher encouraged, again playing the doting local figurehead.

'Your boys. They took a liking to LeBron. Would they have... you know?'

Fletcher flushed purple in an instant, unable to believe the affront. Yes, his boys were a pair of socially-remedial fuckwits—but this kind of accusation could not stand. Then he said, in a tone that was not very parliamentary: 'I would be very careful with what you say next, Peter West. Boyd and Burnett, my boys, are *good* boys.'

Peter looked shocked and apologised profusely. Fletcher piped up a sing-song farewell into the kitchen, and even added on a whim that he'd pray for the family that evening. It sounded like the kind of thing he should say, and he liked it. He'd use it again. He always felt smart with his ad libs.

As he left, he looked at the street, and laughed to himself. The street was empty, and stone silent. *As if this place needs a Neighbourhood Watch*, he thought with glee. It was just another brick in the wall.

21

CHRISTIAN SNAPPED AWAKE, and put an arm out. He felt nothing but space. Remembering that since the move, he and David had swapped sides in bed, he rolled back over and checked the other way. David was there, his body slack and pliable with sleep.

The room was jet black save for the faint square of orange where the streetlamp beyond the window bled into the room around the edges of the blackout curtains. Everything appeared as it should, but something must have jarred Christian awake. He lay there, listening, feeling the comedown after that strange tug of something had dragged him into consciousness.

Usually it was David coming to bed. They were creatures of tried and tested habit. Christian preferred to get to bed earlier to read by lamplight, while staunch non-reader David would sit up watching television until his eyes couldn't stay open any longer. David often made quite a bit of noise getting into bed, stumbling about in the dark if Christian had already turned the lights off and gone to sleep.

But David was long asleep, his breathing even and deep. He had been in bed for some time.

So what was it? What had woken Christian up?

He wondered if it was a noise from outside, so he got up and carefully parted the curtains. The streetlamp outside was so bright that at night it flooded the room—a little inconvenient surprise they'd come across when moving in. Christian's eyes had swept the street in a swift moment.

Nothing.

The baby monitor suddenly came to life, hissing static into the room. The penny dropped suddenly—it was the baby, rustling in the night, that had woken him up. They always kept the damn baby monitor on too loud, but somehow always forgot about it. *Still getting used to the routines*, he thought.

Christian sighed, sitting back down on the edge of the bed. Olivia didn't sound unsettled, and was probably just rolling over. He'd give it a minute to see if their daughter calmed.

Daughter. A word for so long he hadn't thought he'd ever get to use. A word that was taking some getting used to.

As he sat there in the darkness, pride popped happily in Christian's chest. Yes, it was taking some getting used to, but they had done it. They had adopted a baby girl. They had become parents. They had pushed and fought, jumped through every hoop that had been placed in front of them, and were actually *doing it*. They were exercising the rights that should come so naturally and freely, and it felt great.

Olivia gave a high-pitched groan, bringing the baby monitor back to life. She's up properly, thought Christian. The groan continued, then dramatically lowered in pitch and tone, to a level surely impossible for a child, before finishing with a scratchy, deep voiced, unmistakable word.

'OOOOOO*oooooo baba*'.

Christian jumped up, chilled to his core, and terrified to the farthest edge of his mind.

Someone was in there. In with their baby.

'David!' he shouted, as he bolted from the bedroom into the darkness of the landing, sprinting along the long upstairs hall to the nursery. As he ran, he cursed their decision to put the nursery so far away. Within seconds, he could hear David behind him.

'What?! Chris, what?! Is it Olivia?!' he was shouting, his feet thudding.

Christian got to the nursery and immediately put the light on.

Olivia simply lay there, blinking her eyes at the sudden brightness. On seeing Christian, she gurgled and put her little arms out.

'It's okay, sweetheart, I'm here,' cooed Christian, as he scooped up the child and checked her over. She was fine— sleepy and surely soon-to-be irritable—but fine. And there was nobody else in the nursery.

'What happened? Is she alright?' asked David as he ran in.

'She's fine, she's fine,' replied Christian, confused and confounded. He looked around again, but everything was as it should be. The changing unit was in the corner as usual, the bears at the foot of Olivia's bed arranged just as they had been the night before, the roadmap rug sitting under the radiator waiting for Olivia to be old enough to play with cars. The curtains were shut, just as Christian himself had left them hours earlier.

Then one of the curtains moved ever so softly—so softly that Christian, for a brief fleet of thought, assumed he'd imagined it. David pulled it back quickly, that damn streetlamp raining halogen right in their eyes—but unmistakably, uncontrovertibly, the window was a couple of inches open.

22

QUINT FENCHURCH WAS a man of very simple tastes and even simpler routines. He liked getting up in the morning before everybody else. It made him feel strong, ready, like he'd got one over on everybody else before the day had even started. He liked sitting in the quiet with a bowl of muesli. Alpen was his favourite, preferably sugar free. Doctor's orders and all that.

He sneaked downstairs to the front of the house and the kitchen, before pouring himself a bowl, adding just a splash of skimmed milk. He put the kettle on, popped a tea bag into his mug, and sat down. The spoon had just made it into his mouth when he glanced out of the window.

His eyes widened, and the spoon just sat there.

Rage boiled in him quicker than the water in the kettle, and he coughed oats and nuts down his flannel pyjama top.

'Wendy!' he bellowed up the stairs, as he ran to the front door and unlatched it hastily.

Outside, the smell hit him immediately. It smelled just how it looked. Of *shit*.

The two big front windows of the house, one on the left for the kitchen, the other for the living room, were streaked and blobbed with faeces.

Quint struggled to keep his breathing regular, rasping in anger as he stepped barefoot onto his carefully manicured and spotless lawn. He couldn't believe what he was seeing. He couldn't believe the *affront*.

He turned, and looked straight at the smaller house on the corner of Lance and Broadoak. Grace Milligan's house.

That spineless, stupid little bitch, he seethed inwardly. *I'll show you.*

23

THE POLICE CAR arrived soon after seven in the morning, and when Fletcher saw it from his ensuite window, the razor at his cheek in the mirror, his mind jack-knifed, falling over itself trying to work out which of his loose ends had come finally undone. He abandoned his shave and threw a suit on, ready to face whatever music they were bringing with denials and spades of outrage. He couldn't see any press yet, which was a good thing.

He had just made it down to the front door and stepped into his Oxfords when he saw Joyce watching through the kitchen window out at the street. Dressed in a dressing gown and cradling a mug of something steaming, she was transfixed by whatever was happening. And their doorbell hadn't rang. Confused, Fletcher joined her.

'Any tea in the pot?' he pretended while glancing out. 'What's going on?'

'It's coffee, and I haven't a clue,' his wife replied. 'Looks like they are going to the one down there.'

Fletcher watched the two young police officers ringing on the doorbell of the house furthest up the street to the bend. 'The one with those retired folks in it, isn't it?'

'Is that what they are… I know the feeling,' she said. Fletcher didn't have time for her surgical sarcasm this morning, so he ignored it completely. His wife's ship had sailed, and frankly, *bon voyage.*

They watched in silence for a couple of moments, as the

older male resident of the house (again, with a name that Fletcher just couldn't bring himself to recall) animatedly showed the two young coppers the state of his windows, which Fletcher noted looked like someone had sprayed them with mud.

'He's really going for it, isn't he?' he said, through smiling lips. This was *perfect*. Exactly the kind of thing the Neighbourhood Watch needed. The timing of a police visit for some kind of disturbance was exemplary—nobody would question its creation at all. And as long as it wasn't his house that had been vandalised... well, he couldn't care less.

'He probably flicked that all up his windows when he was mowing for the six hundredth time this week,' Joyce said, then blew on her coffee.

'Maybe,' said Fletcher, his voice already returning to calm, collected, assertive politician mode. It was the voice he saved for his constituents.

'What have you got on today?'

'Public surgery over in Chorley to hear what bees are in whose bonnets. Then it's over to Manchester for a few planning meetings. Some bigwigs want my approval for a regeneration project. Probably be a late one I'm afraid—where are they going now?'

He was transfixed on the movements of the police, one woman, one man, both mid-to late-twenties, as they crossed the road to the little house opposite.

'What the hell do they want with her?'

24

GRACE WAS RELIEVED she was already dressed ready for work. She'd have hated being questioned on her doorstep in front of the neighbours in her pyjamas. It was bad enough already, and even now she could see her denials were falling on deaf ears. It was taking some real restraint to maintain an air of professionalism.

'I will, of course, answer any questions you might have. It's quite easy when you're glaringly innocent of any such accusations,' she said, court voice back on and locked in tight.

'Can we come in, Miss Milligan?' asked the female bobby.

'I'd prefer not, PC...?' *Always get their name*, she thought. It put the fear of God into them. Kept them behaving to the letter of the law.

'Gibson, Miss,' the young woman replied, a hand resting on the cuffs secured to her belt in a subconscious assertion of just who she felt held all the cards.

'PC Gibson, this might sound trite, but I do have a sick dog inside. I'd much rather we had our conversation outside. I'm not afraid of anyone seeing us, as I have nothing to hide.' Grace was all business, her tone even, measured and forthright, but inside she was quivering like a reed in a stiff breeze. The other officer spoke with a slick delivery.

'PC McIlroy. This would be the dog that relieved itself on your neighbour's lawn yesterday?' He looked at her with a smug flicker of satisfaction.

'No, it would be the dog that did no such thing. I'm afraid if you'll excuse the pun, you are barking up the wrong tree here.' Grace eyed McIlroy carefully. He clearly fancied himself a fair bit, carrying himself with a *nightclub five minutes to closing time* swagger. She was already thinking of all the ways she could trip him up and bring him back down to size.

'Jokes aside, Miss Milligan, it's a complaint about your dog that has brought us here today… and the subsequent behaviour of said dog's owner.'

Grace iced over in an instant. 'Exactly what is being implied here?'

'Madam,' leered McIlroy, pointing back across to the Fenchurch house, 'the substance on those windows certainly didn't hurl itself. And considering your neighbour complained to you about your dog's antics only yesterday, it's not the daftest assumption that you might have taken the hump and chucked your dog's next product at his house in revenge. You might even have saved quite a bit of it up, by the looks of things.'

The anger that flooded Grace felt beautiful to her. It was like a drug. Answering allegations on the spot like this, when she knew she was in the right, was nothing but fuel.

'PC's McIlroy and Gibson, can I get this right… I stand accused of throwing canine excrement at my neighbour's windows. Is that correct?'

Their looks confirmed that, but hearing it put in such a way seemed to deflate them a little bit.

'Please let Mr Fenchurch know, even after his crude outburst yesterday, I had no intention of taking things any further in the name of neighbourly spirit. It seems my hope that this would blow over has been unfounded. I will be making a complaint about the antisocial behaviour of Quint Fenchurch, and a separate complaint about the unprofessional behaviour of two police constables, both of which I'll be taking to your superiors this morning. Now if that's quite enough, I've got to get to work.'

McIlroy and Gibson were stunned into silence. Grace went for one final push.

'You have no evidence, aside from hearsay. I have asserted my innocence, and in such case you have no cause to be here any longer. Goodbye.'

She shut the door, having gone from hoping nobody saw the police at her door to wishing everyone had seen the way she dealt with them. Her buzz soon dissipated. Dewey genuinely was ill, or at least a bit offside. And this problem with the Fenchurches was shaping to be exactly the kind of window-twitching numbskullery that she had been hoping to avoid.

With sudden sadness, and the hopelessness that immediately followed it, the thought she'd been suppressing finally reared its ugly head.

I wish I'd never moved here, she thought.

25

DAVID WANTED TO go out and see what was the matter, but his innate Britishness, his built-in sense of *make-no-scene*, seemed to step in and stop him. He watched the police return to their car through the half-closed slats of the kitchen blinds. The kitchen was dimly lit, with the early sunlight flaring into the room through the slats in a jarring grid of harshness.

He was knackered, plain and simple, but more than anything he was confused. So, it was good to be alone while he worked his thoughts out. He sat on what had become Christian's chair at the countertop, and watched the street covertly. From what he'd seen, everyone spent great portions of their day like this, one eye out there at all times. It was nothing more than curtain twitching, and he resented himself for following suit, but plain fact dictated that everyone's kitchens seemed to face the street, and, well, it was suddenly so damned *interesting* around here.

Olivia and Christian were still asleep upstairs, and the house was quiet. After the disturbances in the night, they had found themselves, all three, huddled in the king size bed in the master bedroom, Olivia swaddled between the two men. Neither adult could sleep, and Olivia was delighted at being with them, cooing excitedly instead of dozing off, so it had taken a until at least five in the morning before any of them had got back to sleep again.

The toaster popped, but David didn't rise to get it. He decided to have it cold in a bit—his appetite felt long dead. So he sat there, and watched as the police car left the street, and

Grace Milligan closed the door.

The visit from the police certainly seemed to corroborate that something had happened on the street the night before, and that their disturbance was not unique. But it still didn't sit right with him.

He had been with Christian for eleven years, and knew his husband well enough to know that Christian was not prone to flights of fantasy, hysteria or paranoia, all of which made the nocturnal events even more disconcerting. However, David couldn't shake the feeling that it was all too far-fetched, all too clichéd. He hadn't heard anything in the night, save for Christian's upset. For all he knew, his husband might have woken confused from a nightmare, having accidentally left the nursery window ajar.

They had met in halls at Liverpool University, and had both arrived on Merseyside as two straight lads going to further their educations. They had been firm friends right through their three-year degrees, but at some point in their final year, the possibility of them going their respective ways triggered something which made them, however surprising to both of them, fall in love. It was something neither could explain. As trope would dictate, it just... happened. Their mates, largely, were staggered, but in recent years some had come around. It was a hugely difficult, revelatory, challenging, liberating time. But they had stood by each other, steadfast in their love.

And they knew what they were going to get from each other. When you've been barracked and bullied for years, you close ranks, and come to rely on each other in very fundamental, deep-rooted ways. They understood each other, and to David's understanding, panic and flights of fancy were not in Christian's wheelhouse at all.

But the whole thing, it seemed to David so... silly. And

hopeful. And silly again. It was ridiculous, a voice on the baby monitor. An adult voice speaking words in a room that patently had no adults in it—apparently. He hadn't heard anything himself.

David acknowledged that the mind sometimes played tricks on its host. He had experienced enough paranoia when he'd first come out—thinking that every half-heard whisper was about him—to know that sometimes, when you were on edge and fraught, your brain can have a rather rude tendency to fill in the blanks. And the logical corners of his head urged that that was what had happened here.

But Christian was adamant. Completely certain. He said he was going to canvas the neighbours today and ask if anything had happened to them. David had thought he was mad even thinking of phrasing a question like that, and cringed at the thought. Old fires of anxiety had been stoked back to momentary life.

But now, seeing the police leaving Grace Milligan's house? He wasn't so sure any more.

26

AT FOUR THIRTY in the afternoon, after spending most of the day gearing up to it, Peter knocked on his boss's door. He was beckoned inside in a sharp, rude tone, as if the audacity of requesting a brief audience with him was just another affront in a long, sad string of them. Peter had been expecting it, and had prepared accordingly by bringing a cup of hot coffee, one sugar and a thimbleful of semi-skimmed milk. He opened the door.

Paul Threlfall was a man seemingly made from bits of coat hangers arranged into a wiry, angular scarecrow. His skin was the colour and consistency of chicken nuggets, even across his hairless skull. He perched on a desk chair behind his workstation, hunched over his PC keyboard as if he was about to dissect it.

'Can I have a minute, Paul?' asked Peter. The last thing Peter wanted was any of Paul's time, but circumstances dictated otherwise.

'If it's a quick minute,' replied Threlfall, without looking up once. Peter walked the coffee to him and made a point of placing it in his eyeline.

'I know I've had some time off recently for the move, but I wanted to ask if I could step out early today?'

'How early?' replied Threlfall, ignoring the coffee and flexing his jaw.

'Like… now early.'

Threlfall paused and finally looked up. 'And pay?'

'Keep the pay, I just need to nip off. I need get somewhere before five.'

Threlfall pushed back from the table and animatedly chucked his pen at his work. He stared at the coffee like the cheap bargaining chip it was. 'You are aware of how difficult it is to get wages to just divvy up half hours here and there?'

'I understand.'

'You are aware of how flexible the company has been with your recent *house move arrangements*?' Those last three words carried the acerbic bite of a sceptic referring to the idle predictions of a tabloid horoscope.

'Yes I—'

'And I know you are aware that you have already asked myself, the department and the company to review your wage in the hope of a promotion—which I assume has something to do with the new house you now need help paying for?'

Peter gave up there and then. He hadn't had a raise since he'd agreed, in that stupid spin of bravado, to buy that infernal new house, and now that it was here, he had chanced his arm. The extra cash per month was far more valuable to him than the half hour now. 'Forget I mentioned it. Please, forget it.'

Before any more could be said, Peter reversed out of Threlfall's office and back into the main mess area of the PR firm's offices. He retreated to his corner desk, which had been management's idea of an upgrade, out of the hubbub of the middle of the room.

Foolishly, he had booted down his computer in the false assumption he'd have been able to leave. Tail betwixt lower limbs *á la* scolded dog, he turned it back on.

It was the local pet shop—that's what he wanted. He wanted to make it before five, which was its traditional closing time. He had got his pets there as a kid, and that's where LeBron had come from. He trusted them. Of course, he could go to the late-night pet supermarket at the industrial estate on the way home, but the animals there all looked confused. Like they were all one or two chromosomes shy of a full set. And local reports had suggested that they often had a habit of dying unexpectedly and without much reason.

Oh well, he thought, knowing that was exactly where he was going. *Better it's a defect if it's only going to end up in the washing machine again.*

27

QUINT'S FURY HAD bubbled along all day at such an unpredictable rate that he kept finding himself short of breath and flushed. Little things that didn't go his way became huge indignant, obstinate obstacles that pushed at his patience. The traffic lights weren't playing ball. The paper he bought from the village shop had a wet patch on the back page. The crease on his carefully ironed trousers forked off and skewed midway down his left shin.

And it was all that stupid girl's fault.

And the police? Piss-ups and the inability to get one going in a brewery sprang to Quint's mind. Not like in his day.

But the reason he'd endured the traffic and even put on his slacks was to go to the local camping store, which was about the only thing today that had been a roaring success. And he was looking at his prize now, sitting on his back porch where nobody could see it, turning it over and over in his hand.

He didn't really know what he was looking for *per se*, save for the fact that he'd heard mention of them on those television wildlife programs he enjoyed. The ones where they fly a chap into the deepest Amazon or onto the highest Himalayan peak, with nothing but a Swiss Army knife and some camera gear to survive. He fancied he'd have a good go at that. And the godforsaken wilderness they ended up in sounded a lot simpler and quieter than the Blackstoke estate. Maybe they should have retired *there*.

There was a battery pack on the back of the unit, a fiddly little thing that needed a tiny screwdriver to get at. Quint liked that. He liked that it needed a unique tool to get at it—a tool that he, ever prepared, had. It meant nobody would be able to just wander up and rip the batteries out either.

This would be perfect. After the electric fence had failed its remit of prevention, he had to up his game.

A hunting camera, the salesman had called it. Eighty quid all told, with a spare rechargeable battery and a memory card, which apparently took the place of a conventional tape. It had a motion sensor too, so that when anything tripped it, the tape started rolling. Or memory card started rolling. Or recorded. Or whatever the hell it did.

Point was, whoever had been chucking shit on his lawn and windows would be caught in the act.

He turned it on like the salesman had shown him, and looked at the green images on the screen on the back. Night vision. Excellent.

Quint smiled at the thought of Grace Milligan caught red-handed, bathed in that luminous glow, her eyes glaring jade-green like a caught cat's. He couldn't wait to hear her denials, only to produce this. The mere thought of it made the hairs on his arms stand on end, just like they always had in his police days when irrefutable evidence was put to the accused.

Justice. Incontrovertible justice. Quint fucking loved it.

The back door clunked open, and Quint hunched over to hide what he was doing. The drone of television voices escaped the open door.

'What are you doing out here, darling?' said Wendy.

'Just enjoying the evening,' Quint said.

'Okay, well, supper's nearly ready. Could you come in and set the table?'

'Of course,' he said, tucking the hunting camera behind one of the large plant pots either side of the porch's top step. *Later*, he thought. *Later.*

28

THE BASTARDS JUST wouldn't die. Their spawn point had to be nearby because they kept reappearing near this spot—and if he didn't find it and camp next to it, killing them as soon as they appeared, they'd never get a handle on them and keep the flag. If he just hid behind this crate, tight to the wall…

BANG. The view shook and tilted downwards, and the screen took the hue of dark claret.

'FFS,' muttered Jacob, enunciating each letter with relish, then tossing the PS4 controller down. 'I'm out boys, sick of it—this is why this map sucks.' He took off his headphones and unlooped his school tie from around his neck. He hung it on the wardrobe handle, ready for the morning, and did the same with his crumpled white shirt.

Don't think of school.

His new room was so much bigger than his last one, with a flatscreen TV wall mounted over a desk, a double bed—which he couldn't believe he had, and equally couldn't wait to introduce the girls at his new school to. There were a couple of girls from his old school that he would have liked to have over here too, but that ship had sailed now that they'd moved. He'd kept in touch with his old mates, via their online nightly *Call of Duty* matches, but considering he didn't know any girls who did any of that sort of thing, they'd have to slip into the past.

Maybe, he thought, there'd even be a girl at his new school who was a gamer. Now that would really be something.

Don't think of school.

He grabbed a T-shirt from his bed, and tugged it on, inevitably now thinking about his new school. It had seemed okay, he guessed. Kind of alright. Much of a muchness, he told himself. On balance he preferred his old one, but this new school meant they could move, and the move meant he got a double bed and 42inch flatscreen, so… you know, compromises. And everyone seemed pretty interested in the fact that he lived on the new estate. Even some of the girls.

Jacob had never been particularly popular. He wasn't an easy fit for popularity, with his apparent late-blooming, and his habit of playing benign lingerer—he was always present at things, but always in the background. He was privy to what went down, but never part of it. And that made him socially malleable. He was never in trouble, but he had the gossip. And his interests in gaming—or generally anything that wasn't sports—meant that he could bounce between both the cool and not so cool camps. And happily, that was what was appearing to happen now, in his new setup.

He swapped his already dusty trousers (from crawling around on the art room floor) for some joggers and made his way downstairs. Tea should be ready soon, and his pre-pubescent stomach was rumbling.

When he got into the kitchen, he came to a stop. Nobody was about, but there, on the kitchen island, was a cardboard box peppered with holes. The kind you got when you went to the pet shop. He hurried over and held his ear next to the cardboard, listening.

A popping sound, then a rustle.

There was something in it.

Warm elation flooded Jacob from his calves to his shoulder blades. He tensed on the spot, and pulled back the lid of the box, immediately smelling wood shavings and urine. As the light from the overhead LED's poured in, Jacob could see a small, round, fat, dazed-looking guinea pig—all black apart from an orange streak from its nose across its left eye, right back to its left hind leg. It looked up at Jacob, sniffing the air.

Jacob's heart filled at the funny little creature, and put his hand in to give him a stroke. The animal backed up into the corner, but Jacob managed to get his fingertips to the animal's spine. 'That's it. That's it.'

The rodent relaxed a touch, and sat still while Jacob's fingers traced wide circles in its fur.

'LeBron 2? TwoBron?' he said, in a hushed voice. The animal started sniffing the air again. 'Or how about something else, like Snuffles or Shuffles or something.'

The animal arched its neck back so it could sniff Jacob's fingers, and before he could pull them away, the guinea pig bit sharply into Jacob's middle digit.

'Ouch!' he shouted, pulling his hand away, looking at a neat drop of blood on his finger tip. 'FFS.'

He ran his finger under the kitchen tap.

'Nibbles it is then.'

29

DEWEY SAT OBEDIENTLY, watching Grace intently through the straggly fur that hung over his deep brown eyes.

'Paw,' Grace said, crouched in front of him. She had put a wind cheater over her office suit, and swapped her patent leather heels for a pair of bright blue Nikes. Thanks to Dewey's size, their eyes were on the same level, and he lifted a big weathered front foot up to her.

'Good boy,' she said taking it. 'Walkies.'

She lifted the loop of the rope lead over his head, but only got it as far as his forehead before he shook his head and ducked backwards.

'Dewey, heel.' The dog bowed his head, almost in shame, and edged forward again. Grace tried again, the routine from start to finish.

'Paw.' Dewey shook her hand diligently. 'Good boy. Walkies.'

This time, as soon as the rope appeared anywhere near Dewey's head, he snatched it with his jaws and tugged it away from her. Grace tried to pull it back, but she suddenly felt the tears go. He was losing it.

'Please, Dew,' she said. She held a finger underneath each lower eyelid and blinked a couple of times, then wiped the mascara that had caught on her fingers across her coat.

Dewey watched her for a moment, his own gaze a primitive mix of defiance and confusion, before walking back down the hall to the kitchen, dragging the lead as he went. Grace heard the tinkle of the metal clip on the kitchen tiles as he dropped it on the floor.

She'd have to ring her mum and dad, she thought. They deserved to know. Dewey was theirs originally, and now that the baton had passed to Grace, she should take responsibility.

It was supposed to be the other way round, she thought bitterly. *He's supposed to be looking after me.*

She knew such petulance was only a refusal to acknowledge that the dog was in sharp decline. It was a common thing wasn't it? Animals not surviving major upheaval in their lives, like moving home?

And now she felt obscenely guilty.

The doorbell went, just behind her head, causing her heart to hammer up into her throat. She stood immediately and pulled on her professional veil. *Please don't be Fenchurch. Not now.*

She opened the door to one of the men who lived over the street, but not the one she was trying to avoid. It was one of the guys from the house opposite, with the cute baby.

'Hello,' she said, almost too jauntily, as she valiantly tried to paper over her own cracks.

'Hi,' said the man. 'It's me, David, from across the way. David Lyon.'

'Of course, hi. How are you?'

'Fine thank you. You settling in okay?'

Grace noticed he had a very laid-back demeanour, even from this small exchange. It was all in the confident posture and the easy, non-judgemental, friendly eye contact.

'Yes, I think. It's going so quickly though. Blink of an eye and weeks go by like that—it'll be Christmas before we know it.'

'I know what you're saying! I can't even remember what it's like *not* to live here!'

They both laughed in that convivial yet ultimately contrived way that signalled that the readily available amount of small talk had just expired.

'I'm sorry to bother you in the evening like this,' he said. 'But I wondered if I could come in for a minute?'

'Of course,' she replied, immediately trying to think of what state her house was in but realising at the same time it was too late to do anything about it.

'Great, thank you.' He crossed the threshold.

'Just pop to the kitchen at the end of the hall,' she said. He did just that. Grace followed and saw with mercy that the kitchen was just fine, with just a couple of dishes in the sink. The kitchen was small yet perfectly formed, with whitewashed walls and chrome appliances, and a window over the sink that overlooked the back garden.

'Like I said, I'm sorry to just barge in,' he said, standing near the back door. 'But we had a... how do I put it... a little disturbance at home last night, and, well, I saw the police car here this morning and I wondered if anything had happened here too? Christ, when I say it out loud like that I sound like the nosiest man alive.' He blushed intensely and looked at the floor.

Grace saw in that very honest moment that he was a very attractive man—not just physically, which he undeniably was, with his six-foot frame, broad shoulders, trendily styled hair and thick designer glasses, but also in his mannerisms. His character. Caring and honest. She liked him, immediately. Embarrassingly.

'Of course,' she said. 'Although I'm afraid from my end there's not much to tell. The disturbance was over at the Fenchurch place.'

'Oh,' David said, genuinely surprised. 'Well, that actually makes more sense given that we live next door to them.'

'What happened, if you don't mind my asking?'

'My husband—sorry, we—heard something on the baby monitor in the middle of the night that was a bit strange.'

'Well, if it helps, it might have been linked. Someone defaced their property—their front windows specifically. It's just that Mr Fenchurch is convinced it's me.'

'Oh. And it's not you?' David asked with a playful smile. Grace couldn't help but smile back.

'No, it wasn't I'm afraid. But any more early wake up calls from the police and it might be.' They both laughed.

'Well, Olivia's room is on the front of the house, and the monitor could very well have picked up something from outside if it was loud enough. I think we have our answer.'

'Yes, but it doesn't answer *my* question. If it wasn't me, who threw that crap up the windows—'

'It was *crap*?'

'Yes. If it wasn't me, or you or your husband… who was it?'

'The plot thickens,' David said, his eyes glazing over slightly, his thoughts gunning elsewhere before he looked straight at Grace. 'If you ever need anything, give us a call, okay? We are only there, and we'll be over in seconds. Although with this fellow I don't think you'd need much help.' He gestured to Dewey, who was sat at the foot of the oven.

Grace laughed, but still felt the tang of bittersweet. 'Dewey, despite his looks, is less of a menace and more of a loveable oaf.'

'Well, then give us a call if ever you feel Dewey isn't up to it. Please.'

It was an earnest remark, and Grace felt warm all over. *The best ones are always gay*, she reminded herself, before chastising herself for the very thought.

30

JOYCE CHECKED HER watch, which was also her pedometer, GPS unit and heart rate tracker. Four and a half miles done, heart rate at a hundred and ten beats per minute, and only half a mile from home. It even told her that it was about to turn seven o'clock. All in all? Perfection.

She'd just about got her route right and was happy. A small thing, but important to her. It came out of nowhere tonight, and, looking back, was so easy to follow. On leaving the estate, turning left outside the entrance gates, she followed an old fence on her left that must have been left there from the building days when the site was fenced off. Keeping the fence visible through the trees on her left, she circled the entire estate property, before returning back to the entrance—which was just ahead.

The air had dropped in temperature with the onset of evening, and there was the softest sprinkle of rain in the air. The sky above was pockmarked with briskly-speeding clouds, buffered by high wind overhead. Whatever this rain was going to become, it would be short lived.

The gateway to the Blackstoke estate was ornate and imposing—a twelve-foot-high arch of wrought iron, predictably in black, with metal lettering over the crest of the arch reading BLACKSTOKE. It reminded her uncomfortably of the gates outside Auschwitz, the Nazi concentration camp in the forests of Northern Poland—only the phrase '*Arbeit macht frei*' was gone. If it was a homage, it was a bizarre one—humanity's atrocities reinvented as kitschy architecture. She turned left under the archway and picked up pace.

On the left-hand side as she passed through, was a small cabin, presumably where the gate attendant sat. The brochures promised a *gated settlement with round the clock security,* which had to be here somewhere. They were paying for it, after all. Or maybe it hadn't started yet? There were only five houses occupied here, after all.

She felt the burn in her thighs, as the road gradually inclined uphill. She pushed harder, trying to think of other things.

It must have been a large plot of land, all told, if the fence around it spanned five miles, yet she'd only spent any time in that one corner which was theirs. She reached a roundabout, which had four exits if you included the one she was approaching from. Left was down through the hastily planted sycamores to Broadoak and their cul-de-sac. Straight on and right led to the next stages of the development, due for building and completion in the coming years. Their corner was the only one inhabited, and it gave her a sense of pride.

We were the first. The originals.

She turned left, as the young sycamores stood in neat rows, accompanied by evenly sequenced streetlights. She saw the glow in the sky over the trees where their cul-de-sac was, and tried to up the pace further. She always aimed to hit sprint by the end of her runs, and at their old house she had thrown up through exhaustion in the bushes on the drive more times than she could remember.

The trees parted, she saw the houses, and she began her charge. Head down, long leggy athlete strides. Freedom. the sense of being all you can be. Giving it your all.

Approaching the Fenchurch place. Their own house on the corner beyond, opposite Pam's. Go. GO! Passing the Lyon's place. Last fifty yards. The burn howling all over. It was *great*.

Something caught Joyce's eye, a white object in the bushes outside the Fenchurch's house. She slowed, as the object seemed to glow a little, but it was only a trick of the light as her eyes had been getting used to the darkness. The bushes outside the Lyons' house were a box hedge about three feet tall and two feet across, right the way around the front lawn, and the object was poking right out of the top. It was so out of place in the clean, freshly prepared neighbourhood. Snared by curiosity, she went to it.

It was made of light-coloured fabric, which even in this light, was quite visibly dirty. Mud and assorted dark streaks marked the fabric. She touched it. It was some kind of starchy cotton. When she pulled it out she saw, amid the mud and dirt, it was emblazoned with little, pale blue anchors all over. She stretched it out. It was a babygrow. Filthy, and foul-smelling, but still a babygrow.

Joyce looked around the street. It was empty and quiet. Lights were on in the surrounding homes. She looked at the Lyon's house. *They must have dropped it, or it must have fallen out of the window*, she thought. She looked at it again, trying to envisage the size of the garment in comparison to the Lyons' baby. It looked about right—maybe? It was a long time since she'd had a one-year-old of her own.

She took it with her, and walked round to their front door, giving it a couple of knocks and thumbing the bell once. There was no answer, so, in a fit of neighbourly pique, she decided she would wash it for them and return it later. Having a young baby was hard enough without things going missing, and this thing stunk to high heaven.

31

THE FEELING OF guilt had assaulted Pam so fiercely all day, that she was bursting for a glass of wine to smooth the edge off. However, such was her occupation of the doghouse, she was determined not to touch a drop. Peter was still in a funk, marching about quietly, trying to mask his blame for Pam (she was sure of it) with silence.

What he had done was nice, replacing the guinea pig like that, but they had barely had a chance to even discuss what had gone wrong in the first place. And now, she was too scared to. It would only eventually lead to another pointless rerun, another spat with no true purpose other than to properly dole out the blame for the damn guinea pig's death.

But, for Pam, that didn't come near the question of what they should be talking about—namely how the animal got in the washing machine in the first place. Peter had handled it, pulling it out, and all the clothes that had to go with it (nobody wanted to wear anything that had been saturated in LeBron's blood, no matter how many times it was going to be put back through the machine).

She was on the kitchen floor messing with a small remote control, trying to work out the LED strip lights that ran around the base of the island, which, when illuminated, gave the central unit a strange Blade Runner illusion that would have worked perfectly if they hadn't have opted for the traditional country kitchen look. Now, it just looked ridiculous, but at least they gave off a nice glow.

The doorbell chimed again, as it seemed to do all too often, and Pam worried if the constant stream of visitors was going to be a feature of living there. It had never happened in their old life—but then she thought of how remote they were in the grand scheme of neighbours. There was them, some half-built houses and dirt tracks mapped out where roads would eventually lay, and that was it. No wonder they all kept checking in on each other.

Before Pam could get to the door, Peter had marched across from the living room, where she assumed he had been working, watching television or just fuming quietly, and opened it.

'Hi Joyce,' she heard him say, with a hint of exasperation in his voice. He must have been thinking her partner in crime had returned, and to save him saying anything embarrassing, she was up, dropping the remote on the counter.

'Hi Joyce!' she shouted as she got there. Joyce was sweat-sheened and lycra-clad, her cheeks rosy and her breath puffing around her head, mingling with the steam rising from her scalp. She smiled.

'I've just knocked on the Lyons' place,' she said. 'But they're out and considering this place has got quite the neighbourhood clubhouse vibe at the minute, I thought they might have stopped by.' She held up her hand, and in it was a dirty babygrow.

Pam looked at the thing. It was a mess, and something about it was off. It was a baby's vest alright, short-sleeved, but the cut was kind of weird. Olden. Not super old, but not something you'd see these days. And the patterning, those anchors...

'They're not here, I'm afraid.' Pam said. 'It is very vintagey, and they are quite cool, so it could well be theirs.'

'Hmm. It's just weird. I found it in the hedge outside their place. You know, *their* place.' Joyce bent her knees and pulled a sarcastic face as she said it.

'I can't picture the Fenchurches having a baby over, even if one was jammed through their letterbox. How weird.'

'Yeah, I saw it while running, and was going to take it in to wash it, but I saw your door opposite and thought I'd just check. Things… alright?'

Pam suddenly felt acutely aware of just how 'not alright' things were, but just as quickly realised that Peter had gone.

'Yeah fine,' she said hurriedly. 'New guinea pig, so big news.'

'Oh lovely. I heard from Fletcher—'

Pam smiled as she interrupted. 'Don't ask.' She liked her new friend. Joyce was a nice buffer zone to the upheaval and strife, and she smiled back conspiratorially.

'Shouldn't smile,' Joyce said. 'Should definitely shower though.' She turned to go, but someone else was walking up the drive past the parked cars behind them. Both women turned to see Christian, looking somewhat tired and more than a little haggard. The usual precision of his appearance seemed off, but Pam couldn't pinpoint exactly what it was that gave her this impression. Maybe it was just his posture, which was both stooped and wrought jagged at the same time.

'Hello there, wanderer,' Pam shouted, and he waved a pursed smile in response. *Definitely something up*, Pam thought.

'Aha,' said Joyce. 'The very man.'

'Evening all,' he said.

'You've saved me a visit,' said Joyce, thrusting the babygrow at him with an outstretched arm, which Christian looked at with an immediate frown.

'Ugh, where did you find that?' he asked. The closer he came to them, the more Pam was shocked by his appearance. Gone was that crisp poise and confident contentedness. This man was exhausted and had the air of deep unsettlement. 'Looks distinctly unhygienic.'

Confusion passed across Joyce's face, as she lowered the item. 'So it's not yours?'

Christian smiled softly. 'No, thank God.'

'It's so strange then,' Joyce said.

'Where did you find it again?' asked Pam, touching the material again. Now unclaimed and thereby certified at least temporarily mysterious, it felt like a foreign artefact.

'In the hedge outside the Fenchurch place. The far corner of the garden, the bit that looks out into the street. Only one little one in our midst, so how the hell did it wind up there?'

Christian eased it from her and held it up to the overhead porch light. 'That is strange. Maybe there's a label, or a name written on it?' He turned it over and checked the inside collar.

'Have we had any high winds or anything? Anything that would send it blowing over here from somewhere local?' asked Pam.

'Not that I can recall,' said Joyce.

'Maryland Fabrics,' announced Christian, as he showed the women the garment. Through the neck hole, he poked the back panel of the vest through to show a small stitched-on label which read the name he had just mentioned in pale blue thread.

'Never heard of them,' said Joyce.

'Sounds posh,' said Pam, but she suddenly felt aware that she may have just exposed her less than aristocratic roots. 'In a boutiquey kind of way.'

'It's filthy though—and smells awful,' Joyce said.

Pam hadn't actually caught that, but now Joyce mentioned it, it did. She'd thought it was just an extension of that low-level pong the area seemed to carry, but no, now she thought about it, it was definitely stronger and coming from the garment.

'Doesn't look new,' said Christian. 'Could have been there

ages.'

'No—he'd have noticed. The old geezer, I mean,' said Pam. 'He spends all day tending to that bloody garden, I'd be amazed if he hadn't seen it.'

They spent a moment of quiet silence as they wondered how this item of baby's clothing had just dropped into their midst, before Christian seemed to remember why he'd come over in the first place.

'Oh yes,' he said. 'You've saved me a job too, Joyce, I was coming over to see you as well. Did anyone in either of your houses hear anything out of the ordinary last night?'

Joyce stuck out her bottom lip. 'Aside from Fletcher's night-time routine which has been out of the ordinary for so long it has become ordinary, no.'

'Pam, anyone here?' Christian looked at her and she could detect a hint of pleading in his gaze.

'Nobody's said anything,' she said. 'Why?'

'We may have had a bit of a disturbance last night,' he said, then blinked slowly. 'But we aren't sure.'

'The police car? But it was over at that girl's house wasn't it?' She didn't like the way she had said *that girl*, but it was out of her mouth now.

'Yes, but that's the thing—'

'She's a lawyer isn't she? I just assumed it was something to do with her work,' Joyce said as she folded her arms. She was no longer steaming now, and just looked damp and cold.

'Right,' said Christian, 'but it wasn't her that called it. It was that *old geezer*.' He nodded at Pam. 'He's been finding... *shit* on his property, and he thinks it's her dog going about marking its territory in very uncompromising terms. He confronted her about it yesterday, next night, his house is covered in shit. Sorry.' He glanced over Pam's shoulder into the house. 'Poo.'

'She threw poo at his house?!' Pam's voice rose with incredulity. 'You're kidding.'

'No, no. Well, I don't really know. David went to see her, and she denied it, of course.'

'Well, I never,' Joyce said, almost to herself.

'So, nothing weird happened over here then?' Christian asked.

Something ticked in Pam's head. 'Actually, now we're on this track, we had a guinea pig end up in a washing machine yesterday. I've no idea how that happened.'

'It ended up *where*?' Joyce said, with her and Christian's eyes widening in unison.

Pam just nodded with a resigned, regretful smile.

'Well, that's a bit weird isn't it?' said Christian.

'Yes, but it was only during the afternoon. Late afternoon I think. Not overnight like the other stuff.'

'Hmmm.'

'Maybe,' Joyce said, 'a neighbourhood watch group isn't such a bad idea after all.'

'If Fletcher has the paperwork, I'll sign,' said Christian.

'Peter already has,' said Pam, finally feeling like she could support his decision to get involved.

32

BOYD TURNED OVER, and noticed that when his cheek brushed the pillow, he felt a little friction. Growth, perhaps. Maybe he'd have to start shaving soon. He'd noticed his voice unreliably wavering, occasionally deeper, so much so that he felt a humorous uncertainty whenever he opened his mouth.

'Do you feel that?' he asked out loud. He knew his brother wasn't asleep, even though he had been still for ages.

'What?' answered Burnett, on the other side of the room, himself having been waiting for his brother to speak, aware he was on the edge of breaking the silence.

'You got any facial hair yet?'

'What do you think?'

'What are you going to do about it?'

'What are *you* going to do about it?'

'Ask dad?'

'Well, we could get some hair removal cream. I saw that on TV. Like a wax.'

'Do men wax their faces?'

'I've no idea.'

'Let's ask dad.'

They fell back into silence. They never meant to mirror each other in the way that everyone assumed they did, but it was just convenient to copy each other—although they did love playing up to it to freak people out. Their behaviour and confidence in their own skin had emboldened over the years because of their innate strength in numbers, mimicking each other in solidarity, so they had become their very own pair quite naturally, despite the obviousness of their shared womb.

What people didn't tend to get was that when they were on their own, completely in control of the terms, they *were* different. Their characters didn't entirely look back at each other with identical gazes.

They had their own rooms, off along the corridor, opposite each other. Their own spaces, which they would get to eventually—but for now, they weren't quite ready yet, so they slept on couches in the newly designated playroom (which is where the Xbox lived, while the PlayStation resided downstairs). Their rooms were ready for them—both furnished, both beds made, both sets of (*very* similar) clothes in both wardrobes.

There was a distant rumble which they both felt deep in their guts more than actually sound in their ears.

'A car?' said Burnett.

'I think so.'

'2 litre?'

'2.5. Maybe even three.'

They waited as it grew.

'Definitely 2.5,' confirmed Boyd with authority. 'Dad.'

The growl turned up and abruptly increased in both volume and clarity, and thin shafts of light spun on the ceiling after sneaking through the gaps in the curtains.

Burnett checked the clock on the wall, but had to wait a second until his eyes adjusted enough to see the dull hands. Two forty-five in the morning.

'He's early,' said Boyd.

The car slowed, the growl paused, a car door clunked. There was a moment of calm, then a plant pot broke.

'Oh God,' whispered Burnett. A sigh accompanied the

words.

Both boys were out of bed in a second, and heading for the window, each one grabbing an end of curtain and peeling it back. The shafts on the ceiling widened.

The scene they found outside was a familiar one, although the smashing of a plant pot suggested that this was a particularly extreme variation of the norm. Sure enough, their father, his tie loose, his hair mussed and his shirt untucked, stood with his legs wide apart and one of his feet buried in soil with shards of terracotta poking out at all angles. A two-foot palm tree lay prostrate, its roots still hidden in the mound of earth. All of this was laid scant by the unforgiving glare of the security light by the guttering over all their heads.

The twins watched as their father's long-suffering driver, Mike, ran around the bonnet of the car and grabbed Fletcher's outstretched arms before he toppled, his eyes casting around the street in concern. Mike held his client up and cleaned his foot off, ushering him to the house. Even without Mike's arm around him, it was clear that Fletcher Adams was in a hell of a state.

'Will mum get up for this one do you think?' asked Boyd.

'She might,' replied his brother, and as he spoke, Mike's eyes suddenly darted up to the window, and registered the boys. His expression spoke of exasperated apology. The boys waved in unison accidentally.

The sight of their father in a state of disrepair was not a new one, nor one that inspired anything in them other than a non-committal 'huh' and shrug of the shoulders. There was no shock, sadness, amazement, betrayal—all of that had been eroded by the frequency of its occurrence. Now though, thanks to the transformative qualities of time, it had metamorphosed into something akin to fascination. This was their patriarch, their leader, and he caused such *drama*.

Everywhere he went, furore seemed to follow. They knew they were expected to follow in his footsteps, and in turns were both daunted and couldn't wait. He did whatever he wanted without recompense, and when they sat there to enjoy his latest escapade, it was with the amazed gaze of children who know this shouldn't happen but reacted in wonder that it did—although being *here*, in their new home, he was clearly ahead of the curve. None of the other dads did this, that they could see—even that house over the road that had two of them. Although the other boy's dad did have a moment when he stormed out, angry. They had heard the door slam and done just the same thing as now—leapt up to the window to watch. They'd seen the one from the little house come out, with that amazing dog. They'd watched the dog tear off, and them follow.

It was drama. It was what they were used to.

The voices started downstairs. Loud, over the top. Well, one of them was.

'I'm sorry, so sorry, that it's got so late.' The voice was muffled, through layers of plywood, paint and wood facias, but it belonged unmistakably to their father.

'She's already there?!' asked Burnett. Boyd didn't answer, as their eyes drifted to somewhere around the door. There was a moment of silence, so protracted that the boys were unsure if their mother was there at all. They edged closer to the door, on a soft subconscious tide.

'Are you going to be sick?' they heard their mother ask.

'Don't be daft, I...' Something caused their father to stop speaking.

'I don't care about the process behind it. I just want to know if you're going to make a mess somewhere in our new home.'

There was another gap of sound while the boys stood in their pyjamas staring nowhere in particular.

'I might,' their father said, so softly they weren't sure they'd heard it. Burnett's eyebrows rose softly. There was a resigned, defeated quality to his voice that they seldom heard. Meek and spanked. Boyd's jaw dropped slightly, and he looked at his brother. He was met by the same reaction, and though they didn't know it at the time, they were struck by the moment's weight. Their father, chastened.

'Needless to say,' they heard their mother say, although she was sounding less like their mum and more like a sergeant major, 'you are not to come upstairs. I don't care what you need. I can smell the cheap perfume on you, and even that's stronger than the booze that's dripping out of you. The camp bed is in the downstairs study, pull it to the downstairs loo if you have to. In the morning, you're going to be sober, whether you like it or not. I'll come down and kick you at seven fifteen, and if that doesn't get you up, the tabloids get a phone call. And if you try to come upstairs with any amorous intentions, I'll make sure you regret it more than anything you've done yet. Just try me—okay?'

'Affirmative,' Fletcher said.

'Just in case you were wondering how good you have it,' Joyce said, 'I would have left you long ago if it wasn't for the boys, and your behaviour has always repulsed me to the point that I even loath myself for letting you get away with *this* for so long.'

No answer for a moment, until. 'Aye aye, *capitan*.'

Footsteps started plodding up the stairs. There was no urgency, no angry stomp. But then the steps paused.

'Did you remember to bring that cash home for the boys' lunches?' Joyce asked.

'Ah…'

'No, of course you didn't. It's folded neatly in a stripper's knickers, isn't it? Which one was your favourite again—Sandy wasn't it? Well, maybe she wouldn't mind feeding your children.'

The footsteps resumed, and after a couple of seconds, they could make out their mother's shadow under the crack of the door. It paused outside their room.

They froze, the air between the boys crackling with the excitement of what they'd heard and the fact that they definitely should not have heard it. There was a standoff for one long moment, an unspoken, silent balancing act. The boys held their breath in unison.

Their mother moved, and the boys ran for their beds, hyped up and buzzing.

Drama. There'd been so much in their lives that it was now a drug to them, the days monotonous unless there was some kind of a fall out or incident.

And this was one to savour.

33

QUINT WAS UP with the larks, with a Christmas morning-level of excitement he'd not felt in years. He'd left Wendy in bed, one curtain open just how she liked it in the mornings so she could gently pull back to consciousness with the rising of the sun. Now, he was bounding down the stairs with a bounce that served primarily to remind him just how dour his life had become—not because of what was in it, moreover thanks to his outlook. He was aware he'd become a bit of a git, and he'd embraced it, furrowing the rut of gittishness ever deeper with each mope, frown and sneer.

He didn't even pause for coffee, or venture into the kitchen, rather heading straight to the front door and throwing it open, embracing the gold dawn light as it crept over the treetops around the estate. The day was starting beautifully, with just a hint of frost on the lawn grass at the bottom of the porch steps and either side of the path, lending a jewel-encrusted sheen. The houses around were quiet, dormant, still asleep themselves. It was pleasant, and he stuck to the porch, not needing to venture any further from the house.

The front of their house was wrapped by a well-appointed, American-style porch, about five feet deep, across the entire frontage—except that, unlike a traditional wooden-style porch in the US of A, this one was made of red brick pillars to match the house itself, and grey stone slabs. Quint walked briskly to the farthest pillar, on the corner of the front of the house, where seven feet up he had hung the hunting camera by passing the attachment loop around the column. It had been positioned out facing the front garden and the street, its unblinking lens watching all before it dispassionately. He reached up, unclipped the loop buckle, and eased it down with the kind of care that would suit an injured bird.

He checked to see if he'd been seen, and once noting the coast was clear, marched back inside.

BACK IN THE kitchen, the kettle on and bowl of sugar free Alpen poured, he checked the rear monitor on the trail cam, powering it up. He had set it up to be motion-activated, so that anything that passed in front of its field of vision would switch it on and start recording automatically. He thumbed the menu button, and navigated to last night's recordings.

There were two of them. Two video files, with dark thumbnails, peered back up at him from the tiny screen.

He felt a tingling surge from the back of his scalp to the base of his balls, a crackle of excitement and glee. This was evidence collection, just like the old days. And he had *something*.

The kettle clicked off, the water boiled, but he ignored it, and pressed play on the first recording of the two. It immediately began moving, the screen filling with grey shapes. Quint was momentarily crestfallen, thinking that something had gone wrong, but he soon realised that the grey shapes on the screen was his front lawn, the road beyond, and on the left side of the screen, the next pillar along. And as soon as he realised it, a pair of bright lights swung left to right across the screen. A car, navigating the road.

The instincts of Quint's former profession sprang back to life, as his police-hewn attention to detail started noting the cars vitals. Dark, four door saloon, nice body shape, possibly a Mercedes. He couldn't make out the registration number, but was sure he'd be able to if he put the video on a bigger screen and paused it at the right time. The speed it was going suggested it was rushing past and headed to the end of the street. The penny didn't even need to drop, as it was already there.

This was just that damn politician returning home.

Perturbed and a little disappointed, he waited until the end of the clip, which finished after five further seconds of inactivity on the screen, and immediately started the second one.

It was identical in composition to the first, with nothing obviously amiss. Quint's excitement restored with every passing second of anticipation. He waited. Nothing.

He was about to turn the machine off when something tiny on the screen caught his eye. A slight fluctuation right in the middle of the screen, off down the street. A second passed, and it grew ever so slightly, the bobbing becoming more pronounced. It was coming towards the camera, down the street along Broadoak. He waited further, and his breath got caught in his gullet when he saw that the thing jittering along the street was somebody's head. Somebody, in their corner of an uninhabited estate, with no reason to come in unless you lived there, was walking down their road.

As the person got closer, it became obvious that the head was bald, and the person it belonged to was marching with a purposeful yet odd gait, as if one leg was slightly shorter than the other. The right leg was overcompensating for the left. The clothes on the person were barely discernible thanks to the low light conditions, but they wore a dark jogging suit. And as unclear as a lot of the physical details of this visitor were, it was clearly not someone who lived on Broadoak.

He ran through all the residents in his mind. Definitely none of them. When the figure had walked across the screen and was out of sight, and the usual five seconds of stillness ticked by before the clip ended, the screen went back to the menu.

Confused, Quint found himself back looking at the thumbnails on the screen, and that's when he saw that the file names beneath them included the time and date of recording. The first one was the day's date at 2.32am. The second one with their hairless visitor was at 3.48am.

Quint sat back and assessed the situation. Maybe the bloke had just got lost. Maybe he was the site security which they'd been promised, which would be somewhat underwhelming, especially if they wore such unofficial attire. Maybe it was one of Fletcher's angry constituents. Quint knew just how bad his press was. He gradually came round to thinking it was interesting and nothing more, and was quietly disappointed he hadn't caught that bloody Grace or her stupid dog doing something they shouldn't.

He resolved to have another go later, after dutifully filing the evidence on his home computer. Once a cop, always a cop.

34

ON THE PATENTED Fletcher scale of shocking hangovers, he was enduring a solid 9.8 out of a possible ten. His skin felt like he'd been smothered in chip fat, and he could smell his own foul fug of BO and part-digested liquor, despite the shower he'd already had. And atop it all, seared into the very capillaries of his nostrils, was the stink of that godawful Poundland body spray Sandy liked to wear—which he found profoundly arousing despite himself. He'd bought her some more up-market Armani stuff, but she never wore it at The Sin Bin, the club she worked at, telling him: 'that'd be like putting on your best knickers to nip to Tesco's'. He hadn't pressed her on it, nor was he thrilled by the implications of her comment, but that other *odour* she used was so strong with citrus and musk, that it turned him on at a moment's notice—so much so that he'd once got a raging boner at a fruit stall. Not very ministerial.

He'd got four hours sleep before dragging a razor over his cheeks and leaning against the bathroom wall while searing hot water singed off the top layer of his epidermis. Teeth scrubbed (amid a few gags when he prodded a bit too far back down his throat thanks to his shaky hands), new suit back on, and out the door he went—stepping over the downed plant pot fragments. He'd become a master of hiding hangovers, and like an elite combat operative scopes out all the possible exits on entering a new environment, Fletcher did the same with bins, bathrooms and bushes in case he needed to skip off for a tactical vom. He knew where every trash can and toilet was in Westminster. Tic-tacs always in his pocket, covering a multitude of sins.

He marched straight across the empty street to the West's house, and rang the bell. He'd tried yesterday to get the neighbourhood watch approved, which was all fine, but it turned out they'd have to wait a month or so for the start-up cash to be released. That wouldn't do at all—not if nights like yesterday's were going to be a regular feature. The wet rag man-of-the house answered, looking very much like he was about to head out also, and would be in a rush.

Perfect, though Fletcher, flashing his best polling-station grin.

'Morning,' said Peter. 'All ok?' His hair was freshly styled and toast crumbs hung perilously at the corners of his mouth.

'Good morning, Peter. I'm so sorry to disturb and won't keep you long—I'm just after another signature?' replied Fletcher.

'Another?' said West, insecurity obvious. Fletcher loved it and pressed on.

'Yes, I'm terribly sorry to put you out, it's just that I missed something at our previous signing session. About ensuring we are up and running with the support of the national network as quickly as possible. Or have I misunderstood your enthusiasm for the project? I'm very sorry if I have.' *That's it. Make them want to please you, no matter what it is.* 'It's just admin, and if we are partners, you and me, I need both signatories for it to be official, remember?' Fletcher wasted no time in switching from apology to dejection. 'I must have misunderstood, please forgive me, I will take no more of your—'

West mellowed immediately, yet still retained the fraught shoulder shape of a man in a rush. 'No, of course, I remember. Do you have it on you?'

'Of course. If it's no trouble, and I assume it won't be.' Fletcher brought his hand up, holding an envelope. 'Right there.'

A pen soon followed, a document was withdrawn and pressed against the door frame, as Fletcher pointed to a line below his own signature—on a council chitty for the two grand bursary. Two signatures meant two grand cash to be picked up at Fletcher's discretion. A much more satisfactory result.

It was only when Peter saw that line did he seem to pause, a hint of indecision creeping in. *Bring it home, Fletch.* 'I'm so sorry for the intrusion. But we will all be so much safer.' He hadn't needed to say anything further than the word *sorry* - as soon as he got there, the pen was moving again. The psychology of the deal always fascinated Fletcher, but more than that, the buzz of getting what you wanted was like the greatest drug, and now sat in his head along with Sandy's cheap body spray.

'Thank you,' Fletcher said, taking the paper and turning briskly. 'I'll let you know when the first meeting is scheduled, partner!' he shouted over his shoulder. A couple of seconds later, during which time he could feel Peter West's bemused stare on his back, the door shut. Job done.

As he crossed the tarmac, Fletcher adjusted himself. Seemed he'd got excited again.

35

THERE WAS NOTHING else to say—this buggy was proper shit on unpaved roads. Unless the tarmac was spirit level smooth, or the gravel fine as sand, it bounced about like poor Olivia was strapped to a pneumatic drill. Christian knew there were fancier buggies—had known it when they bought this shoddy thing— but budget constraints, especially with the big move on the horizon, were a genuine thing for he and David, and no longer just ghostly concerns of those in distant social circles.

Served them right for buying a fancy new build before a referendum on the country's continued inclusion in the European Union—and especially before anyone in the country (or the government for that matter) knew what the true implications of leaving the EU would be. Pennies suddenly had to be counted, while everything felt just that bit more expensive.

Christian quickly cast the thought aside—he and his husband had had countless conversations, done endless sums and debated the matter back and forth from all viewpoints they could think of. Too much brain power had been wasted on the topic of Brexit, and nothing would become clearer stewing on it now. What was done was done.

Besides, Christian had a mission. Against all possible odds granted by her mode of transport, Olivia was asleep soundly. Whisps of blond hair danced around the edges of her woollen bobble hat. Christian had wrapped them both up accordingly for this father-daughter day, which was four days one week, one the next, and repeated onwardly. Their employers had been excellent, extremely considerate and only too happy to help the men achieve their goals of finally managing to have a family and juggle their careers. Today David was in work, and it was to be a late one too, with his bosses giving him a chance of some much-needed overtime.

The frost of the morning had lifted, and as soon as it had, the pair had taken to the pavements of the estate, some finished, some like this one definitely not, and set off to find out just what the security of this place truly was. They knew they were paying for some, but just what service it was, Christian wanted to know—especially in light of things being not quite as serene as they had hoped. Something was amiss, definitely.

Words don't just appear on baby monitors.

Baby clothes didn't just appear in hedges.

Shit didn't just fly up windows.

The words he'd heard were bothering him most because even he was beginning to doubt himself now, so much so that, with his memory of the moment scarred by tiredness, he was no longer entirely sure what he heard. But his first instincts—of fear, panic and somehow *revulsion*—remained the strongest. And if he couldn't get answers as to what had caused it, he wanted answers as to what was being done to keep them all safe. This was what he hoped to find in the hut dead ahead, in the central reservation of the entrance road to the estate, directly beneath those grand gates.

The hut was little more than a wooden box with windows on three sides and a door on the last, wide enough for a chair to sit in—but he had never seen anyone either inside, by or around it. The wood itself was unfinished, unpainted and gave off a temporary air. Christian didn't expect anyone to be there, but he thought, given its unimpressive condition, he could get in and find something with a phone number on it. There'd have to be something there—something he could use.

The central reservation was a muddy strip held in place by curbs on either side, and paving slabs up the centre. It was a poor excuse, and the whole thing looked like it was merely a placeholder for a much more impressive edifice when the rest of the estate was finished. It filled Christian with approximately zero confidence.

As he got there, the mist finally lifted, and he could see that, true to form, it was empty. He looked left and right, and checked on his daughter—still sound asleep. With his right foot, he clicked the buggy wheel brake on and checked that it wouldn't roll anywhere on the pavement. He then hopped across the empty road to the hut, and looked through the windows.

Inside was not nearly as bad as the outside, and came as somewhat of a surprise. There was a small desk built into the wall, albeit out of that same shitty crumbling wood, yet above it was a bank of four plug sockets, some of them in use. Overhead, there was a dim, dangling bulb. This thing had power.

The air was still and pensive, but that could just have been Christian's heightened sense of anxiety, knowing he was about to do something he wasn't supposed to.

He tried the hut door, and the cheap black metal handle clanked. Somewhere, in the trees beyond where Olivia was parked up, a bird responded with a soft coo. Christian couldn't help but pause. He was freaking himself out.

He blew air out, creating his own little mist cloud, and opened the cabin.

There was a chair. Nothing on the little drop-down desk. Two of the plugs were in use, and he followed the black snaking cables down into the recess beneath the table top, right through the partially closed zip of a sports holdall. There was nothing else in sight.

Plumbing the depths of just how naughty he felt he could be, he reached for the zipper on the bag, and pulled it to the sharp *strip* of metal teeth parting. Inside, were a couple of torches, and a load of batteries. One of the cable ends led to nothing, plugged into nowhere, but was clearly a phone charger thanks to the obvious connector on the end, just like Christian's back at home. The other was plugged into a black box with smooth edges and a green LED blinking in the corner, next to an unlit red one. The front of the box slid back, and revealed batteries— green, rechargeable ones. And underneath them were other packets, a black fleece, a couple of spare torches and a head torch. It looked like the tool kit of an overnight security guard, which heartened Christian a great deal.

So there was someone here. And they appeared to be doing something at least. But where the bollocks were they?

Christian had one last look for paperwork, a quick rummage through the bag, but found nothing, although he conceded that the phone itself would have been nice, and if it were here he'd have to go through it if it was unlocked.

Christian caught himself. *The phone. The bag.*

Whoever it was must be there somewhere—nearby. Maybe they were even patrolling the site.

He was suddenly all too aware of his minor wrongdoing, so he hastily put everything back where he'd found it and shut the cabin door. Back at Olivia's side, where she was still merrily miles away, Christian took in the surroundings.

He didn't know for sure just how big the Blackstoke site was, but if the advertising bunkum were to be believed, there was room and scope for two hundred homes to be built, similar to theirs. If their little corner had five houses on it, and that was of a fair size as it was, then simply multiplying that inhabited area by forty, well, you had… a big area. A needle in a haystack kind of size, when it came to trying to find a solitary person.

Reluctantly, Christian turned back in the direction of Broadoak and home—but stopped in realisation.

He could take the car.

See how many roads they'd managed to get finished.

36

WITH A MORNING off for a dentist appointment, Alice had never been in the house by herself before. She was old enough, of course, but with everyone out at work, the shops and school, she felt that solitude with a surprising keenness. She had been left alone at their old house so many times, but that was then. This was unfamiliar, strange, didn't feel like home yet. That would change very soon, she felt.

She stood on the top floor landing, looking down the gap between the winding staircase, all the way to the bottom. Whenever, as a family, they had stayed in a hotel, which admittedly hadn't been that frequently, she had done this exact same thing. Ask to go to the highest floor the hotel had, and look down the stairwell drop to see the bottom. Sometimes, the sights had made her dizzy, and she remembered one particular hotel in Newcastle where the mosaic tiling on the bottom floor had been so far below she couldn't even see the grouting that held it in place. She held the bannister extra tight that day. Consequently, it was with a sudden wash of pride that this was her home now. Her family, lived in a place that had its own high coiling staircase down which she could ponder.

Suddenly aware that she had the run of the place, she moved down the stairs to go and have a proper snoop around. She'd barely been in any other room than her own bedroom on the top floor (her choice) and she wanted to have a good snoop. Where was her brother's porn? For example. She heard that all teenage boys had porn stashed somewhere, and Alice had never actually seen any yet. She didn't know whether it would repulse her, or if she'd find it interesting. She had no basis for comparison in this regard, aside from the notion that she felt it may carry some sort of instructive quality—far more informative than the oily music video obviousness and crass suggestion of the news media. She obviously knew all about reproduction and its mechanics, she just didn't have much of an understanding of the fine details. This accompanied an obvious recognition of feelings within herself that she was scantly able to admit. But they only got so far, ending with a question mark. What did it all mean? Why was it such a preoccupation? And why was she, so steadfast and bold in so many other areas, bound by the same inevitability? She was aware that some other girls her age had done stuff by now, but on this topic, unlike some others, Alice was fairly happy to be behind the curve.

She bounded down the steps two at a time, suddenly dizzy-headed with the freedom of such a large space, and all the secrets it may contain. First stop, her brother's room.

It was about three times as big as his old one, in a similar upgrade to Alice's own circumstances. Massive telly being the new addition. Double bed too. The walls were white, and he hadn't bothered putting up any posters yet. It felt clinical to Alice, as had her own room when she'd first entered it. Since then, she'd put her own aesthetic slant on the space, almost covering every square inch of white with postcards, photographs, posters, and those off little corners of white she couldn't manage to cover with her mural-work, she Blutacked bright feathers from an old feather boa she found in one of the boxes. She had no idea whose it was, but the odd feather really wasn't going to make a difference.

Where would I hide something if I was Jake? If I was a daft little boy who'd just opened his eyes to grown up things?

There was a bedside table in an expensive looking oak. Two drawers under a square table top, and under that, a little smooth-edged opening where the stunted curved legs emerged from.

Big sister was confident she'd worked little brother out.

She put her fingers under and into the gap, and her fingers immediately grazed paper. She grabbed and pulled them out, as her mind raced as to what the title of the magazine might be. Something astonishingly crass and childish no doubt. Big Jigglers. Or Whopping Boobers. She laughed, despite herself.

But it was none of these things. It was a sheaf of papers, rag tag, folded in an array of ways. Different sizes too. She pulled them out. The top one had a crudely drawn tombstone on it, with RIP WEST written on the front. The grave below was marked out in that same blue biro, tufts of grass around the edges, and sat on the supposedly freshly moved earth, were a pair of round spectacles.

37

CHRISTIAN WAS AMAZED, now that he'd taken the time to investigate the streets and turning circles of Blackstoke, that nothing else was even remotely ready. On the roads close to their cul-de-sac, homes were half built, scaffolding in place, with no workers to match, while the further he drove away, the less and less was done, until there were merely dirt tracks with plots marked out in the grass. And then it was acres of untouched woodland.

It's a weekday, Christian mused as he peered through the windshield. *Where are they? And what have they been doing all this time?*

These roads, only a couple of moments' drive from his home, didn't look like a development years in the making. It looked like everyone had downed tools, or that the COMUDEV money pit funding this whole thing had abruptly run dry. Christian couldn't make head nor tail of it, and before long, the road surfaces themselves reflected that abandonment.

Tarmac became rough stone, then dirt. He was a mile from home now, he could see on the onboard satnav, which showed him as a red arrow in a vast green space. It clearly needed updating, but what would it be updated to? There was barely anything here. He followed the dirt road he found himself on, as it began to wind its way through high old trees, and it struck him that the extent of the roadway planning here was merely driving some kind of earth mover through the undergrowth, shifting it to one side so machinery could pass through.

Christian's car, a sleek Mercedes built for a smooth commute, wasn't suited to the terrain, so he stopped, and tried to take in his surroundings. There really was barely anything on this huge patch of development aside from their beautiful little road. The rest was good intentions at best.

Intrigued despite the nudge of disappointment, he wanted to press on on foot—then remembered not just baby Olivia snoozing in the back, but the crap buggy that wouldn't get them anywhere.

He squinted through the trees down the dirt road, deep into the heart of the vast acreage he knew the development comprised. He'd come back another day. He'd have to.

He started a three-point turn, and as he spun the car sharply to the right on the first of those three movements, he noticed something shimmering beyond the tree tops. Of course, the shimmering was merely breeze giving life to the leaves of the canopy, but he could clearly see something solid beyond.

It was high and angular. His interest hooked, he pulled the car straight again, and forged slowly ahead along the dirt track into the trees.

It didn't take long before he came upon another car. To his amazement, it was a white van with the word *security* printed on its panelled flanks, alongside mud sprayed up from the track itself. He pulled up behind it, and got out, taking a quick glance at Olivia. Fast asleep.

Christian glanced around. There was nobody here, although the trees were close on either side. Could never be too careful, and he was on edge enough, so he pulled out his keys—when his eyes caught up with what was on the glass his daughter was beyond. The reflection of what was in the sky behind him.

He turned, craning his neck upwards. Tall, and cresting the peaks of the surrounding greenery, in long-faded whitewash, was an observation tower.

38

LITTLE SHITS, she thought.

Alice checked the other papers, and it was suddenly crystal clear and staring her in the face. Her little brother had been in school a mere couple of days, but he was already the target of relentless bullying. She felt an immediate boil inside.

She'd kill them. Whoever it was.

There were over twenty sheets in her hands, all different pens and handwriting. So many kids were in on it. This was supposed to be an elite school, where only high achieving kids went. What on earth were they teaching them there? It seemed that money couldn't buy class, no matter the price. Alice was suddenly filled with a sibling pride she'd never known before, in an urgent rush. He'd simply shouldered it, her brother. He hadn't made any fuss whatsoever. You wouldn't even know anything was wrong, but of course, it had got to him. You didn't keep reams of stuff that didn't matter to you. And he'd just kept a lid on it.

Alice felt for him. Felt his pain. In the hurdy-gurdy churn of the day to day, where every device, large or small, yelped and bleated for your attention, it was easy to let the important bits slip by. Let the real fundaments of humanity float along with nary a glance. Her and her brother kept themselves to themselves, but their bond—or at least Alice's with him, in that particular direction—had solidified quietly in the background.

She resolved to pay more attention, and offer him support. What big sister wouldn't? And she'd also properly fuck up the kids that were sending him this crap. To that, she was committed.

She made sure the evidence of Jacob's torture was in the right order and stashed just as she'd found it, and walked out of the room. She didn't want to snoop anymore, and now felt bad for even contemplating it. Heading down to the ground floor, she took the last flight of stairs, then noticed something through the window on her way down—the back window, which gazed over the rear aspect of the house. The garden was unimpressive, especially in the grey morning light, which in itself could knock the sheen off anything, and was waiting for the stroke and sweep of landscaping. It was a mere three-sided square attached to the back of the house, walled by freshly-creosoted fence panels.

It was none of this that had caught her eye, however. Her attention was caught instead on the thing that had appeared in the middle of it all. Something about a metre tall, a thin pole, like a bird table—except there wasn't a cheery little feeding station on the top. No, there was something off about the shape that sat there.

Alice ran down the stairs, straight into the kitchen and out of the back door, tiptoeing onto the cold patio flags in bare feet. She was drawn to it, whatever it was, and without thinking found herself walking onto the fresh turf, the morning dew needling the soles of her feet.

As she got closer, her stomach roiled, as she processed the three colours of the shape, dangling on top of the pole. Black. Orange. Vivid red.

She stopped a yard from the obscene monument, feeling suddenly too young to ever see such a thing.

It was a black strut from a metal fence railing, exactly like the ones which lined the estate, pushed into the turf to stand upright. At the top was a sharp point, rendering the pole a solid obsidian spear, and on that point was a blood-soaked tangle of twisted fur. She could make out a tiny foot on a leg that was bent impossibly upward, and a pink marbled section that looked like uncooked chicken. There was a shard of face, missing parts, but she could see one little jet-black bead embedded in the hair. An *eye*. The fur itself dangled loosely, an orange stripe right through it, dripping blood onto the grass in fat drops.

It was Jacob's latest guinea pig. Half-skinned, half-twisted apart, skewered on a spike.

Alice's world span with sudden violence, and before she could even compute her shock, she was on her knees expelling her breakfast onto the cut green grass.

Gasping for air, choking the bile back down, she suddenly felt very alone and exposed. It was the quiet. Everything had gone so still. No sound from the rutted field behind, no rustle from the trees. No bird song.

And then a low hum, behind her. A murmur, on a solid note. Deep, but not too deep.

She began to tremble.

She wanted her mum.

The hum quickly dropped into something guttural, primal. A growl.

And she felt a thud on the back of her head, heavy and deep, which immediately brought a sensation of strange detachment.

Then nothing.

39

CHRISTIAN SKIPPED ACROSS the mud to the driver's side of the van, parked at the bottom of the tower, and peered inside—only to find it empty. A handful of newspapers rested on the passenger seat, but there was nothing else in there to indicate signs of life.

He turned to peer up at the tower. He guessed it was maybe fifty feet in height, with a small room on the top, lined with windows, and a railing around which one could walk and peer out on the open air. Below, and reaching all the way to the ground, was a spiral staircase, tightly wound.

Suddenly begot by nerves, he took a second. What on earth was this all about? What was it for?

It looked old, the white paint on the little shack up there dirty and tired, while the metal work propping it heavenwards was chipped, scuffed up. It had been there a long time, quite clearly. Decades, at least.

Christian suddenly felt isolated, and very uneasy. So he shouted, as loud as he dared.

'Hello?'

No response, just the shush of the breeze. After a moment, he tried again.

'Anybody there?'

He waited as his thoughts drifted to climbing the stairs and going to have a look for himself. Just because the car was here, didn't necessarily mean that the driver was up there, right?

Christian looked around. There was literally nothing else here. Just a big tower in the woods, next to a dirt track.

Then he heard a door open with a squeak of hinges, and a clunk of footsteps. He looked up, and a man appeared at the nearside railing of the tower platform, gazing down at him.

'Hello?' the man shouted.

'Hi, yes!' Christian shouted, waving his arms. From what he could see, the man was grey-haired and moustached in the same tone. Sixties, maybe—and he wore a blue shirt. Jowls for days.

'Can I help you?' the man shouted.

'I'm a resident here, just wondering what was here, and… well, I was looking for you, if I'm honest. Are you security?'

'That's me,' said the man. Christian couldn't get a good look at the guy, because the bright greyness of the sky behind offered him a soft silhouette.

'Great, can I come up?'

'No, health and safety. I'm just observing from up here.'

What he was *observing*, Christian didn't know. The completed part of the development was a mile from here, but yet again, his interest was sparked, snagged and he found himself walking to the bottom step. 'I'll only be a minute,' he said. He was good at this, getting his own way. Sometimes, if you wanted to do something, the best way was with a grand smile, a happy demeanour and to just do it anyway.

'Wait a minute…' shouted the man at the top, but Christian couldn't hear any more over the clang of his footsteps. It took him longer than expected to reach the top, such was the tight coil of the staircase, but within a couple of minutes, he found himself emerging onto the platform, to be met by the man himself, who had been waiting for him. 'You shouldn't be up here,' he said gruffly, the moustache quivering side to side as he pursed his lips and worked his jaw. 'What do you want?'

Christian gave his brightest smile, and stepped out towards the railing. Suddenly aware of the height, he grabbed it with both hands wide apart. 'Wow,' he breathed, as he gazed out. You couldn't really describe the view as impressive, but the height gave a perspective of the area Christian simply hadn't experienced before—and in turn this brought understanding and comprehension to the development's geography. 'I didn't know it was so big.'

The other man sighed and joined him, but Christian was already moving, walking around to take in the views on the other four sides. Trees in most directions, but they were punctuated by clearings. 'Blackstoke is a big area,' he said, when he finally caught up with him.

'Sorry, I just… I've been trying to make sense of the layout of the place, then I saw your van, and this… Oh, I'm Christian.' He offered the security guard his hand, which the man took.

'Jeff,' said the man, taking his hand. He wasn't smiling, but he wasn't cold in his demeanour either.

'I live on Broadoak.'

'Settling in alright?'

'Yes, so far so good. For the most part.' Christian's mind was racing now, that childlike sense of story coming alive like it so often did. 'What is this?'

'It's exactly what it looks like. It's where I come and watch over things.'

'And, where are our houses exactly?'

Jeff pointed off in a north easterly direction, and, with a squint, Christian could make out the roofs of Broadoak. 'Ah I see. Thank you.' Questions sprang forth in his head. *Why on earth would you come way out here to keep an eye on something that's all the way over there?* He didn't ask that one, but did ask another. 'How long has this been here?'

'Years. Like I said, it's a big property.' Christian regarded him properly. He was weathered and portly, his powder blue uniform shirt gripping him snugly. But there was a cast to his gaze. A veil over it. Suspicion.

'We've had a couple of things been going on, over our way. I wondered if you could come take a look, put our mind at ease.'

The change in Jeff was as obvious as night to day, with no time for dawn in between. 'What?' His eyes were suddenly bright, and wider, revealing they were as grey as the strands on his head.

'Yeah, I wanted to see if there had been any other reports, anything else out of the ordinary?'

'Not that I know of,' he said. The answer didn't tally with his sudden animation.

'Are you sure?' Christian felt stupid asking it, but found he simply couldn't avoid it.

'Of course I'm sure.' Jeff's tone darkened, and became more dismissive.

'Well would you mind coming over and letting me talk you through our concerns?'

'Our?'

'Yeah, there's been more than one… complaint.'

'Oh.' That seemed to trouble Jeff, whose expression adopted a sudden hangdog quality.

Christian's eyes were drawn to a vast gap in the trees, behind Jeff's shoulder. 'What's that?'

'What?'

Christian pointed with an outstretched finger. '*That.*' There was, a few hundred yards away, a huge clearing in the woodland, and, although from this position he couldn't make out the ground, he saw that it was a gigantic space that had been cut away—and further to that, he could just make out the peaks of piles of rubble within that space. A number of them—a miniature mountain range of discarded stone and upheaval.

'Ah, that's—'

Jeff's words were interrupted by a car door closing, a soft thunk-click of metal and catch carried forth on the wind. Christian's stomach dropped, and carried on falling.

The car. He'd locked it. *Hadn't he?*

He sprinted over to the other side of the watchtower platform, overlooking the car below, and looked down. The car was sat there as normal.

'What?' said Jeff, catching up with him.

'Who else is out here?' Christian stammered.

'There shouldn't be anyone.'

Before the words had left Jeff's mouth, Christian was sprinting down the steps—why were they so close? *Why so tight?* In a couple of agonising moments, he'd reached the bottom. He didn't pause, running straight for the car, his shoulders wracking with tension.

He saw his nightmare through the window before he threw open the rear door anyway.

Olivia was gone.

40

WENDY FENCHURCH PICKED up the tin bucket at the back door, and ambled round the side pathway of the house to the back garden. It was half-full of potting compost, not too heavy, but she still perhaps should have asked Quint to come and take it for her. Shouldn't take too many chances with her back, not at her age. He'd brought it to the back door for her initially, before retreating to whatever scheme he was working on in his office. He thought he was being so clever with that new camera of his, and it made Wendy smile. The fact that it was Wendy herself letting him feel like that, by not saying anything to burst his bubble, made her smile even more. He'd gotten himself in a tizz, and he needed to work it out, plain and simple. Burn off that excess energy. Besides, it kept him busy.

She wandered down the pathway, leaning heavily to one side to counter the weight of the bucket, taking easy sure steps. She'd been sat on the back step, using the compost to pot a set of indoor house plants in quaint ceramic planters. It was the perfect spot, where the soil could be swept out the back door easily enough. She surveyed the back garden as she walked, looking for potential, rather than the present. There was a lot they could do with this blank space, but it was definitely a question of first things first. Come summer time, it would be a wonderful project to bask in.

She reached the back potting shed, which she had specifically asked to be installed before their arrival, having paid a rather handsome premium for the privilege, and opened the door. Out wafted an earthen smell of freshly coated timber, compost and engine oil—all the key ingredients for an outbuilding such as this, and a fragrance of comfort for those green-fingered enough to recognise them. They promised solitude and honest work.

She was so happy it was theirs. Their previous terraced home hadn't offered much opportunity for her to practice any truly ambitious horticultural exploits, but now, the gloves were off. Unless they were green, in which case, they were certainly *on*.

She walked to the right-hand counter, over which a window looked out upon her fledgling domain, and placed the bucket on top with a heave, sitting it alongside the carefully laid out rows of pansies they'd bought only yesterday at the local garden centre. They all still sat in their plastic nursery planters, waiting to be given their proper homes. It made Wendy smile.

As she began pulling out yet more little pots, and filled them with soil from the bucket with a small trowel, she noticed a second odour. A sickly sweetness. Just a soupçon, over the other notes in the shed. She moved to check the pansies, one at a time, sure that she must have been sold a rotten one accidentally. However, they were all in perfect condition. Some looked a little withered, granted, but on average, they were a good-looking crop.

There was a sharp scrape behind her, like a shoe on gravel, and abruptly, she felt a sharp pain in her neck. It was there only an instant before the pain gave immediate way to a dullness. It moved to numbness, which flooded up the back of her head, and round to her jaw, which she felt sag—just like her knees, which promptly buckled. She folded onto her back, and felt no pain from the impact either. Lying there, on the floor, she couldn't feel a thing—but she could hear a *spurt spurt* just below her chin. With every spurt, she detected a disembodied pressure, somewhere around her.

Her eyes could still move, and she looked as far down her body as she could. The handle of the trowel—the brand-new trowel she had excitedly bought last night to plant her pansies with—was sticking out of her neck. And the spurting was blood, her own blood, gushing out in streams up past the handle, steaming mid-flight as it hit the crisp winter air.

As she watched it go, she saw something else, hovering above her—but she couldn't focus on it. It moved towards her at speed, before she realised it was a bare foot, filthy in a way she could barely imagine. As soon as she worked out what it was, it connected with her face, right in the centre, and everything went numb and off centre, a shattered kaleidoscope of nerve-endings. The foot came down again and again. And again and again. Until all she could think of, was her pansies.

41

PETER HAD ONLY just got home from work, he was immediately met on the drive by Pam, who came out of the house to see him. This never happened. Or hadn't happened in a long time, so it took him by surprise—so much so that, he found himself on edge before he even exited the car.

'Have you seen Alice?' she asked, her eyes stricken. Her posture was wrought with tension, her shoulders jutting her arms out at near right angles. Shouldering his bag, he stepped out onto the driveway.

'No, I've been at work all day,' he said, glancing at the house behind, his eyes scanning the windows as if his daughter might just be sat there looking at them, enjoying this sudden fuss.

'We've been back a couple of hours, and she hasn't come home from school.'

'Did you call the school?' Peter walked to the house, the first prangs of anxiety taking root and blooming.

'Of course, but the office was shut. She usually gets back about 4, I gave it until 4.45, but they'd obviously gone.'

Peter checked his own watch. Five twenty. 'Okay, well, have you tried her phone?'

'No answer.' Pam's voice was breaking.

'Shit. Ummm…' He stood there on the step to their house, running a hand through his hair. 'We need to go looking for her.'

'Do you think I should call the police?'

Peter thought about it. Teenage girls and lengths of time

missing and all that. The telly shows always said something about them not being able to declare someone missing for yadda yadda however long—but this was a teenager. And it was *his* teenager. Fighting against the innate Britishness of not wanting to cause a fuss, he nodded. 'I think it couldn't harm.'

There was a screech and a sweep of lights swiped across them both, and they both turned to see a car appear coming down the street at speed. It was plush with a luxurious black paint job, going far too fast, and stopped outside the Fletcher house opposite. The politician himself immediately hopped out. This conspicuous entrance had a hypnotic effect on the Wests, who could only stand there and watch. Fletcher saw them and immediately crossed the road and walked up their drive.

'I've got it!' he said, pulling some paperwork from his inner jacket pocket. 'All approved!'

'What is?' asked Peter.

'The Neighbourhood Watch of course, partner!' Fletcher smiled and clasped Peter's shoulder holding the piece of paper out like the Olympic torch. Peter absent-mindedly reached for it, but Fletcher whisked it away straight back into his pocket.

'Oh it's just admin Peter, nothing to see,' he shushed, and Peter wondered if this man ever did anything that wasn't deeply embellished in political flourish.

'Okay, well—' Peter said, but Pam butted in.

'Have you seen Alice? On the road, walking up here?'

'Alice…' Fletcher let the word hang, his eyes asking the question.

'Our daughter. Fifteen?'

'Oh yes, the eldest, yes?'

'Yes.'

'No, I'm afraid not.'

Pam ran her own hand through her own hair this time and

muttered: 'Jesus.'

'What would you do?' asked Peter, stepping forward, his arms and appealing in a question of his own.

'How do you mean? What's happened?'

'She's missing,' Pam blurted, urgently.

'She hasn't come home from school,' Peter clarified. 'She had a dentist appointment at lunch, then was supposed to come straight there. But she's not here.'

'Well, did she make the appointment?' Fletcher asked.

Pam and Peter looked at each other, epiphany dawning across each mind simultaneously. 'I'll call the surgery,' said Pam, turning to the front door hurriedly, when another screech, and another set of headlights carved the street in two.

This time, all three turned to see what was happening, and watched a silver saloon race down the cul-de-sac. As it got closer, Peter could make out mud on the flanks of the otherwise plush vehicle. It paused for a second outside the Lyons home, but then sped up and pulled to an abrupt stop outside the Wests.

Christian Lyons got out, sodden and muddy, his face caved by panic, his teeth bared, panting near maniacally.

'She's gone,' he panted. 'Olivia is *gone*. She's been taken.'

42

QUINT EMERGED FROM his office when he realised the sun was setting, having spent the entirety of the afternoon combing through each and every trail cam video file at double speed— looking for any sign of that bald headed figure, scampering through their neighbourhood. Alas, there had been nothing, and the evening had drawn in regardless, leaving him sat alone in darkness in the upstairs office of their home. Shutting down the computer, he rubbed his eyes with a finger poked behind both frames of his spectacles, and rose.

Emerging onto the upstairs hallway, he was confused to see that the lights were off everywhere—and with the landing carrying somewhat of a mezzanine design, offering views of the open-plan living area below, it gave him the distinct impression that the whole house was in darkness.

'Wen?' he shouted. 'Love?'

The only thing he could hear was the low hum of the fridge in the kitchen below. He shrugged, and realised she mustn't have realised the darkness herself. *I bet she's in the potting shed*, he thought, with a smile to himself. He liked the idea of that for her—that they'd have such activities to keep them occupied in their new lives here. A life with no stresses as they sailed into serious old age, or at least that was the idea.

After a brief fumble for the light switch, having failed at first to remember where it was, Quint flicked it live and the house suddenly popped to life and brightness. No Wendy in sight. He took the stairs, remarking to himself that he hadn't quite found that peaceful comforting hobby of his own yet—and he certainly hadn't managed to assuage the stress. He'd merely upped sticks and started a new investigation.

Downstairs, he entered the open living space, but couldn't find any sign of his wife. Their chairs were empty, the TV was off, no cup of tea sat half-drunk to suggest recent hospitality. He was confused, and went to the kitchen, flicking the light on as he entered. Nothing there, but even more tellingly, there weren't any of the usual things he'd expect to find. He checked his watch, the gold retirement effort the constabulary had given him. Five thirty.

They always ate at six, hell, high water, rain or shine. Forty years of it. Yet there was nothing here to suggest that. No cans out, no vegetables prepped, no chopping boards with meat prepped and diced. Just bare counters.

Except the back door was open.

Quint had attended enough burglaries to make assumptions in his head, yet couldn't make the leap to believe it. He'd been upstairs, surely he would have heard someone in the house? He checked the door. The lock was intact, the frame was spotless. Nothing had been forced or jimmied. He was confused, until he saw the light on in the potting shed, glowing softly through its windows. His chest eased, his heart fell back into place, and he smiled. Wendy really was enjoying it here. His wife was happy.

He walked down the path, smiling, with a spring in his step. 'Hey, you! Stop-out! Leave those pansies alone and let's get some tea going!'

He pushed the door of the potting shed open, and saw a sight he couldn't make sense of. His wife, Wendy, was on the floor. Her blue blouse was soaked in dark blood that had dried in parts to a dull brown. A wooden handle was protruding from her neck—above which was a pile of gristle, bone, pink jelly, blood and chunks of grey hair. A scream left his throat, a noise he had no control over, nor had ever made before—as if the horror of the sight had unlocked a new vocal capacity.

The sound was cut off, as a sort of cage was thrown over Quint's head. Short, small, like a budgie cage, but tight to his skin. It cut and scratched as it was pushed on. He tried to yank it off, but he suddenly felt a jolt of such explosive fierceness, his head and hands felt like they'd burst simultaneously.

As suddenly as it started, the assault ceased, and he found himself on his knees, his head, hands and shoulders in agony. He shouted again, and tried to pull the cage up and off over his head when, with a spasming jolt and a hiss, the shock returned. He clawed at the metal, which seemed to be exploding all around his head, but his hands exploded in a pain so severe he couldn't fathom it.

And then it stopped again, and he lay on the floor, panting. He opened his eyes, and found himself next to the remnants of his wife's head and, as the horror and revulsion hit, the assault started again. His brain began to separate from what was happening to him, such was the severity and agony of the experience, and in that brief numbness he realised that it wasn't a cage at all that he was caught in—it was the spare roll of electrical fencing that he hadn't got round to using yet. It was being turned on and off again, in some sort of sick torture.

This time, the pain and shock did not relent, and he found himself clawing maniacally at the coil, the hissing growing louder and a smell of sickly burning growing in his nostrils. Both of those things, he realised as his brain loosened him from consciousness, were down to his hands and face melting against the current surging through the very frame of the prison he found himself in, and, as he felt and smelled himself cook next to his savaged wife's body, he pleaded for it all to end soon.

With a loud bang and a sudden dousing of darkness, the assault ceased. And as Quint dropped from the waking world for good, he could have sworn the last thing he heard was a sigh of disappointment, before the black hit at last.

43

PAM HAD THE phone in her hand, ready to call the police, when the power cut struck, and the West home was plunged into a darkness that was cave deep, thanks to its suddenness.

'Is everyone alright?' Peter shouted from the hall and, at the kitchen counter, she replied in the affirmative. Just to be sure, she pulled the handset to her ear. No dial tone.

She went for her mobile, but as expected, no bars. That damn phone mast, slighting them all once more.

'Jacob,' she shouted, rounding the kitchen corner to move into the hall, guessing where she was going and doing a half decent job of it.

'Power cut?' he replied, from his bedroom, where he'd been sadly convalescing since he'd come home and found that his second guinea pig had disappeared.

'Seems that way, do you want to come down?' she said, and heard her son take the steps out of sight above her. 'Take your time, don't trip.' She was trying to stay calm, but having heard the story Christian just told them outside, it was getting harder.

'I've got a torch in my room,' Jacob said, and turned around. 'Be right down.'

As he carefully climbed back up the stairs, Peter appeared through the front door. She recognised his shape in the doorway, framed by the deep black-blue of the sky. 'Lights out on the whole street. Streetlights too. And… there was a shout. A scream maybe. Just before it. I… don't know.'

'What the hell is going on?' asked Pam, of herself, God, anybody listening.

'We need to call the police.' It was a male voice, owned by the person following Peter into the house. Christian. 'That security guard said he'd go looking himself. Said he didn't get reception either.'

'Didn't he have a radio, or something?' asked Pam.

'Said he carried it but didn't have anyone to call. He's the only security staff member on the site.'

'Well this simply will not do,' said Fletcher, another large figure entering through the doorway—one figure which Pam, frankly, could have done without. 'When I agreed to live here, I was promised a round the clock security team. Not some old fart in a cabin.'

They turned into the kitchen, Peter guiding them. Pam caught up with Christian and took his arm. She wanted to tell him that everything would be fine, but what the hell was possibly fine about a baby going missing? And not just missing—taken. In the woods right here on their estate. It made her skin crawl.

'Have you spoken to David?' she managed, trying to keep the tremor in her own voice under control.

'No, I...' Pam, with her hand on the man's back, could feel his shoulders quake. 'I wouldn't know what to say... I... I've fucked up so badly, I forgot to lock the car!'

'It's not your fault, it's not your fault,' Pam said, shushing him as she would one of her own children. One of whom was missing too. A teenage girl, and a female infant. Both missing. Was there a connection? She didn't want to think about it. Couldn't let the thought race, so she clamped it off. Alice would just be out with her new friends. Surely.

'Time for clear heads I'm afraid now, Mr Lyons,' said Fletcher, as he took a spot at the kitchen island, once again like he was the man of the house and the belle of the ball in one big queasy go.

'Fletcher, that's not helpful,' said Peter, and Pam was suddenly proud. That was the Peter she had fallen in love with. The one with backbone, and principle, amongst all the other qualities she had found so attractive.

'On the contrary Peter, it's exactly correct,' Fletcher admonished.

'Still unhelpful,' Pam interjected, backing up her husband. The fact that they were on the same team suddenly buoyed her, flushed her with hope.

They *would* find their daughter. And they *would* help Christian find his.

'Here we are,' said Peter, as a small white light appeared from his midriff, casting deep shadows off everything in the room. The silhouette of the centre island tap stretched and span on the ceiling, same with the clawed hand of bananas, as Peter placed the phone face down on the table, using the torch on the back of the device as a mini lantern, which bloomed a soft glow around the kitchen, and settled.

That's when she saw them, over by the fridge.

Two other men were in there with them. Or at least, she thought they were men. Pam screamed.

GRACE HAD BEEN walking Dewey on the entrance road to the cul-de-sac, coaxing a mile out of those shaggy old legs, when she heard the first scream. Both human and canine stopped in their tracks, and found themselves looking at each other—before they sprinted to the patch of houses on Broadoak, Dewey's exhaustion immediately forgotten.

'You heard that, didn't you, Dew?' she said, mid-stride.

They pounded the pavement until it narrowed and became easier for them both to run in the middle of the road, and round the shaded corner into Broadoak, where again, they paused, caught and confused.

Every light was off. The cul-de-sac was dead. The only light was from a silver car, down at the bottom between the biggest two houses, which had its door open, emitting the soft warmth of an interior light. The vehicle itself looked empty.

'Well that's a bit disconcerting,' said Grace. Dewey huffed in reply, before they started walking. 'Where do you think it came from?'

As they walked, and the houses shifted to meet her perspective, she could see that not one house had a light on. She fought unsettling waves of anxiety, and appealed to her sense of logic and cool.

But this didn't feel right at all.

Dewey barked and abruptly picked up speed, straining at his lead.

'Wait, wait,' she said, and pulled him back. The obedient animal paused, even though, as they both knew, if Dewey wanted to go, he could just *go* and drag Grace behind like an urban water-skier.

He barked again, and looked up at Grace.

'What is it, mate?' she asked. They were stood outside the Fenchurch house, looking up at its vast darkness. Nothing about it was inviting, but Dewey was pulling towards it.

Grace was indecisive. The neighbourly thing to do was to check on them, make sure they were alright given the obvious power outage. And dogs had that innate sense when something was amiss.

But… Quint Fenchurch had been a right twat.

To her and to Dewey.

Yet the dog was straining on his leash, looking at the house expectedly, eyes wide with concern.

'You really want to go and have a look?' she asked.

Dewey humphed again, and pulled forward slightly to emphasise the point.

'Jesus,' said Grace with resignation, looking dubiously at that short, electric fence that now ringed the lawn. She unclipped the lead. 'Just don't shit anywhere. And don't go anywhere near that fence.'

As soon as Dewey felt freedom, he was gone—but not to the front door. Instead, he took the side passageway, which led to the back of the house.

Grace panicked, and ran after him. If Quint Fenchurch saw Dewey off the lead and in his very garden, that would be that. And as she rounded the corner, she realised why Dewey was so excited—and her panic doubled. There was the growing odour of grilled meat coming from the back garden. The quaint little Fenchurches must be having a barbecue—and her giant dog was about to bound straight into it.

'Dewey,' she shouted. '*Dew!*'

Images appeared of her wolfhound crashing into their happy al fresco dining scene, snatching sausages like a ravenous scraggly grey horse with sharp teeth. They disappeared just as quickly—when she found the rear garden empty. It was dark, and the smell… wasn't right.

Dewey was heading straight for the shed at the back, while Grace pulled out her phone to activate the torch app. Something was very wrong. And the darkness wasn't helping.

As Dewey got to the closed shed door, she called him off with a firm command of 'stop.' The good dog sat on his haunches, looking at the door and whining.

Grace stood next to him, and gingerly tried the handle. A

simple drop lock, she twisted, and it opened—as tendrils of smoke eagerly fingered through the opening gap, reaching into the cold night air. With it, came an unholy stink.

Grace felt a dread she had never experienced before, as if she was brushing alongside death, in perilously close proximity to her own frail mortality. She felt like prey.

Dewey pushed forward again, and she commanded him to be still once more.

She cracked the door open, and looked inside, pulling the torch light into the slight gap in the door frame to see the most unholy sight she'd ever witnessed.

PETER WANTED TO ask who they were, but found the question pointless. What he really wanted to ask was *what* they were. There was something altogether animalistic about the two men in the kitchen at Iron Rise. Animal and predatory.

'We can work something out,' he said, raising his palms.

They didn't reply.

Their faces were cruel and off-kilter. A pair of Picassos come to life, certain things in the right place, other things slightly off or misshapen. Eyes so dark they were almost black, skin pale as emulsion. One was the size of a regular guy, maybe five ten or so, while the other was bigger by some way. Basketball tall. So tall, in fact, that his face was high in the shadow, almost at the ceiling. Wide in the shoulders, although lanky. Physically terrifying. They both wore filthy jogging suits, with the size emblazoned on the breast in black letters reading BIG.

'Man,' the smaller one said abruptly, in an unsure rasping gurgle, as if he was trying out the word for the very first time. He looked directly at Peter, the blacks of his eyes unnaturally wide and searching, so much so that Peter could make out no iris. The word chilled Peter to his very core.

The smaller one shifted gaze in a reptilian slide to Pam. 'Woman,' he said in that same hiss. Suddenly, Peter began to feel abject dread regarding the whereabouts of his daughter.

'Man,' said someone else, and it took Peter a second to realise it was Fletcher, stepping forward. 'Yes, we are men. You and me, men.'

Ever the politician, Fletcher somehow could see an angle here and stepped forward to press the flesh.

'Chaps, entering homes is a serious business, but I'm sure we can work something out.' He brought up an envelope from his jacket pocket—the envelope that apparently contained Neighbourhood Watch approval—and, to Peter's amazement, started pulling notes from it.

'I'm sure reasonable fellas like us—'

His words were choked off by the huge behemoth, who grabbed Fletcher around the throat with a hand so big the fingers almost touched the thumb on the back of the politician's neck. Fletcher couldn't get a breath out, never mind another word.

'Man,' the big one said, in a voice that sounded like earth moving. A tectonic plate shift with words attached. He abruptly hoisted Fletcher up dangling him like a scarecrow effigy, raining a handful of notes which fluttered in the thin light—and slammed him onto his back on the kitchen island, bending the once proud tap out of place. The grip from his throat was released and Fletcher screamed in pain and terror—so much terror—before the big one pinned his shoulders to the countertop with splayed hands.

'God, let me go!' howled Fletcher, as Peter and Christian stepped forward.

'Stop,' Peter commanded, but a flash of metal in the torch

light stopped him. A cleaver—their meat cleaver, new and unused—was being brandished by the smaller one—held out in a stark warning.

'Man,' the smaller one said again—then raised the long square blade high over his head, before crashing it down, burying it into Fletcher's groin.

The scream that burst from the MP was otherworldly. 'No man,' the thing said. The cleaver went back up, then down again with a wet thunk.

Peter stepped forward, but Pam grabbed his arm, screaming. He was speechless. They were frozen. The horror of the assault just too… The *gore*. Watching a man being as good as quartered before their very eyes. Reduced to screaming for his life in vain.

As the strikes rained down, and Fletcher's trousers were reduced to blood-soaked rags, the howls transformed from desperate to plaintive, and it reminded Peter of a badger he'd once hit with his car. Moaning, knowing its race was run, insides now on its outsides. At the end of the day, we're all animal. Flesh, blood, bone, gristle, the chance nuisance of consciousness the only difference in the human case.

Christian started pushing Pam and Peter out of the kitchen, just as the big one let go of one of Fletcher's shoulders, reached down to the gaping maw of what had once been Fletcher's groin—and began pulling at the flesh, ripping it loose from the rest of the body.

The last thing Peter saw as he turned to run for his life, was the big one holding what must have been the remains of Fletcher's manhood, which he then threw at the escaping party. Something hit Peter on the arm, soft like squashed fruit, but Peter didn't allow his thoughts to venture any further as to what that might have been.

As they entered the hall, Fletcher's howls decreasing with

every step, Peter's mind went to base functions and, following that, his parental responsibility. 'Where's Jacob?', as he started up the stairs. All he could think about doing was putting a barrier between his son and those things in the kitchen—even if the obstacle was him.

'In his room,' replied Pam urgently, but her words were drowned out by the thump of footsteps coming from what felt like the back of the stairway. All three of them realised what it was at the same time. The big one, had worked out the geography of the house and was coming around the central column to meet them at the other side. They all began running up the stairs, when the big one stormed through the living room launching after them. They were in a standoff, the three on the stairs, and the one at the bottom—who was suddenly joined by the smaller one.

They faced each other in the darkness, unsure of exactly where each party was, but sure of their invaders' intentions.

The front door suddenly opened, and all paused. The blue night framed the square, but it was suddenly filled with a leaping shadow, which bounded into the hall with a vicious snarl, and immediately went for their assailants. Peter gasped with pure relief at the sudden lifeline, that this surely was the greatest gift from God. It was a dog—big, angry and fighting for its life— for all their lives. When the ponytailed figure appeared in the doorway, he knew for sure—it was Dewey.

Good fucking *dog*.

'Get 'em Dewey, get em,' Grace was shouting, and Peter— life on the line, human survival in the balance—threw himself down the stairs. He dived into the two men, themselves fighting the giant dog, as it clawed and lashed and bit in an astonishing act of offensive force. The dopey lumbering hound was no more—although Peter had seen the suggestion of this before when, the other night, Dewey had smelled something he hadn't liked.

The smell. As Peter landed on them, the sudden closeness with the men sent his nose into uproar, as he started thrashing and kicking and hitting as hard as he could. Dewey had torn the big one's jumper, revealing jags of pale white flesh in the torch light. Christian was suddenly in the melee too, and Pam started throwing kicks from the bottom step. After a few more frantic seconds, the outsiders retreated to the door, Dewey snapping at them.

Peter noted that during the exchange, the intruders couldn't have cared less about the attentions of the humans. It was the dog they were bothered by, twisting this way and that to avoid it. Dewey chased them out of the front door, passed Grace, who stepped aside to let them flee. Outside, without the confines of a ceiling, the big one looked especially huge—as Dewey chased the two off into the night.

44

JOYCE HADN'T BEEN bothered remotely by the power cut, and if anything, enjoyed the quiet it gave. She knew the twins would probably be losing their minds over it, with no XBox to play, no electronics to gaze upon. So she sat in the living room, waiting for the power to come back on, enjoying the darkness. Nobody could see her. She was invisible. Just like she always felt.

A creak on the dark stairs behind gave her gooseflesh, and she turned in her chair to look back into the hallway. 'Boys?'

'Power's gone,' came a voice.

'My God, boys, please don't creep around like that.'

'But the power's gone.'

She couldn't see her sons, Boyd nor Burnett. Couldn't even tell which one she was talking to. 'I know.'

'What do we do?'

They'd got bored even quicker than Joyce had thought. 'What do you want me to say boys?'

'Nothing works.'

'That's the general result of a power cut.'

'How long will it be gone for?'

Joyce sighed. This was genuinely like talking at a brick wall, but again, the experience was proving an ample metaphor for the way she felt about her existence in general. Just pleading into the void. 'How do you think I would know?'

'Your phone?'

'And the wifi? Connected to a router? The router that needs

the mains? Catching on yet?'

No answer.

'There are some candles in the kitchen cupboard, the one by the fridge. Why don't you get them? Use the lighter that's in there with them, and go upstairs and read?'

No answer.

'Boys?'

Joyce got up, and walked into the hall. Even in the darkness, she could see the stairway was empty. They had gone. She shook her head, and walked into the kitchen. No peace, even when the planets aligned to make sure you couldn't even do anything.

She went to the cupboard, that store every house has, where the odds and ends of a functioning family were kept. The cast offs, the things you might need one day but not immediately, all of that existence detritus. She reached past the Sellotape, the batteries, the coils of ribbon and string, the unopened packet of screwdrivers, and grabbed the box of tea light candles, put there by herself for this exact occasion.

That's when she heard snarling, shouting and screaming.

Her heart beat with sudden bedlam, clattering around in her chest, and she looked out of the kitchen windows. She couldn't see anything, everything being so dark. But it sounded... yes, she thought. It's coming from the front of the house.

She walked into the hall, using the gas lighter to ignite one of the tealights, and as the soft orange glow caught and flourished, she almost walked straight into a man.

Standing there, in the dark, in her hallway—looking like a living nightmare.

She didn't have time to scream before the man grabbed her, clamped a hand over her mouth, and hit her so fiercely on the top of her head that she wasn't even awake by the time she started to fall.

'BACK DEWEY, BACK! *Here!*' commanded Grace, as she held the door open for him. Within a few seconds, the wolfhound lolloped around the corner of the hedges, panting heavily, and trotted in through the front door of the West's house.

'Who were they?' asked Grace, as she closed the door behind her, and stood in the dark, all of them panting.

'I've no idea,' said Peter, as he emerged from the kitchen, bringing light with him from his phone. 'Don't go in there,' he added gravely.

'Why?' she asked.

'Is he dead?' blurted Pam.

'I think so,' said Peter, a thousand-yard stare locked in tight.

Pam ran upstairs, shouting the name Jacob. Grace bent to calm Dewey, whispering what a good dog he was in his flopped ear. 'I think we now know who's been causing us so many problems around here.'

'If those things have my daughter…' Christian jittered. 'I have to follow them. I've got to find her.'

'We need police, out here now,' said Peter. 'And an ambulance for all the good it will do.'

'Who is in the kitchen? Did you say dead?' Grace asked, trying to catch up. The logic part of her mind was desperate for answers, in a battle against the flight mode that was pressing for her attention. She turned to Christian, as though hearing his words for the first time too. 'And they have your daughter?'

'I don't know,' he replied desperately. 'She disappeared from my car a couple of hours ago. I was by a watchtower right back in the estate, and… I heard the car door shut, and that was it. She was gone. We looked everywhere.'

'We?'

'I found the security guard, fat lot of good he was.' They fell quiet for a moment, all minds churning, reeling. 'He's a little old guy with a gut, what good is he gonna do?'

After clipping Dewey's lead back on, and since no one had answered her first question, Grace edged to the door frame of the kitchen. Peter put his arm out, and looked at her dead on. 'Don't,' he said.

'I'm a big girl, mate.' She peered into the kitchen. In the dark, she could make out a form splayed on the kitchen island, which was enough. 'The Fenchurches are dead too,' she said, turning back round. 'And it was… well, it was bad.'

Peter looked at the floor, his frown belying the puzzle he was trying to unravel. 'They… castrated Fletcher. I think.'

Pam appeared on the stairs. 'Jacob's in his room, I've told him to stay there.'

'What was that all about?' Grace burst. 'And this security guard has no back up? What's he going to do, come over here and give those maniacs a talking to? We need to get some reception. And we need it now.'

'What happened to the Fenchurches?' It was Peter. He looked beaten.

Grace didn't really know how to put it. She hadn't even come close to processing what she had seen. 'Similar to what happened here. It was gruesome.'

'Was he… you know?'

Grace looked at him, unable to decipher his meaning. He slowly raised a hand, and with two fingers, mimed a snipping motion of scissors—which sent the penny dropping. 'He, umm… I don't know. I don't think so. The rest of him looked okay, it was all mainly … here…' She motioned to her own face and head in a circular sweep of her palm.

'What do we do now?' asked Pam.

'We need to go and find my daughter.' Christian walked to the front door.

Peter looked up at Pam. 'And we need to find ours.' She choked back a sudden sob and nodded.

'Right, then we need to tool up and get after them,' said Grace. 'They didn't like Dewey, so he's coming with us. And I'm thinking he'll be able to point us in the right direction.'

'I'm coming too—' Pam said, but Peter held up his hands.

'You need to stay and protect Jacob. I'll get Alice back. We'll get the children home.'

Christian opened the front door, the cold night waiting for them beyond.

'Meet back here in five,' Grace said, stepping through. 'Grab anything you can use as a weapon. Let's go and find them.'

45

ALICE HAD BEEN in shock since she'd come round in the dark place, drifting in and out of consciousness, as if her body was protecting her with a failsafe shutdown, keeping her from using all her energy up in one frantic go.

The smell in here was oppressive to the point of suffocation—musty, rotten and fetid—but it wasn't her sense of smell that had prompted Alice out of her most recent exhausted slumber. Instead, she could hear something. An urgent back and to, a constant whisking. She opened her eyes, and tried to see. She'd been stuck here for long enough to lose some of the feeling in her legs, and had no idea what time it was. At best guess, it was evening time, but it was impossible to tell.

The darkness was almost complete, but a flickering light, almost candle-like, was glowing at the far end of the tunnel, allowing her sight of the concrete tunnel walls and the damp coursing down them in a slick sheen. But as her eyes adjusted, she could see that the reflection was broken by the shape of a man.

It wasn't a tall man, although he was slightly crouched, hunched even. She could make out the paler outline of his hairless head and those godless eyes. And that sound—that *shapshapshapshap* which had woken her this time—was coming from him.

She lifted her head, righting the image, and it caused the man to step forward and the noise increased in volume—and thanks to her world being now the correct way up, she could see in full what was happening.

The man was staring at her, his eyebrows raised high and expectant. His sweatshirt was pulled up to reveal the palest of bare skin, while his hand was jostling forward and back inside his jogging bottoms. His breathing was urgent and building.

Fearful and confused, she pulled herself up, but because she was already backed up to the wall, she couldn't put any more distance between her and that man. It was the little one, she could see now, when she could pull her eyes from his frantic hand. The youngest one she'd seen yet.

She expected him to come nearer, such was the fervour in his eyes. Gone was the anger, gone was the savagery. In its place was hope, and something akin to prayer. But he didn't move, keeping an almost respectful distance from the bars.

Alice didn't know how to feel. She was perplexed and revulsed, an obscure fascination holding her, preventing her from doing anything at all. She'd heard about this kind of thing, but never seen it. She was aware that this was what boys sometimes did, but only through the ruder channels of the playground grapevine. She'd never thought it would be in front of her, and it left her with an additional deep sense of shock.

Abruptly, another sound joined in. A shuffling, which grew in speed. Then a chattering voice, echoing along the tunnel to Alice and her young captor. The owner was agitated, there was more shuffling, and then, in the tunnel behind the small man, two bald heads bobbed towards them. It was the other two, carrying lanterns made of burning firewood outstretched. She thought of them as brothers, because that's exactly what they looked like.

Disturbed, the young one looked behind and saw them approach, then turned back to Alice, his eyes wider, his hand now moving quicker than ever. Alice didn't know what she was watching, what was happening.

The two other brothers shouted something in that deep, abbreviated chit-chat, like a pair of baritone crows, and as they reached their little brother, the light from their lanterns illuminated him fully for the first time.

His head was now thrust back, his eyes jammed tight and his jaw locked in a meshed grimace of filthy teeth.

His hand was pumping, and something flicked out of it. It was thick like mucus, and it gobbed on the floor at his feet. Alice was lost for both words and thoughts.

The tallest brother started berating the little one as he was still convulsing, while the middle one put his hand out to catch some of the liquid as it fell, like it was possessed of deep value. The tall one slapped the little one, as the fever seemed to ease, and barked into his face. He then pulled his little brother's now-stilled hand up from his midriff, which, Alice could see in the lantern-light, was slick with a pale oil—and licked it off angrily.

The other one, the middle brother, fell to his knees and tried to scoop some of the fluid from the dirty floor, slurping the spoils from his fingers—in between angry reprimands directed at the sibling that had put it there.

Alice shut her eyes as tight as she could, her young mind having finally reached capacity, but her stomach lurched regardless and the tunnel echoed with her own violent retching as she was thoroughly sick all down her front.

46

AS CHRISTIAN RAN back to his house, a curious sense of cold autopilot descended upon him, and the more it tightened its hold, the more he wished David were here. His unpreparedness and inadequacy were feelings he had been loath to admit to, but both had been growing spectres in the dark corners of his mind since fatherhood had arrived.

He and David had waited and waited, fighting relentlessly to become parents. They both knew that, and they both knew the joy of the moment had been earned. But in that patient battle, Christian wondered if it had prevented them from truly becoming ready for the actual experience itself. Most couples watched the mother's stomach grow, and attended regular scans and appointments, were granted ultrasound images of what was happening within the expanding belly—and with that, Christian was sure, came an understanding of the additional life that would soon be entering their worlds, a comprehension. The baby was there, after all, in their midst, albeit safely in the womb.

All Christian and David had been able to do during this time, was attend classes and get funny looks from the apparent myriad of bigoted loons that also attended, leaf through paperwork, and eventually contemplate getting a nursery ready. That was it.

Then suddenly, they walked into a hospital with a brand new, empty car seat, and walked out shortly afterwards with a baby in it.

A living, breathing infant.

They were largely silent on the drive home, shock setting in. They'd actually done it. They were parents now.

The first week was frantic and happy, but shock was the underlying bass note.

They'd come to terms with it, quickly enough. They'd fallen in love with the child herself, and the label of daughter took unbreakable root. Indecision had held them from naming their little girl for the first week, but it was also through the thought that something might present itself more naturally. And it did.

The fighting was over. The scrabble to exercise their right to become parents was done, and with that the men, with their brand-new beloved daughter, had found *peace*.

Peace.

Olive branch.

Olivia.

And it stuck.

And now Christian, in his rank stupidity, had lost her.

As soon as he unlocked the door to his house, he'd sat on the bottom step of the stairs and cried. Sobbing snottily into the crook of his arm, lamenting his unpreparedness and cursing himself.

He had to get her back. He just had to.

And then there was his husband, David, at work on the late one, blissfully ignorant of the whole thing. Christian couldn't even call him if he tried. Literally no way to get through to him at all.

He'd been wrestling with it since the awful moment he'd found the car seat empty. Drive back to the house and use the wifi to call for help. But that meant leaving her in those woods with whatever, whoever...

He stopped the thought dead. Seeing those things, and what they did to Fletcher Adams, turned his stomach to rot and ruin in a hot heartbeat.

Marching into the kitchen, he emptied out drawers and cupboards, looking for that one particular item he knew he had somewhere, stashed for emergencies. While he was turfing pans out onto the plush tile, and their loud clatter seemed to bounce off every surface in the damn house, he cursed further his continued lack of readiness. Why couldn't he ever find anything? Why could you never find anything when you really needed it? He felt more useless than ever, and gave up, going for the thing he wanted next.

The biggest knife he could find.

He knew exactly where the knife block was, on the counter to the left of the sink, and as he reached for the handle of the carving knife that he knew was top left in the block, he remembered.

Yes! Of course!

He had got something right. There it was at last, the big Maglite, the one he'd loved ever since he was an X-Files devotee in his teens. It had been stood behind the knife block, in the corner where the counter met the fridge. He reached for it and actually felt something like a smile creep across his face as his fingers closed around its sturdy metal grip.

And then the sound of glass breaking, somewhere above him.

Upstairs. Something was upstairs.

THE CRASHING SOUND of a large piece of glass shattering was heard all around the inky cul-de-sac, followed by the wandering tinkle of settling shards. Pam even heard it on the stairway, and crept down. Something about a loud noise, unexpected in the dark... it was designed through force of evolution to upset you.

Peter emerged from the under stairs cupboard, holding a bigger torch that looked like a battery with a cone of light firing from one end. In his other hand was a cricket bat. 'Did you hear that?' she asked him.

'No, I was under there. What was it?' He lifted the bat up, nerves frayed on the assumption that anything could and *would* happen any second.

'Glass shattering. Somewhere in the street,' she said, walking to the front door, but Peter put a hand across her path.

'Let me,' he said. And he kissed her. Pam was taken aback. It was a kiss with actual feeling. He meant it. She sank into the embrace for just a second, before releasing him into the void.

Watching him walk carefully into the centre of the cul-de-sac's turning circle, she noticed Grace appear outside her house on the corner, with a torch of her own. She immediately looked further down the street.

'The Lyons' house?' shouted Peter. Grace nodded in response, and her, Dewey and Peter started running to the grand black house—but not before Peter shouted 'Love you Pam!' over his shoulder.

'Love you,' she shouted back. Maybe there was hope for them after all. She wanted to tell him to be careful, not to take any unnecessary risks, but this was it. The chips were down. It was survival time, as only a few unfortunate souls got to truly experience. You fight this, or it kills you.

And she was going to live. Her family were going to live. She was determined of both.

She could do nothing to help Peter now. She had to protect Jacob first and foremost, so Pam ran back into the house, and shut the door quickly, locking it behind her.

It was dark. Way too dark for her liking, and she wanted to

get the candles from the kitchen. But that would mean going in there were Fletcher was, laid bare and flayed on the kitchen island, like one of those old pictures of Victorian medical lectures, with the large operating table sat in the centre of an auditorium, so all and sundry could get a good look at all the blood and gubbins.

No. She needed to protect Jacob. That was her job—her immediate objective for survival for her and her family. And that was best served by acquiring light.

Big girl pants time, Pam.

So she couldn't talk herself out of it, she marched straight into the kitchen for candles, which she knew to be in the drawer next to the sink—the sink that was embedded in the central island worktop. The worktop on which Fletcher Adams had been killed.

Big. Girl. Pants.

Head down, she walked to the unit, determined not to look at it. There was a smell—a medical, human smell, rusty, visceral.

Don't look up.

She dipped low, in a crouch, to avoid the temptation of allowing her eyes to drift to the body, and in the dark found the candles with ease. She turned, and stood, buoyed by the small success and headed back to the hall—clicking the candles on as she went. Smart cookie, she'd bought battery operated candles which gave off an immediate soft glow without the need to fumble about with matches in the dark. Her planning had been perfect.

But when she clicked it on, she passed the integrated kitchen units, which included the cooker, and in its glass door, unintentionally, she saw the reflection of the worktop.

No. It couldn't be.

Pam spun around to make sure her eyes weren't playing tricks on her, but sure enough, the reflection in the cooker door hadn't lied. She needn't have worried about seeing anything untoward when she came in for the candles.

Fletcher's body was gone.

47

DESPITE THE THINGS he'd seen, despite the horrors of those men in their weird outfits and their awful glares, and what they'd done to poor Fletcher Adams. Despite the darkness and the growing dread he felt spiralling through every fibre of his person, Christian clicked on the Maglite and sprinted up the stairs, two at a time. He prayed that Olivia had been returned. That the glass smashing was those bastards breaking back into the bedroom to return her to her crib.

The crib. The bedroom.

The dread spiralled in Christian as he realised. How foolish he had been, how blind. He'd been so frantic while searching earlier, his brain tumbling in all directions but the right one, he'd failed to make the link.

Ooh baba.

Olivia wasn't a chance abduction. She had been watched. She had been chosen.

Please, Christian begged inwardly. *Please let her be in the crib. Please let her be safe. I will never let her out of my sight again, I will never ever take having her for granted.*

He got to the top of the stairs and raced down the hall, throwing the nursery door open, not caring if one of *them* was in here—he was ready to do anything it took to save his daughter.

The sight he found, as he pieced it together through the searching circle of light from the torch, was not comforting. The nursery had been ransacked. Toys tossed everywhere, things launched this way and that. Glass from the shattered window glinting in the torchlight.

Olivia wasn't here, but only moments ago, someone else had been. And they'd smashed the window in escape—all while Christian had been downstairs, feeling sorry for himself.

He felt anger billow as he marched around the wreckage of the nursery they had so carefully and lovingly put together. Tears resurged down his cheeks.

The front door clunked downstairs, and someone shouted into the house. 'Christian?'

It was Peter West. 'I'm up here,' he replied, hopelessly.

As he heard footsteps on the stairs, he crouched and sifted through some of the wreckage. Broken drawer bits, blankets strewn.

'What's happened?' asked Grace, appearing at the nursery door. The massive dog was at her side.

'The clothes. A lot of Olivia's clothes are missing.'

'That was them, in here?' It was Peter again, joining them in the room, sliding in next to the massive dog that was taking up most of it.

'It must have been,' Christian replied.

'Wait clothes, clothes,' said Grace, with sudden animation. The mere energy in her voice gave him a surge of hope. 'Do you have a laundry basket for Olivia?'

'Yes, but it's not here, it's downstairs in the utility room.'

'Is it clean?'

'I was going to wash it tonight.'

'Perfect, where is it?'

A moment later, Christian walked Grace and Dewey into the utility room and pointed to a white wicker basket that was stood next to the washing machine.

'Dewey, get your head in there,' Grace said, taking the lid off the basket and shuffling the contents as if it contained something of great canine worth. Dewey obediently put his whole head in, and snuffled, licked and shoved about with his great snout. 'Get a good noseful, mate.'

Christian caught up, and that slight waft of hope returned. 'Her scent.'

'Dewey will take us right to her. Let's take a couple of these babygrows and go and find her.'

NO MATTER HOW long Pam stared at the kitchen island, marvelling at the sheer quantity of blood that was smeared and pooled all over it, the mutilated body of Fletcher Adams would just not reappear.

Fletcher was tall. Solidly built. Easily over fourteen stone in weight. How on earth could someone that big be moved so quickly, so easily, so quietly?

As soon as she thought about it, she knew the answer. That big one. He could do it. No problem. He manhandled Fletcher when he was alive and writhing, chucking him about like a ragdoll. It would be even easier with him dead and lifeless.

With a shudder, she was forced to acknowledge that those *things* had come back for the body, and taken it. And worse still, they had gotten in the house so quietly, so easily, that they could surely come back anytime.

Jacob. Family survival.

Protecting him was number one.

How could she keep them from coming in? The front door was locked, which left the back door. She had to go and lock it.

The quicker she did, the better. Don't dally, just go.

She grabbed a knife from the kitchen drawer, and followed

her synthetic candle light around the island unit. The back door was through the kitchen by the utility room. Of course. All this time. They'd been coming and going through the back door.

Treading as quietly as she could, she rounded the island, and caught sight of blood spatter on the white floor tiles. It wasn't a smear you'd associate with a body being dragged. It was more of a trail of droplets—some small, some fatter. The body had been carried out. Pam could only imagine Fletcher's mangled corpse placed over the crook of that giant's arm like a coat on a warm winter night.

She shuddered with how small she felt.

But she was a mother. And that counted for a lot when it came to any physical discrepancies.

She tiptoed around the blood, keeping careful not to disturb any of it, although not really sure why. It just felt like the wrong thing to do, like standing on somebody's grave at a cemetery.

The dark opening of the utility room yawned at her, and she strained to see if anything or anyone was in there. Nothing. But the blood pattern on the floor led neatly to the back door, which had been left open aimlessly. Her fear spiked, but she knew, if she could get that closed and locked, she was one step closer to safety.

But what if they're just outside the door, waiting to pounce?

She forced herself to cast the thought as far away as she could, and ran on her toes to the door, throwing it shut and locking it tight.

Once the latch had caught, she couldn't resist a look into the garden, but nothing was there. It was dark, granted, but the garden was doused in a soft blue moonlight which outlined just the bare grass and the fencing that boxed it in.

But amid the stink of Fletcher's death, another smell emerged. Filthy, morbid, and somehow *alive*. The utility. She hadn't checked the utility.

A massive impact on the side of her head cut dead the sudden regret, and she fell knowing she had let Jacob down.

48

DEWEY PULLED AT the lead as if he was suddenly years younger, and Grace had to repeatedly command him back—not because she was slow, but because he was at risk of pulling her off her feet. Christian and Peter ran behind, as they followed the wolfhound and its nose into the night.

When they'd opened the front door to Christian's house, and Grace had said 'Go, go on boy, *go*!', Dewey had led them back to the bottom of the cul-de-sac, past Christian's car (the driver's side door to which he finally shut while walking past), beyond the Adams and West homes, and down the dog walk track Grace and Peter had followed Dewey down, only last night—a point in time that felt like lifetimes ago now.

The fronds of ferns and nettles reached out to them on both sides like admiring fingers caressing their pumping calves, while their bouncing torchlight showed Dewey's ragged grey hindquarters as he bounded along the trail.

Grace kept encouraging him, not as if she needed to, until they came out onto the grass of the fallow field, and Dewey stopped, as before, to take in the trees opposite. They loomed, portentous as ever, although now, because the threat within had been experienced, and had even claimed a few of them, the malice dripping from those trees felt much greater.

'In there, Dew?' Grace asked, as the three of them cast their torchlight along the trunks. There was nothing obviously amiss about the woodland, save for the fact that it was hardly inviting, and the wet bodies of the trees gradually rose to sparse wintery boughs and the heavens themselves high above. Dewey barked in response, a huge gush of steam escaping his mouth as he did so.

'Okay, let's go folks,' she said, and led them across the field. It was heavily rutted, and the humans had to take their time—something Dewey was respectful of. As the trees drew closer, the atmosphere followed it, suddenly becoming close, tight and strange as they entered the woods. The air was thick with a wet, mulchy smell, like a bog, and Grace soon found her trainers sodden. The trees overhead cut out the deep indigo of the sky, and the only illumination was fully man-made. There was no obvious trail, so they followed the dog step for step, casting shafts of light this way and that. Grace, at the front of the human part of the group, shining her torch over Dewey's bobbing head, saw their destination before anybody else.

'What the hell is that?' was all she could say, and within a couple of moments, they were there, surrounding this construction that was so out of place in its surroundings, even though its aged appearance suggested it had been there for many years.

Embedded in the ground, in the middle of the trees, was a tubular stone cylinder, four feet wide, and four feet high, made of brick. Dewey jumped up and placed his paws on top of the brickwork and peered down.

'Jesus, what is it?' asked Christian.

Tentatively, the three of them followed Dewey's lead and peered over the ledge. A dark drop presented itself, and their torchlight showed no sign of the bottom. It did, however, show a rusted steel ladder leading all the way down.

'My God,' said Peter. 'It's an air vent.'

'A vent?' said Grace. 'What for?'

Peter stepped back and looked at the structure, before eventually pacing around it. 'I've seen these before. On railways. Old steam train systems used to have them, for allowing the steam up and out of the tunnels.'

'Are you saying there's a railway down there?' asked Christian, the disbelief in his voice so obvious.

'Not necessarily,' Peter clarified, still unable to take his eyes away from the structure. 'For railways they'd be three of four times bigger than this, to handle the amount of steam. But this is definitely for a similar purpose. It's an air circulation vent. For tunnels.'

'Are *they* down there?' asked Christian, as all three people turned to look at Dewey, who hadn't moved. He was still staring down the vent, into the black space, gazing with focus, a low grumble seeming to warn them of what he was thinking.

'Down there, Dew?' asked Grace, joining him.

Dewey barked twice, and Grace turned to the men and nodded.

49

JACOB HAD LAID under the bed, alongside the boxes he still hadn't opened yet, let alone got round to actually unpack, and waited for ten minutes after he last heard something. His mum was supposed to be there, protecting him from whatever that shouting downstairs was before. He felt alright though, because after the shouting, his mum had come to see him, told him to hide out under here. He was cool with that—he had his phone, preloaded up with games, so he'd have plenty to do. Couldn't get on Roblox though, which was a serious bummer—needed wifi for that. But focussing on something else was a help. It diverted his thoughts from confusion, put them onto something more normal than whatever was happening in the street.

He still didn't know why his mum was being so quiet though. He'd heard Christian, his dad, and the absolute babe from over the road leave the house together. Had even heard his mum and dad say goodbye. But then nothing. His mum shuffled about for a bit, then went quiet.

Should he shout for her? Make sure she was still there?

That's what he'd done when he was a kid, suddenly woken in the middle of the night, and his instincts suggested it was the right thing to do. But something wasn't right about that. Something was more serious now, as if all those times when he was little, he knew full well there was nothing to worry about, whereas tonight, the threat was very real. All of that was training for right now.

This, Jacob resolved, was a grown-up situation that required a grown-up course of action. So he pulled himself from beneath the bed, shuffling on his belly, and out into the centre of the room, where he stood, listened and took stock.

Nothing had changed during his commando manoeuvre. The house was still quiet.

He edged out of his room onto the landing, all his senses on the highest of alerts, receptive to the smallest sound.

But that coast appeared to be entirely clear.

He padded down the stairs in his socks, one careful step at a time, pausing halfway down to peek through the bannister at the darkened living room. He expected to see the shadowed form of his mum in one of the armchairs or on the sofa, but there was nothing and nobody there.

He wanted to shout for her, now more than ever before, but no, this was grown up time. Taking the quietest deep breath he could, he crept to the bottom of the stairs, and into the kitchen.

First thing he caught was the soft glow coming from the utility room, which caught him off guard, because he didn't know they had a lamp in there. He thought, as he walked across, was that it could even be one of those little plug-in nightlight things with a sensor in, that switch on automatically when it was dark. He had one of those in his room growing up, and thought it was a good idea.

Then, he remembered why it was dark in the first place. Power cut. As in no power.

The mystery was solved when he saw the flickering battery-powered candle on the floor, but it was fact that it was on its side he didn't like, its little fake flame dancing against the tile. He doubly didn't like the fact that it was lying next to a lot of dark drops. Drops that looked eerily like blood when he picked the light up and shone it properly on the splatter.

'Mum,' he whispered hoarsely, his mouth suddenly sub-Saharan. '*Mum!*'

He stood and turned back into the kitchen to resume the search for his mother—when he saw the central room of the house now resembled an abattoir. There was just so much blood.

He felt the heave of nausea, the grip of his throat tighten as his mouth pumped full of saliva, and he started running. Anywhere, not here, go, front door, yes.

It was locked, so he had to unlatch it quickly, a quick flick of the lock lever on the inside and he was out the front of the house into the cool fresh air, gasping, his head spinning.

Darting out of the door, he ran straight into the low hedge that framed the porch, and dumped himself onto the grass, knocking the air clean out him. He lay there, on the wet turf, feeling his T-shirt begin to soak, and rolled over. He stared at the stars. He searched for the dimmest one he could find, as his breathing returned to normal—then wished as hard as he could to be on it. Far away from here. Eons from whatever was happening on Blackstoke tonight.

As he sat upright, Jacob started to feel more exposed, just sitting there in the front garden, out in the cold night, and began to think leaving his hiding place under the bed had been a really bad choice—even if the house was a bloodbath.

He begged that the blood wasn't his mum's. *Please, mum. Please don't let that be you.*

He stood, and tentatively walked down the path to the concrete roadway, careful not to make any noise—which was easy considering he still didn't have any shoes on. The dark and the quiet was so strange, so off-putting. He found himself walking past a silver car that had been parked in the middle of the road, and went to the exact middle of the cul-de-sac's turning circle.

Something about that central position appealed to his sense of balance, his perception of calm. He was on autopilot but didn't know it, his young mind clambering to reject what he had seen in the kitchen, and what it might have meant for his parents and protectors.

Once he'd reached the centre. He took in the darkness and tried to make order of it. Each house was a black mass, crouched in wait, troll-like. The street itself took a hazy shape in lines of the deepest purple, thanks to light from the moon and sky above. The quiet was fixed in vacuum, as if every resident and the very remnants of their existence—the echoes of their lives—had been sucked clean away from this place.

Blackstoke was a ghost town.

A sound burst out, and Jacob was surprised to realise it had come from him. As if the need to fill the void had suddenly become too great, he found himself bellowing: 'Hello!'

He dragged that last vowel out as long as he could, letting his voice die on it, then listened to it resonate off into the estate.

No answer.

So he tried again. 'Hello!'

As he let the word play out, and enjoyed the catharsis the scream offered, he brought his head down as his lungs expelled the shout, and on opening his eyes, saw the shadow of a person.

He strained to see, but felt hope take flight within him.

'Hello, yes! Over here!' he shouted.

The person was standing on the edge of Grace Milligan's garden. It was so hard to make out the definite edges of the silhouette, but he definitely saw it move—given away by the shifting of the softest reflection on the top of the person's bald head.

Bald.

Jacob wracked his brain to think of who he knew who was

hairless up top, and, on finding no obvious answer, considered every resident on Broadoak. The old man with the leccy fence obsession, he was thinning, but he wasn't like this. Maybe it was the politician over the road? Maybe he wore a wig, and he'd come out to see what was happening and plain forgot to pop it on. The thought forced a delirious smile from Jacob.

'Who's that?' he asked though the grin, and the person suddenly started running.

Sprinting.

Straight at Jacob.

'Who are you?' he shouted, the grin long gone. 'Who *are* you?'

The figure made astonishing speed, making the fifty yards or so in long loping strides, and Jacob felt a surge of panic. This was all, horribly, wrong. This wasn't someone he knew. This person wanted nothing more than to hurt him.

'No!' he shouted, as the person appeared just yards from him, and Jacob felt the threat and presence of something akin to a predatory beast. He screamed, as the man entered the small circle of light from the candle, and revealed height, long outstretched arms and bared teeth. An animal snarl erupted from his jaws, when another light shone directly in the man's eyes. Powerful, strong and blinding.

'Get back" came another pubescent voice. 'Back, back!'

Jacob in his panic couldn't work it out, but he was sure those saviour's words came from two separate sources. The words sounded the same, but overlapped.

A burst of torchlight, which put Jacob's flittering candle to shame, and a dot of darting green both shone at the man, who covered his eyes with a loud howl.

'Back!' said one of the voices. 'Get back!'

'Jacob, here,' said the other.

Jacob ran to the voices and saw the twins. The Adams boys,

one with a heavy-duty torch, the other with a green laser pointer. He wanted to hug them both.

Moving behind them, the man tried to follow, and Jacob got a good look at him as he struggled. Completely hairless, which went for eyebrows and beard too, and in a filthy grey jogging suit. There was something weird about the way he looked and carried himself, belying a horrible life journey that was beyond Jacob's comprehension. The man reared back suddenly, less phased by the bright lights, and dove forward like a wolf—and stopped abruptly. He paused mid-movement, staring, his jaw hanging, the hate in his black eyes bleeding to confusion.

The man screamed, but it wasn't off murderous rage—it was borne of a lack of comprehension.

He looked from one boy to the other, confusion writ large in every bent feature.

'Go!' commanded one of the boys.

'Away, back, away!' hollered the other.

Jacob worked it out when the man took a confused backward step. Twins. This man had never seen identical twins before, and it seemed to terrify him. He took two steps back, then three, then started to scamper away, turning back to look every few strides. They followed him with the torchlight until he took one last look, at the entrance to the dog walking trail, before disappearing into the brush.

The boys doused their lights in unison, and Jacob grabbed the twins, holding them both tight with a shaky arm round each neck.

'Thank you,' he whispered. 'Thank you.'

50

DEWEY WAS HEAVY, but the three were unified in their resolution that the great wolfhound had to go down into the tunnel with them. Peter offered to carry him on his shoulders, not quite aware that the dog was getting on for eighty kilograms in weight. Christian had gone down the ladder first, shining the torch into the black depths, and Grace followed Peter and Dewey closely, so that the big dog could see her, and hear her coo calmness to the shaking animal.

Peter's shoulders heaved, and felt like they might just break, but he wouldn't relent—they were almost there. He was finding new depths to his endurance, new places he could push to. Alice's life, he was sure, was on the line. As was Olivia's. And Dewey's presence was their best bet at combatting these creatures.

They inched for what felt like an age, one step at a time, and such was the tightness of Peter's grip, with the dog's front quarters on one shoulder and its hindquarters on the other, he was pressed tight to the ladder rungs and the wall itself. The brickwork was musty, aged with mould, and the steps were crusted with rust. He didn't give light to the nagging idea that he, at a hundred and ninety pounds with a dog almost the same on his back, might be too heavy for this particular route—they were already way too far down the air vent to turn back.

Mercifully, his concentration was broken not by a missed footing or a crumpling shoulder ligament, but a hushed exclamation from Christian below.

'I'm at the bottom.'

Within a moment, Peter's soles hit solid brick, and he let Dewey hop down, feeling the muscle tension dissipate in one glorious moment of release. The dog's claws clicked across the floor, as he got to sniffing around straight away.

'Wait, Dewey,' said Grace. 'Lead.'

Dewey returned to the bottom of the ladder for a congratulatory pat from his owner, as she too hit floor and clipped the red rope lead back onto his collar.

The bottom of the vent opened out directly into a tunnel, with two simple directions to pick. Left and right. Both was as dark as the other, with a wide curving roof drooping down into walls ten feet apart. Peter took one step, before slipping, landing square on his arse.

'Careful,' said Christian, helping him up. 'The rain water from the opening above has made this part really slippy.' Once on his feet again, the seat of his once-cream chinos now sodden a dark green, he shone his torch left, then right.

'Any ideas?' he said. 'Dewey?'

Grace unzipped her jacket pocket, and pulled out one of Olivia's babygrows, and offered it up to Dewey's nose. He nudged it with his snout, turning it over in her palm as if he was trying to fold it, then pulled to the right-hand section of tunnel.

'Makes sense,' Peter said, as they followed the dog.

'I think this way leads us back under our houses.'

'And deeper into the heart of the estate,' added Christian.

'Let's go,' said Grace, starting to jog. Within seconds they were all running into the murk, torches swinging.

'MRS ADAMS. Mrs Adams. Please wake up. Joyce. *Please.*'

Joyce's head hurt. A whirling black migraine punctured by words she just about recognised. A name she could latch onto. *Her own.*

'Please Joyce, it's me, Alice.'

She pulled herself out, and opened her eyes. 'Yes, I'm here.'

'Thank you, *thank you.*'

What Joyce saw made no sense. The room she was in was dark, but an amber tint washed bare brick walls, beyond the cage wall. At least, she thought it was a cage. Thin coils of wire lashed to metal, densely packed. Three sides of it. Behind her was brick again. And in the structure with her, was the eldest West child, Alice.

'Where are we?' asked Joyce, sitting up, the world spinning again before it settled.

'I don't know,' replied the teenager, who Joyce now saw was mucky, with dried blood matting one side of her hair to her head. 'I've been here hours now.'

'Jesus. What happened to you?'

'I think the same as you,' Alice said, pointing to Joyce's own head. The woman put her hand in her hair, and was alarmed to find her palm sticky with blood. 'Hit on the head and put here.'

Put here.

Joyce remembered.

The face in the darkness, a jump-cut nightmare.

'Who put us here?' she asked.

Alice's eyes abruptly filled. 'Those men.'

Joyce suddenly remembered. The commotion outside, the candle-lit man in her house. 'Who are they, Alice?'

'I don't know,' she said, now whispering. 'But I think they live here.'

'And where's here?'

'I don't know that either.'

'We can't have gone far.' Joyce checked her wristwatch, which she was pleased to find intact. Small mercies. It read 6.06pm. 'We really can't have gone far. Last time I checked it was about half five.'

Alice shuffled back and sat against the wall where the caging and brick met, and it gave Joyce pause to actually look at their prison. Yes, strong wire had been strung between three-foot posts, with more across the top. The more she looked at it the more she thought the tension of the wire looked quite springy, and the frames they hung upon were about six feet high and three feet wide rectangles of steel. Each frame was held together with more wiring. She touched the wire and it gave considerably, but not enough to let her through—and when she looked to the other side of the structure, she saw something she'd missed. Each frame had a short pole jutting out from each corner, suggesting this wasn't their primary purpose.

Joyce stepped back. Amazement and realisation washed over her.

'This cage is made from old hospital beds,' she said. 'What the hell are they doing here?'

As the questions flowed from her, a clank from the darkness down the corridor paused them both, and the light shifted.

'It's them,' said Alice, backing into the rear corner of the cell. Joyce joined her and placed an arm around her shoulders, pulling the girl into her. She didn't want to cower, but felt unable not to, as heavy footsteps approached. Joyce found herself squinting at the source of the light, though it was blocked by an approaching form, getting larger with every step towards them. Its shape was hard to pinpoint, with thick legs topped by an impossible breadth, and it was only when she clocked the dangling, swinging tail of hair behind the figure's back that she realised that this was a large person carrying someone over their shoulder—someone who, from the shape of it, looked like another woman.

Alice caught on quicker. 'Mum? *Mum!*' The girl scrabbled out of Joyce's embrace, and pulled herself to the cell's makeshift wall. 'Mum, are you okay?'

The large man used a giant hand to unwind the wiring of the corner post of the structure, and opened a small gap, through which he deposited Pam West. Joyce and Alice were there to catch her.

The giant eyed them bleakly, and unleashed a volley of harsh clicks with his tongue, interspersed with a snarls and huffs of breath. It seemed like to Joyce like the crudest of languages, as they cradled Pam and lay her in the centre of the cell, her head propped up on Alice's crossed legs.

'Mum, I'm here, it's me Alice,' said the girl, openly weeping.

'Pam, it's Joyce, are you okay?'

They huddled around her, listening as the giant retreated back down the tunnel, before Pam finally spoke in a low murmur. 'They smell even worse up close, don't they?'

The three women embraced, as humour dissolved to tears.

51

PIPES COURSED ALONG the left-hand slope of the tunnel roof. Two large and one small, unbroken since Grace first noticed them moments earlier. Intermittent bulbs hung, dead. Dewey had been cautious but steadfast. He wanted to go this way down the tunnel, and never once paused or wavered.

'Any ideas?' she asked as they marched.

'Not a clue,' said Christian. 'But we've walked what, a few hundred yards?'

'I think so. What are you thinking Peter?'

'I think it must be something to do with an old industry, but I can't think what,' he said, then pointed at the floor. 'If it was for mining or something, there'd be tracks in the floor for the mining cars, but there's nothing like that at all. It's just smooth concrete—which suggests it can't be that old.'

'There's not much damage down here either,' Grace mused. 'It's all a bit gross, but it's not even in disrepair or anything.'

'Almost as if it has been maintained,' said Christian.

A couple of seconds passed. 'That money, that Fletcher had, it was for the Neighbourhood Watch wasn't it?' Peter said.

'Yeah,' said Christian.

'He was scamming us, wasn't he?'

'Looks that way.'

They walked in a line, a redemptive wave, on their way to bring the missing children home, when Grace stopped.

'Look, there,' she whispered. 'Right hand wall.'

They slowed and focused their torches on the emerging shape. It started as a black stripe, which broadened on approach, and eventually revealed itself to be a doorway.

'Shit me,' said Christian. Strangely, Dewey was disinterested, and remained poised forward in the archetypal hunting dog pose, as if, like his ancestors, he'd spotted a distant wolf on the emerald fields of historic Ireland.

'Dew,' Grace said, pointing at the door, but he would not be dissuaded. He wanted to go ahead. Canine instinct butted hard against human curiosity, as the three torch beams settled on the doorway. It was open, the darkness of its shape caused by shadow, and their beams were merely sucked into darkness. As they approached, Grace's stomach roiling, the memories of the last time she flashed a light into a dark doorway all too vivid, scarring and recent, shapes began to emerge within. Lines began to form in the dark, and they all peered in at the same time, torches lighting the room harshly.

It wasn't the biggest room, but it was full. Wall to wall metal stretchers resting on trolleys. Some were rusted, some had lost their cushioning to reveal bare metal slats, some retained a little pole and hook at one end where a drip could be hung for administering medication. As their beams cast over the beds, Grace could see that a few of them were marked by dark stains, and she looked away to the walls instead to save her stomach. Cabinets lined the sides. Steel boxes, with little label cards on the front panel of each door.

'What the fuck is this place?' asked Christian, gravely.

'It looks like a… hospital store room,' said Grace.

'Seriously, why would this be down here?'

'I just don't know.'

'But it's been like this for some time,' added Peter. 'Let's keep moving.'

As they got to walking again, Dewey happy to be going in what he considered to be the right direction, Grace couldn't stop her thoughts from bounding this way and that. 'Let's face it. There was something here long before the Blackstoke estate,' she said, to herself as much as anybody else.

'And they didn't tell us a damn thing about it,' said Christian, anger in his voice.

'Either that or they forgot about it,' said Peter.

Grace didn't like any of those possibilities.

What was this place?

52

THE WOMEN HAD swapped their individual stories as to how they had ended up in the cage made of old bed frames, but Pam hadn't told either Alice nor Joyce what had befallen Fletcher Adams in the kitchen at Iron Rise.

She reasoned this was a time for positivity and pooling information, not telling one of the women that her husband was dead—even if the husband in question was a misogynistic twat. Whether Joyce would appreciate being left in the dark on this was up for debate, and a bridge that Pam would have to cross eventually. The bottom line, however, was the same for all. Someone had crept up on each one of them, and bashed them on the head—but not so much that they'd been left maimed or killed. Then, they'd been brought here and imprisoned.

'But why have they brought us here?' asked Pam. 'Why are they keeping us?'

'Why is it only the women too?' asked Joyce.

The youngest of the group spoke, words that should never come from a fifteen-year-old girl. 'They've been coming to look at me.'

Pam's parental hackles raised immediately. 'What do you mean, love?'

Alice couldn't look at her mother. They'd had the talk about body changes, and the whole puberty chestnut. Mother daughter stuff, essential wisdom passed from generation to generation as it always had done, while the actual nuts and bolts of sex had been well dodged by them both—but there was no time for such prudishness now.

'They've been coming and looking one at a time. One of them touched himself while looking at me. The others came and I think they told him off, and...'

Pam knew there was something else. 'Did they touch you, Alice?' She felt flushed with the spirit of a lioness whose cubs had been fucked with.

'No, no. It just... it was really horrible.'

'I'm sorry baby,' Pam said, and pulled her daughter close. Tears fell from Pam's eyes, and coursed channels through the grime on her cheeks.

'At the risk of stating the obvious, we need to get out of here,' said Joyce, walking to the corner at the tangle of wiring that had been used to bind the cell shut. 'The twins are in the house by themselves. And God knows where Fletcher is. Did you see him, Pam?'

Pam was unsure what to say, so opted for: 'I lost sight of him before I got knocked out.' Every word of that was true, but shamefully omitted some very key details. Again, something for later, she reasoned.

'Has anyone tried talking to them?' Joyce said. 'Like, reasoning with them?'

'They seem to talk in a load of grunts and clicks,' said Alice. 'I haven't heard any words.'

Pam then remembered she had. Loud and clear. When one of them pointed at her in the kitchen. 'Woman.'

'What?' asked Joyce, turning from the binds.

'One of them pointed at me and said *woman*. And he also said *man*.' The difference between the two words, not just in language but in meaning, caught in Pam's throat like a mousetrap snap, her breath suddenly stilling.

The man that thing pointed at was then immediately castrated and killed.

The woman was hit on the head and saved for later. Along with two others.

'I think I know what's going on,' she whispered to herself.

'What is it?' asked Alice.

But then she remembered what Grace said. That Quint and Wendy Fenchurch had both been murdered, man and woman, killed together. Her theories stopped dead in their tracks. 'No, never mind.'

'How do we get out of here?' asked Alice. 'I really want to go home, mum.'

Her bottom lip started to wobble, and the young girl was peeking through the steely reserve she had worked so hard to maintain. She grasped for her mother again, and Pam pulled her head onto her shoulder, and let her cry.

'We'll think of something, don't worry,' she whispered.

'Pam,' Joyce asked, stepping close to the pair. 'What are they?'

'I really don't know,' said Pam. 'But it looks like they've been down here a while.'

The light jangled in the distance, and there was a screech of metal on metal.

The women looked up like rabbits. Between the two older women's concerned faces, Alice peered through, and said, in a quivering voice and rapid breaths: 'That's them. They're coming.'

53

'LIGHT! UP AHEAD,' said Peter, pointing. 'Do you see it?'

'I see it,' replied Christian.

Grace shushed Dewey, stroking his face.

All three picked up pace, while Peter felt his hands pulsing with nervous energy, as if they were readying themselves to be used in the near future. 'Shh,' he said. 'Let's stay quiet, and kill our lights. We don't want to let anyone know we're here.'

The three beams clicked off one by one, and the tunnel was suddenly plunged in darkness, except for the tiny light far in the distance, a bit like looking into a telescope the wrong way round. Peter gripped the cricket bat in his hand, and it made him feel a little bolder. A shade more confident. He didn't want to have to use it at all, but if it meant getting Alice back, he was pretty sure it would hurt whoever he needed to hit with it.

'Do we have any kind of plan?' asked Christian.

'We don't even know what we're walking into.'

'Do you think we could reason with them?' asked Grace.

'I think Dewey might come in handy in the persuasion stakes.'

The light was fixed an indeterminate distance away, but was definite. It was no mirage. The silence though, aside from their obvious shuffling, was deeply unnerving. It felt like they were being pulled towards it, helplessly, antibodies drawn into a syringe.

Dewey picked up pace abruptly, and this time, pulled Grace

to the right-hand side wall. 'What is it Dew?' she urged, matching his speed. The men followed suit, and Peter subconsciously lifted the bat high.

They almost missed it when the dog suddenly darted into a doorway that had opened in the brick, much like the previous one. This one, however, had Dewey's full attention, and Grace had to strain to keep him back from dragging them in.

Christian, however, had no such restraint and bounded into the room. 'Olivia? *Olivia?*'

As Peter motioned to follow him, a wall of stink suddenly assaulted them. It was so thick, so rich, so rotten, he couldn't take another step, and clamped his hand over his nose—before clicking the torch on.

The room was much like the previous one in terms of size and overall decor, but the contents were wholesale different. There was only one bed in this room, in the centre, and on it was a sight that caused Peter to gag immediately.

'Oh *Jesus*,' he said, while Grace tugged Dewey back out of the door. Christian fell to his knees, alternating wretches with deep lungfuls of rank air.

Once his shock was under control, and the desire to lie down had dissipated slightly, Peter tried to make sense of the sight, and in doing so, fit it into the nightmare in which they had been dragged.

The bed was fouled with viscera. Its legs were rusted. It was folded so that the top half was at an angle, so the patient could sit up. The patient was, however, in a state of decomposition, dead for some time. Peter was no expert and had no idea how long the person had been dead for—but there was still skin there, sallow and ashen of hue, sagging against bone. The eyes were sunken, brown teeth and black gums bared, the hair grey and coiled on the head like a brillo pad grown out.

The cadaver stared at the ceiling, arms out either side of the bed, spindly wrists bound by leather restraints. The ankles were treated similarly, pulled wide and bound at the foot of the bed.

'What happened to her?' asked Grace from the door.

Her was correct. The body was nude, sagged and thin, breasts rolling down either side of her mottled chest. The area below her midriff was an unspeakable mess of torn grey flesh, mouldering gore and a sole, dangling rope of tissue, which was severed just before it reached the filthy floor.

'She... it looks like she... died in childbirth.'

Peter couldn't wait anymore. He had to leave the room, and within moments he too was gasping for breath against the tunnel wall. Grace gave him Dewey's lead, and went and had a look for herself.

'She was old,' came the shout from within the room after a few moments. 'Too old to be having kids in a minging tunnel underground at least.'

'What the hell is she doing here?' asked Christian.

'She's filthy. Not the result of decay, but of living this way,' said Grace through the doorway. 'She's been down here a long time. But not dead for all that long. Weeks not years. A month perhaps.'

'How do you know?' asked Peter.

'I'm working to specialise in violent criminal cases. Murder and so on.'

Christian interrupted incredulously. 'So a month ago, a couple of weeks before we moved in up top, this old woman was dying in childbirth down here?'

'Looks like it.'

'So where's the baby?' he asked.

They all went quiet. The notion of infants in peril was something that rattled the innate cage of all human beings, barring those with psychopathic tendencies. A species defence mechanism, that inhabited other creatures in the animal kingdom too. The end game of course, with every living creature on the planet, was species preservation. To keep your kind going. So when a human hears that a baby might be hurt, functioning humans fill with fear and dread—hence the silence that had fallen on them. Peter knew also that Christian's mind would be racing to his own child, Olivia, and what had befallen her.

Grace poked her head out of the room. 'There's no baby in here.' She'd obviously been checking while the men had waited outside, their thoughts quietly turning. To his shame, Peter was impressed with her. She was no nonsense, rational and action-orientated, and proving to be a brilliant accomplice on their journey underground.

'Then let's get moving again,' he said. 'And hope that's the last of the horrible surprises.'

He didn't think for one minute, as they fell into a line again and headed for the distant light, that would be the case.

54

THE THREE WOMEN were ordered, via a procession of furious clicks, shout, grunts, and pointing, to stand in a line. There were four of *them* present, having emerged ominously from the gloom one at a time.

Alice couldn't stop sobbing while they stared. When they didn't comply, they'd been spat at. The fury in the black eyes was impossible to ignore. The clicks came at a torrential speed Alice thought impossible to repeat, let alone decipher—but indeed, they used it to communicate. And they used it to argue. They bickered incessantly, barking at each other, the sounds coming so fast and thick their mouths frothed and sprayed angrily, which they made no attempt to control.

And the worst part about it? They seemed to be arguing over them.

The women.

Alice saw the maths—three into four—and killed the thought before it got any further. It didn't stop the tears coming, and even the obvious fear and sadness of the women in the cell didn't quell the ire of their audience.

As they bickered and the friction ramped, Alice noticed a hierarchy emerge—and amazingly, the giant one wasn't the leader. If anything, he was in third place, next to the smallest—the jostler—who you couldn't call a runt either.

The big one definitely had a place, though. The top two were similar sized, and bickered relentlessly, but the big one had a clear favourite, and this appeared to settle the positions in the food chain. The one that was covered in blood, his sweatshirt down to his joggers drenched in maroon. The big one seemed to favour him, and stood close by, edging nearer to him when the disagreement peaked in animation, as if he was a good back-up.

Maroon had a really nasty bump on the top of his head, which seemed to carry all the way down between his eyes and to his chin, resulting in one side of his face being slightly higher than the other—giving his mouth a lopsided quality that looked ever like a vicious smirk. He was taller than Alice's dad, but her dad wasn't really a tall man. Some of the lads in her class were even taller than him now.

This particular one had the clicking thing down to a fine art, maybe because of the uneven composition of his face, and his advanced grasp of their language seemed to give him an edge. And for whatever reason, it was Alice herself that seemed to be the object of his attention. He gesticulated and pointed at her, and twice pawed at the area between his legs—after which Alice could no longer meet his gaze.

The little one, or littlest, the jostler, didn't enter arguments at all. He merely focused on Joyce, his stringy neck bobbing up and down, the tufts on his head giving him, despite being the only one with hair, the appearance of youth, in that they were downy, like a duckling's tender plumage. The others appeared to leave him to it, locked in disagreement.

The other one, who Alice thought of as Cueball, because his head was a perfect ghostly sphere, was not backing down, and he too seemed to have a twinkle in his dark eyes for Alice. His jumpsuit was filthy, in a deeply ingrained way, and he had very sharp incisors either side of buck teeth. The Giant kept pushing him back when he got close to Maroon, and pulling him away from the cage when he stepped out of line.

Joyce, on the end, was muttering to herself, but Alice couldn't work out what she was saying. It gave Alice an idea. 'What do you want?' she said.

They went quiet, and Alice was initially of the opinion that they couldn't understand her, that their secret language was the only method of communicating that they had. Then a word spilled almost dismissively from Maroon's cruel lips.

'Baba,' he said.

'What do you mean *baba*?' spluttered Joyce as she stepped forward, but it only resulted in eliciting laughter from their chief tormentor, as he stuck his belly out, and patted it. Laughter was a generous word for the sound. It was a horrible echoing bark, throaty and deep. Alice thought she'd never ever forget that sound, that it would be the last thing she'd hear before falling asleep every night, regardless of whether she ever managed to leave this place or not.

Within seconds, the others were barking between bouts of repeating the word 'baba', as if it were the punchline to the funniest joke in the world.

'Why us?' Alice asked. 'Why *us*?'

This made them clam up, and they debated with each other, back to the clicking and rasping. They were on the same page it seemed, it wasn't a disagreement, but they aimed the occasional point back down the tunnel to the light source. The little one then broke away, and looked directly at Alice. 'Mama *oosh*,' he said, and raised his fists and curled them tight on the second word.

'Oosh?' said Alice. 'Oosh? What is oosh?'

'Oosh!' repeated the little one, balling his fists up by his chin. 'Oosh.' There was an inflection of malice in the word this time.

'Dead,' said Maroon, definitively. It shut the chatter cold.

'Mama's dead?' said Alice.

'Mama dead,' said the little one.

The tunnel went quiet as an understanding appeared to have been met between the two groups, however opposed their positions. Alice felt sadness. Had these men lost their mother? But then why had the women been brought here? Was it to bring some feminine cast to their world? Alice's mind was racing.

'No mama, then,' she said. 'Where's dada?'

They started the barking again, dismissively howling, throwing their heads back in apparent disbelief that Alice could be so stupid.

'No dada?' she asked tentatively.

Cue Ball placed a palm with force on Maroon's chest. 'Dada.'

Maroon put a hand on his chest too. 'Dada.'

The little one walked along the line, patting the other's chests. 'Dada, dada, dada,' he said in turn, before going backwards, repeating the word on each. Their howls were loud and incongruous and terrifying.

Alice felt a penny come close to dropping within her, but some last thread of understanding was stopping it from falling completely.

A loud clunk of metal sounded off in the distance, reverberating down the chamber to the two groups. The men all turned to the source of the sound, stunned and wide eyed. They clicked to each other, Maroon taking the lead, before scampering off down the tunnel to the source of the disturbance.

Only the little one paused to offer some chatter at Joyce, before joining the others—who were all at full sprint now, dwindling shapes in the darkness.

55

DEWEY WAS AT full pelt now, the distant light the object of his fixation, while they charged in a silent line towards the growing amber glow. As they got closer, Grace noticed the light was flickering, and that, along with its colour, kickstarted an ancient survival awareness.

Fire.

Buoyed by the idea that they had surely found the missing children, she urged the others to 'come on'. Orange fingers flickered along the walls beckoning them on, as the tunnel opened out into a room.

The space itself was hexagonal, while some of the sides were other openings to inky darkness, or doors embedded in the walls. One wall had a staircase at the bottom of it, a wide set of steps which led up to a door in the ceiling, a door which was iron and oranged with rust.

This had to be the central point of the tunnel system, Grace thought. The original point of both axis and access.

It was obscure, dim and flickering, but she could make out certain features. It had all the hallmarks of a squalid living space around an open fire, with a number of odd distinguishing features, amid a stench so raw it stung the eyes. The fire was a long-established circle of brick with stacked tree branches glowing in the centre, slick with some kind of accelerant. Old cans were discarded next to the flames. The bricks of the circle were black with years of smoke wash.

Grace watched the smoke rise, wondering where it went to, and then noticed that the roof was blackened too. Even the door that was recessed into it was darkened by what had to be fire damage. There was a story here, untold, leaving dangling threads.

Filthy beds, much like the one the woman had died in, were strewn about in an order that wasn't obvious. In fact, there was a general lack of order to what she was looking at, except that one thing was blindingly obvious:

'They live here,' she said, her voice cannoning about in the space.

'I think you're right,' said Peter, stepping towards the fire to warm his hands. 'They won't be gone long, so we best get looking.'

'Smells like a sewer system,' said Christian, as he started walking towards the nearest bed, the swaddling on which was almost black with grime. 'The beds are gross, but surely that's not the smell?'

'Are we connected to the sewers somehow?' mused Grace, pulling Dewey close, after he'd been nuzzling something on the floor. 'Dew,' she commanded.

Dewey pulled forward again, and Grace admonished him softly. 'Come on Dew, there's a good boy.' She absent-mindedly looked at what the dog had been trying to get and saw an object on the floor—and held her breath. Glancing around, she saw similar such items all over the place, which they had clearly overlooked in the poor light.

'Watch your step,' she said.

'Why?' asked Christian, as he walked past the nearest bed towards a door that was recessed into the back wall.

'Because there's human waste everywhere.'

'I'm afraid a little shit isn't going to stop me from finding my daughter,' Christian said, as he threw open the door. The handle came loose in his hand, causing the door to swung inexorably into the wall, where it impacted with a loud metallic bang.

They stood still with sudden terror, as the sound chased down the other tunnels, off into the belly of the underground system.

'Bollocks,' he whispered, looking back at the other two apologetically.

They waited a moment, until the echo of the impact had fully disappeared, then Grace started investigating the space, paying no heed to her own earlier warning to watch her step. 'What's a bit of shit between neighbours,' she murmured.

The place was a disgrace. If this really was their home, these people lived a life of filth and squalor.

People. The word didn't work for Grace. *People* didn't crap all over the floor, and sleep on old hospital gurneys in derelict tunnels. The word *people* inspired civility, thought, craft and cooperation—all notions far removed from what these things had done to her and her neighbours this awful day.

She counted the beds. She knew there were two at least, of that she was certain. But there were five beds—although they were so filthy, she wasn't sure when they'd been last slept in. Could have been last night. Could have been years ago.

'Oh my *God*,' shouted Christian. Grace looked up. She didn't like the tremor in his voice, the give in his words. He was stood in the doorway, shining a torch inside, the room beyond a black mystery.

'What is it?' Grace whispered. 'What have you...'

Her words trailed off, because as she listened to her own words echo around the space, she noticed another sound joining in.

Footsteps. A lot of them.

Drawing near.

56

AS SOON AS David eased the car into Broadoak, he knew something wasn't right. Humans, modern humans at least, react with immediate disquiet when presented with darkness. It's a stark reminder that, no matter how much brain power has put the species at the top of the tree, if you strip that away, there's always something bigger and stronger out there with teeth and claws that would happily rip you to pieces. And darkness gives those things cover. It levels the playing field.

David wasn't ever one for flights of imagination, and the rational part of his brain had been stubborn in its acceptance of events in the last few days. An explanation was there, he just needed to find it, see it, feel it. And he had been convinced that moment was coming.

Until he drove into the pitch-black cul-de-sac of Broadoak.

Every house was dead, the only hint of artificial light coming from the ever-so-soft orange smear in the sky beyond, where the motorway lights glowed heavenwards. He saw his husband's car, parked oddly at the end, right in the middle of everybody else's turning circle. He found that most strange of all.

He pulled up outside their own house, killed the engine and got out.

The night had held a stillness akin to anaesthesia.

His paternal instincts fired, and his mind catapulted to Olivia. He jogged to the parked car. Where were she and Christian, if they'd parked here?

The vehicle was empty and unlocked. Olivia's empty car seat yawned balefully at him through the passenger window. A pang of fear, hot and white, threatened to puncture his shield of rationality—although he still clung to it for now.

The car had been left immediately between the two biggest houses, with the Adams house to the left and the Wests on the right. He looked at each in turn. Black and vacant, the pair of them.

Proactivity was always David's default action, so he marched straight up the Wests' drive. The moonlight was weighty enough to let him see where he was going, and he could even make out some damage to the hedging by the front door. Even though it was somewhat trivial, and could have been caused by any number of things, it was another little tick to add to the column of overall strangeness.

He pressed the door bell and immediately cursed his stupidity. The completeness of the darkness could only be attributed to a power cut—which meant no fancy electronic door chimes. So he banged three times on the door with a clenched fist.

He waited.

Nothing.

So deep was the silence, it felt futile to knock again, so he crossed the cul-de-sac to the Adams', his steps scuffing soil that had been left on the path. He felt like he'd driven back onto an alternate plane, as if the Blackstoke gates themselves had acted as a portal and offered him carriage to a different reality—one of a whistling breeze through woodland canopies and the vacuum of abandonment.

He knocked on the front door to the MP's house, but again, was met with silence. He didn't even bother listening, and turned back to the street. Examining every house in turn, he saw that each front door was shut and all windows were darkened. It was a ghost town, but as he took the first step back down the path, something caught the corner of his eye, bright, and whirling, like a firefly. He turned back immediately, trying to catch sight of it, but it had already moved off.

No. There again.

Either side of the front door was a frosted glass panel, and, beyond the right-hand pane, a pin-sharp light danced a tight jig. He banged on the door immediately, this time much more forcefully.

'Hello? Is anyone in there? It's David Lyons here, from across the road?'

There was silence for a moment, before a muffled voice replied from within. 'David Lyons?' The voice was adolescent. 'Prove it.'

'Prove it?'

'Prove you're David Lyons.'

The youth in the voice made it hard for David to take the request seriously. 'I don't have time for games, young man. I want to know what's going on.'

'Prove it.'

David sighed with exasperation, and pulled his wallet out. He posted his driving licence through the letterbox. 'Happy?'

'Are you alone?' came the voice again.

'Yes, it's just me.'

The door was unlocked, thick deadbolts retracted, and swung open just enough to let David see inside. The West boy was standing there holding a small tea light candle, flanked by the Adams twins, one on either side. They were holding tennis rackets and kitchen knives, and in the dim candlelight, David could see, piled on the stairs behind them, was all sorts of sporting goods like ski poles, golf clubs, cricket bats and so on.

It was a sport store armoury.

'What the hell is going on here?' asked David, as the door was bolted behind him.

57

A WHOOP JOINED the pounding of feet, and the feral, animal sound had Peter raising the cricket bat over his head without a second thought. Suddenly four of those hairless monsters emerged from the right-hand tunnel, howling and bellowing in a baseless rage.

They all paused in unison at the threshold of the room, taking in the intruders one by one. To see them, the size of them, all of them taller than Christian who himself was the tallest, set off a firework of dread in Peter's gut. Their eyes flickered from one to the other with cold reptilian malice—when another metallic impact sound jarred the room. It sounded like the last one, and all turned to look to the door that had caused the initial noise—but it was now shut.

Christian had shut himself in that room, away from the beasts that had come to kill them.

Peter couldn't believe it—*the bastard*—but didn't have time to think, because they were coming for him. The four were stepping into the room, and fanning out, murder and blackness in their eyes.

It was as they began to run in unison when a disjointed fragment of Peter's mind realised why their pupils were so dark and expansive. They were the direct result of a life in darkness, their bodies having adapted to their lot in life to make at least sight a fraction easier.

No time to dwell. Peter wanted to run, and he took two steps back, fully uncaring of what he might be stepping in now. Behind him was the stairway, the steps to nowhere, but at least it would give him the height advantage—so he went backwards, never turning from the oncoming group.

Grace was rounding the other side of the tunnel, with Dewey—but the dog was yelping and pulling to go to Peter. He could see her idea though. Double back around them. It was still strange however that not one of them had gone for her. Was it the dog? Were they really that scared of it?

He started swinging the cricket bat as he reversed up the first three steps, and as the four reached the bottom of the stairwell, they slowed. This was the first time he'd got a good look at them—a stomach-churning group of feral animals that somehow possessed human form. Where had they come from? What was their story?

The biggest one, the one who had held Fletcher down in his kitchen earlier, had taken a step up, the first to make a move, and he walked coiled like a panther, strike-ready. Peter jabbed with the bat, but the giant merely bobbed backwards to avoid it. The smallest one stepped up, a growl escaping his lips. Peter ran up the stairs as high as he could go before the ceiling closed in, and the steps finished at the horizontal door in the roof.

He turned, and tried to push it. It was no good—he couldn't even twist the handle, it was that rusted. He tried to push the whole door from its frame, in the hope that the locking mechanism was so decayed it would crack under stress, but it wouldn't budge. He merely turned and banged the door in anger. It was him versus the hoard.

'Come on then, you bastards,' he shouted, as he saw Grace at the mouth of the tunnel they had come from. She was looking down it into the darkness, then back to Peter up by the roof, all as the four took step after careful step up the stairs to him. 'Go, go!' he shouted to her.

He swung twice, back and to, and connected with the little one, who jumped back a few steps, yelping angrily, clutching its forearm. It gave the big one the chance to grab the bat, which he did with one massive hand, like a normal fist might grip a rolled-up newspaper. He yanked it, but Peter held firm—yet, in doing so, it held Peter in place. The other two saw the chance and moved in. Peter looked at Grace one last time. 'Just go!' he shouted, a tired, sad resignation creeping into his voice.

Grace looked at him, their eyes locking, and she released Dewey's lead—before shaking her head once and sprinting into the blackness of the tunnel.

The dog snarled, darted across the room, and took the stairs in giant bounds, three steps at a time. He was on the men within seconds, and again, all of them span and looked at the wolfhound in pure terror.

It gave Peter the chance to swing the bat as hard as he could at the nearest one's turned head. It was the one covered in blood—Fletcher's blood. He felt his wrists jolt painfully with the weight of impact, and out rang the wet crack of splitting bone.

While the other three addressed Dewey, who was on them remorselessly, pulling and tearing at them, matching them animal for animal, the blood soaked one turned and looked at Peter with something close to confusion. A pure incomprehension at the gall of Peter for even thinking of swinging the cricket bat his way. Its skull was crooked, as if the two halves of the head were being viewed at different frame rates.

Abruptly, the head fell, lolling back while still attached to the neck and the weight shift caused the rest of the body to fall back too—right over the bannister. It fell the thirty feet to the ground, landing with a dull impact somewhere below. One of the others, the smallest, saw what had happened and unleashed a furious howl, agitated, pointing and hopping like a gibbon, all the while trying to avoid the thrashing jaws of Dewey, who simply would not stop.

He was pointing and chirping at the empty space on the stairs where their colleague had been. The big one, suddenly back in the game, stepped forward and grabbed Dewey by the chest and pushed him as far as he could—which was only a few steps back down. This didn't get Dewey off their case, but did give the giant a second to look where the little one was pointing.

The giant's eyes swung immediately to Peter, and he threw his head back to charge—when Dewey jumped on the monster's back, biting at his thick neck.

'Good boy, Dewey!' Peter shouted, as the remaining two went for him, grasping and clawing him to the ground with rough hands, and sharp, claw-like nails. Peter screamed for Grace, for Dewey, even for that coward Christian, then eventually settled on God. His hand was outstretched, fingers reaching white-knuckled to the ceiling, the last remaining part of him free, expecting something awful and deep to suddenly strike and end it—when the ceiling opened, and a shaft of light rained through the gap.

58

CHRISTIAN FELT AWFUL for closing the door on his neighbours, but felt, considering what he'd found in the room off that awful central living area, that there was no choice. The children came first.

When he'd first opened the door, he was awash with the purest joy when he saw an infant on the floor, in a makeshift pen made of over turned trolleys. Olivia. He hadn't had time to fully appreciate his relief, when he saw a second infant had turned to look at his wandering torchlight.

Two children. In this awful subterranean... crèche?

And when his eyes adjusted to the torchlight, and he saw that this other child was far removed from his, that there was something fundamentally wrong with what he was seeing, he couldn't help himself from saying: 'Oh my *God*.'

Then the madness had started on the other side of the door and like any parent, he put a barrier between his child and harm's way. Once it was shut, he searched for a catch or lock by torch light, but found nothing, so he readied himself by the door, prepared to defend the children to the last—his child *and* the poor wretched thing in there with her. But the door didn't open. He heard voices, clattering, shouting, barking, but it was as if he'd been forgotten.

So he went to Olivia, and picked her up. She appeared unhurt, merely dirty, and recognised him instantly. She grasped for him, her cheeks making way for a huge grin. He held her to his chest and gasped a couple of sobs into her curls. The other child, in the pen, looked up at them both, bemused.

Christian couldn't bear the confusion on the other child's face. There was a lack of comprehension, but also a connection to what he or she was seeing. As if the child knew that was the normal way of things. To be comforted. To be nurtured.

'Hello,' Christian whispered, in as calming a tone as he could. As disturbing the child was, with its near-black eyes, pale hairless skull, it was still a *child*.

The child watched for a moment, as Olivia pawed at her father's face, then crawled to the far end of the enclosure. When it reached the barrier, it sat, and reached upwards with one arm, fingers stretched. With the torch beam, Christian followed where the child was reaching, and was almost prompted into heart attack when the circle of light crept up a figure standing at the back of the pen. He saw the face of a man, and another hairless head, before a scream caught in his throat, the terror too fierce to even permit sound.

The man hissed, revealing a disgraceful chasm of brown teeth and black gums. Christian turned for the door, clutching Olivia as tight as he dared, but stopped. The sounds outside were cacophonous, as if a battle was raging. What would happen to them both if he took Olivia out there and *they* saw them? The image of Fletcher Adam's body being hacked to ribbons by a meat cleaver crashed into his mind.

There was only one in here, and in pure numbers terms, one versus one was better odds.

With the torch in one hand, and his daughter cradled with his other arm, he shakily turned back to face the man.

Something about him provoked less fear than the others. The way he was stood. He wasn't coiled and predatory like the others, and the hiss was a bit… half-hearted. It made Christian feel as if he could reason with him.

'Hello,' he said, bringing the torch light up a touch, but not so high that it was pointed at the man. He kept it aimed towards the ground, taking the glare out of the beam. A grunt came back. It didn't immediately fill Christian with threat. It actually made him think they might get out of the room alive.

He turned slightly back to the door to listen, but, while it was quieter than it had been, he still didn't feel he could go out there.

'I no take child.'

Christian froze, half thinking it was he who said it, but unable to remember speaking. But the sound, the scratchiness of it, was nothing to do with him. The voice from the back of the room sounded like it was trying the words out. Like it was a forgotten skill, the communication equivalent of riding a bike after years without doing it.

He looked at the man, offering torchlight for them both once more. He was looking at Christian, who in turn was confident enough to regard the man properly. His eyes weren't nearly as dark and passionless as the others, his head wasn't completely devoid of hair, relegated to a few greased strands like oiled threads across his head. He wore a sweatsuit like the others, but there was something different about him. One of the sleeves was rolled up to the elbow. That was it. It imparted an air of personality, of character. Of human choice, and in turn, a hint of civility. The man held himself carefully. He was older—much older than the others. His pale skin curled into wrinkles and crow's feet at the corners.

'Child. I no take,' he said again, like a broken gear box come to life.

Christian couldn't be sure, but he thought he could detect regret. 'Who take child?' he asked, mimicking the man's delivery.

The man pointed to the door. 'Boy...' He tried again, putting more effort into another last consonant, as if he hadn't put his mouth in such a shape in years. 'Boys.'

'The boys? Out there?'

'Boys. Out there.'

Christian was getting somewhere, and despite the horrors of where he was, he felt hope. He didn't see threat from this man, although he would be damned if he was going to take it for granted. Despite his resemblance to the others, this one was different.

'The boys—who are they?' he asked.

The man thumped his own chest gently. 'My.'

'Your boys?' Christian couldn't hide his shock as his mind filled in blanks and made connections. 'They are your sons?'

'Sons.'

'Where is their mother?'

The man looked crestfallen and confused, as if in his head his mind was a forest canopy and the sunshine rays that pierced through were emotions he was not quite able to handle or process. 'Mother,' he said as softly as his gravelled voice allowed.

'Where is their mother?' Christian said.

'Mother,' the man replied again.

Christian, not for the first time today, was stumped. And in the silence of his confusion, he noticed a greater quiet.

Outside the door, in the main chamber, the fighting had stopped.

59

LETTING GO OF Dewey was the hardest thing she'd ever done—but it gave Peter West the best chance of survival. Not to mention that Dewey had a bit of a rapport with Peter, liked him, even. Dewey, bless him, wanted to go and protect him.

Grace had done fast maths on the subject. What was the best way to create enough time for her to sneak off and find the children? Let Dewey go and occupy them.

As she sprinted into the darkness of the tunnel—the tunnel those creatures had just emerged from—she found herself fancying Dewey's odds. The men clearly didn't like him. They acted as if they'd never seen anything like it, hadn't ever thought such a creature was possible. She could understand. Most people in the street found Dewey a bit hard to get their head around, with his mad combination of size and affability, and many such people had their own dogs. But if you'd never seen a fully grown, grizzled Irish wolfhound before, charging at you in the dark? Nightmarish.

Go on Dew, sort them out.

She ran knowing time was of the essence, and her eyes retuned to the darkness. She didn't want to use her torch, not yet, because, should they look down here, it would be a beacon to call those creatures after her.

That thought caught, however. Why had they all ignored her?

They'd looked at her, then looked at Peter. Then descended on him alone to attack. Why not attack her? She was grateful to whatever quirk had made it happen, of course—but was still none the wiser.

The tunnel began to narrow somewhat, and was soon half the width of the tunnel they had been in earlier. But before she could wonder as to why this was happening, what design purpose the narrowing sought to achieve, a voice cut the darkness.

'Hello?' It was female.

'Hello?' she hushed in reply, a strangled call.

More than one voice replied.

'Grace! Is that you?'

'Grace!'

Grace couldn't work out what was happening, how there were other people down here that weren't the children, when she came across the cage. She finally dared to flick her torch on as she came to a stop, and saw a sight that shocked and appalled her. Filthy, wet-eyed, cowed but unbroken, packed together in a small filthy enclosure of bent metal and wet brick—Alice, Pam and Joyce.

'How did you...' Grace asked, as she reached the bars.

'They took us,' said Alice. 'Those men. Knocked us out and brought us down here.'

'Pam, I left you up there with your son?'

Pam shook her head, her face cracking with worry. 'I've not seen him. They took me soon after you left.'

'My boys are still up there too,' added Joyce. 'I think.' She, too, wore maternal concern like a ten-tonne veil.

'Where are the others?' said Pam, looking down the tunnel to the pinprick of light. 'And what is that noise?'

Grace felt a wave of shame that wobbled her footing. She'd left this woman's husband to chance, fate, luck—and whatever he and an old dog could bring to the party.

'I don't know what's happening.'

It wasn't really a lie, not really, but she could make a ninety per cent sure guess that it was a fight to the death that Pam's husband was a very key part of.

Refusing to dwell on her own indecision, with the time factor an accelerant, she checked over the cage for a lock.

'Over here,' said Joyce, catching on immediately. 'It's held shut by all this wire here.'

Grace followed her gesture to a bird's nest tangle of industrial wire, that was coiled tight. She took the end and started to unravel it, but soon found she could go no further. The wire was thick, stiff, and bent by raw power—the kind of power that the really big one possessed, she thought.

'Have you seen Fletcher at all?' Joyce asked, joining Grace as close to the wire binding as the structure allowed. Grace paused, and met eyes with Pam.

Pam shook her head in a quick jerk. Grace got the message. Not only didn't Joyce know the fate of her husband, but Pam had also chosen not to tell her, and the rub Pam was giving her daughter's shoulder suggested the omission may have, in part, been to protect her too.

'No,' said Grace, careful not to say any more. 'Have they hurt you?' she asked.

'Not yet,' whispered Joyce. 'Alice has been here most of the day, and she seems alright too.'

Grace looked at Alice, who was dirty, wide-eyed, ever-so-young—yet defiant as a tree in a flash flood. Grace nodded at her in admiration. 'Well, we all need to get out. Heads together, what have we got?'

'I've tried pushing the panels,' said Pam. 'But they're all fixed in place with this wire.'

Grace stood back, and traced the edges of the contraption.

She realised, if she could see the brick behind, and that there was no interruption of metal, then the structure wasn't four sided.

'Is it fixed to the wall?' she asked, her torch brushing along the framework edges, paying particular attention to where it met brick.

'I don't think so,' said Alice, having moved away from her mother to look at the brick above. 'No, I can't see any join.'

'So if it's not attached to the wall, can you push it?' asked Grace. Looking at the thing they were stuck in, it seemed more like a pen that you'd use to section off animals. Like livestock. Grace shuddered—that that was most likely *precisely* how those men viewed the women.

Cattle.

The women in the cell looked at each other, as if wondering how they could have missed this and immediately darted to the front wall of the prison, pushing it from the inside.

It clanked, wobbled, juddered, until Grace took Dewey's lead, looped it around one of the bed supports that was part of the frame, and pulled for all she was worth. The whole thing jumped forward a fraction. The promise of hope—the small flash of possible sanctuary—flooded the four women in an instant, and they couldn't help but release small exclamations of joy.

'Wait, focus on this corner,' said Grace, moving her dog lead attachment along to the furthest point of the front panel—where the cell abutted the wall. 'If you push here, you can tilt the whole thing and create an opening.'

The women inside excitedly did exactly as instructed. Pam lay on the ground and pushed with her legs, Alice above over her mother, with Joyce on top, and Grace outside, pulling with her dog lead.

With a scrape, a gap emerged between wall and cage. Just an

inch. Alice's fingers were through. They kept going, and the gap widened with excruciating slowness, until Alice was able to force herself out of the gap. Grace caught the girl, who was immediately overwhelmed with freedom and gripped Grace tight around the neck.

'Thank you,' she whispered with a quiver in her voice.

'Come on, let's get your mum and Joyce out,' Grace said, and Alice turned, grabbed the opening, and really put her back into it. It didn't take long before Pam and Joyce were free too, and the four women were embracing in the tunnel, a tight-knit spark of brightness and joy in the dark.

60

THEY HADN'T BEEN in the house long when David decided that enough was enough, and he had to go and find all the people in his neighbourhood that had gone missing—and find out who these people were that had been causing so much harm. Sitting in the dark, at the bar stools in Fletcher Adams' kitchen, had listened to everything the boys told him with confused horror.

Well, boy, singular. The twins were mute while Jacob West was honest, and told as much as he could, stumbling over the parts which clearly butted against his comprehension. But David had heard their story now. Every last impossible part. That Alice West had gone missing. That there'd been a huge fight in the kitchen in their home, as evidenced by what the young lad had heard while hiding under his bed, and the lashings of blood he discovered in the room when he came to see where everybody had gone. How his mum had stayed with him, until she too disappeared. How he'd almost been attacked by a strange pale man, only for the twins to save him with nothing more than some bright lights and their dual presence.

It seemed these people, whatever they were, didn't like the twins. Couldn't understand their identicality. It led David's mind down a rabbit hole of wide questions, but the big one remained, looming large: what was going on at the quiet estate of Blackstoke tonight, and where was his own family?

'And the power has been out this whole time too?' he asked, spinning slightly back and forth on the bar stool as if he had a sideways nervous tick.

'It went out a couple of hours ago, and never came back on once. Not even a flicker.' Jacob seemed more emboldened and encouraged as the moments passed. As if having an adult in their midst was an offer of hope.

Two hours was a long time for an outage, thought David. It suggested to him that, outside of the estate, nobody knew. 'Stupid question, but no phone reception?'

'Stupid question,' agreed Jacob.

'Then we have to get the word out some other way. Get help. Are you boys happy enough here while I go?' He didn't like the idea of leaving them there, but it was the logical, right thing to do. People were missing, the power was off, and neither of those facts appeared to be about to change without some kind of intervention.

'Yes, we can do that,' replied Jacob, glancing at the twins. They nodded, predictably in unison.

'Can I borrow a torch?' One of the twins stepped forward and handed him one, which he pointed at the floor and gave it a quick click on and off to check it was working. It was. 'Stay quiet, stay safe, alright? Don't open the door to anyone you don't know.'

'What do you think we've been doing these last couple of hours,' Jacob replied with a smile.

They let David back out into the street, which he surveyed with eagle-eyed care, and locked the door behind him. He didn't ignite the torch, but used the moonlight to cross the road to the Wests house. He just needed to check. He didn't doubt the boys, but he was well aware that adolescents were capable of embellishment—and he wanted to be sure before he raced into the night and its supposed nightmares. The easiest way to verify the severity of the situation would be to check the West's kitchen.

The front door to Iron Rise was unlocked, and only once inside did he hit the torch. Within seconds, he was back out of the front door again, gasping lungfuls of crisp air.

The boys were right. The kitchen was every bit as bad as described, although he'd noticed some plasma-soaked money that the West kid hadn't mentioned. On seeing all that blood, and how it was dry in places and congealed in others, the stakes just rocketed. They were all in grave danger, and given the amount of blood loss he'd just seen, at least someone was surely already dead. David breathed, and composed himself.

Where to start? They couldn't be far, and the boys said their attacker ran into the hedges at the back, down the dog trail. David thought that would be as good a place to start as any, but he looked at it reservedly. A dark inlet, into thick brush, it was hardly inviting, and God knew what horrors he would find down there.

And then he heard something. Faint, almost a whisper. On the breeze, coming from the opposite direction. He turned his head, and looked along the entrance road to the cul-de-sac, to the bend that brought cars onto it, then the thick trees beyond.

He couldn't hear it anymore, and for the briefest second thought he must have imagined it.

No. There. Again.

A distance away, but unmistakable.

A dog barking. Deep in the grounds of the estate.

He jumped up, energised, renewed with purpose and direction.

But the question of help slowed him. He was supposed to get some. That was their best bet for survival. Then, an idea lit. He ran back over to the Adams' house, and knocked softly on the door. 'Boys, open up, it's me again, David.'

The door cracked open a centimetre, and three pairs of eyes looked out at him as he spoke:

'Can you all walk?'

'Yes.'

'Then how do you lads feel about saving the day?'

61

PETER HAD SO many hands grabbing him, clawing at him, shoving him, that he hadn't realised that there was one more which had come with light. The strikes of the men had been vicious, his position at the top of the stairs precarious, and the pressure of the life and death balance had been so severe, so much so that when the hand reached down to pull him upwards into blinding light, it could well have been God himself calling time and plucking him from this world with a personal touch.

But it didn't work out like that. There were no pearly gates, unless the doorway was rusted, horizontal and embedded in soil. Because within seconds that is exactly where he found himself. In dirt. Outside. Under the bare sky. With fresh air, which he gulped in mouthfuls that felt so pure and searing it was like chugging bleach.

He had no idea what was going on.

There was a bright light, brighter than any torch he'd seen before, which hit his attackers as he was pulled through, and it kept them oddly at bay, like fire. Like it carried harm to the men.

And it was another man pulling him through—a large man with a pale blue shirt, with a starched collar and navy epaulettes. He was wielding a torch that resembled a briefcase with a colander on one end.

'Quick,' he shouted, as soon as Peter was through, 'close the door.'

Peter crawled in the dirt to the hatch opening, as the man

waved the torch down the stairs, emitting a near-absurd level of white light.

'Back, back!' he was shouting.

'The dog!' shouted Peter. There was no way he was going to leave Dewey down there, if he could avoid it. 'Dewey!' he shouted. The light from the monstrous torch occupied the men just enough to allow Dewey to slip between them. He was big and tightly wrought, but thank God he was slender and agile. He hopped up and out, bounding into the dirt, as Peter slammed the door shut. His saviour immediately slid a spade handle through the metal grip of the door, pinning it closed. There was furious banging and shouts from beneath them, cries of fathomless anger, muffled by the metal doors. Suddenly, ominously, they receded.

Peter lay in the dirt, panting, until Dewey licked his face.

'Jeff,' said the other man finally, through deep breaths. He finally switched the torch off and the darkness crowded in. 'My name is Jeff.' He held the contraption up. 'It's got the power of ten thousand candles. Ebay, in case you need one.'

'Thank you so much, Jeff,' Peter said, sitting up. As Jeff was dusting himself down, Peter took a good look at him, then made the link. 'You're our security guard?'

'That's right,' he sighed wearily.

'I'll make sure there's a good showing for your Christmas collection.'

Jeff remained silent, and appeared not just tired, but troubled.

'How did you know I would be here?' Peter asked, as he took in his surroundings. 'And where is *this*?'

'It's a... complicated story.'

'Please tell me—what do you know?'

'They just came up, started causing trouble?'

He knew, Peter thought. Jeff knew about these people living in the tunnels. 'Yeah, fair to say, there's been some weird things going on these past few days. But tonight it all... went mad.' It was in that precise moment, when forced to try to explain even a scant summary of the night's events, that Peter knew this was going to take a very long time to get over.

'They've been more active, I've noticed.' Jeff still couldn't look at Peter properly.

'You knew about them, and you... you didn't think to warn us?'

'I didn't know they were like *this*.'

'How long have you known?'

Jeff's eyes suddenly became glued to his fancy torch, but sadness was evident. 'Not long. A few days. When I found this place.'

Peter stood, petted Dewey, and looked around. They were at the back corner of a vast clearing, closed in on either side by thick trees. In the clearing, were huge mounds of rubble, made up of masonry, twisted bits of metal, chunks of earth and brick. And here in this back corner, a square of overturned earth with a battered door embedded in it.

'What *is* this place?'

Jeff sat morosely, and looked about. At the mounds and the trees, then eventually the sky. 'It's all going to come down eventually.'

'What?'

'This... this is all that's left.'

'Of what?'

'Blackstoke.' He smiled ruefully, as he rolled onto his hands and knees. 'Come and have a look, you can see through this gap. I found it when I dug the door out.'

Peter joined him, and saw, in the excavated doorframe, that

there was a small opening between the battered metal of the door and its housing. Maybe an inch in width at its widest point, against which he dipped to offer his eye.

It was a top-down view of the chamber below, etched in the flickering glow of the central firepit. The bald heads were easy to make out, white circles moving around the space like moths—except one, which wasn't moving. Peter's mouth suddenly drenched, and he felt faint. He had done that. He had made that happen. One of the remaining three, which he thought to be the little one, was hovering over the body on the floor. Peter was too high to work out what he was doing, what impact the death of one of their own was having. The other two were in the middle, not doing a lot. It was strange. The behaviour, they appeared, if anything, a bit confused. Directionless.

'I...' Peter started, sitting up, but found the words hard to come by. 'I think I've killed one of them.'

Jeff reacted with wide eyes, unmistakably fringed with panic. Between the behaviour of the men in the chamber, and the security guard's reaction, Peter was more confused than ever. 'Which one?'

'I don't know—not the biggest one. The next in line. It was the one who killed Fletcher Adams.'

'The MP? He's dead?'

'Yes. It was... really bad.'

'How many did you see down there?'

Peter counted the ghastly faces that had tried to end his life so savagely. 'Four.'

'Did they all look the same? Same age, I mean.'

Age? 'I mean, it's hard to tell, but I think so. Do you know what they are? What are you not telling me?'

'Was there an older one?' Jeff was shouting over Peter now, his voice urgent and pushy.

'An *older* one?'

'Yes, there's those four who are all about the same age, but did you see another one?'

This was becoming too outlandish for Peter to understand, but the fact of the matter was that this man had been hired to protect them, and the impression he was giving was that he was more interested in protecting the horrors that had come up to claim them.

'I haven't seen any others,' said Peter, hurriedly. 'I've got friends down there I need to help—and my daughter is still missing!'

'Your daughter? I knew about the baby.'

Peter felt suddenly like a failure. All this effort and he still hadn't got his daughter back, nor got any closer to establishing her whereabouts. 'Yes. She's fifteen. Alice.'

Jeff was suddenly quietened, but did let loose two small words. 'A female.'

Peter didn't know what he was suggesting, but it jogged something in his memory adrift, which bobbed to the surface. 'We found a woman down there.'

Jeff suddenly sprang up as if he'd been sharply introduced to an electrical feed. 'A woman?! Where?' Peter saw something new in his eyes now. Hope.

'She was dead. Had been for a while,' he said, without offering any of the additional detail because he didn't want to put words to what he saw in that dank room off the tunnel. He'd have to add those images to the zoetrope of horror that was going to blur his eyes every time he shut them for years to come.

Jeff was quiet, exhaling softly, his breath chimneying skywards. The news was affecting to him, for some reason. Peter ventured a thought, and put words to it.

'Did you know her?'

'What did she look like?'

It was Peter's turn to look into the distance. 'I think she was old. But like I said, she'd been dead for some time. It wasn't pretty.'

'Did you see what had happened to her?'

All Peter could think about was the withered rope, dangling from her midsection. 'We thought she might have died during childbirth.'

Jeff sat down heavily, as if his knees had threatened to give way and he'd pre-empted their failure. He put a hand to the bridge of his nose. He pinched tight and, to Peter's amazement, he started crying in a high-pitched mewl.

'Did you know her?' Peter asked, more forcefully this time.

'Madeline,' the old man stuttered. 'Poor misguided Madeline.'

Peter was lost for words. It was not just hard to swallow, that this man was somehow far more connected to the events at Blackstoke than merely in his role as security guard, but also that that cruel shape tied to the bed down in the tunnels at once been a person. A person with a name as beautiful as Madeline.

Tied. The word that just ran through his head repeated on him. Revulsion cored through Peter once more. 'She'd been restrained Jeff. Tied down while having a baby. What do you know about her?'

Jeff was crying openly now, phlegmy pulls of air echoing in the clearing. 'When I saw all this, I thought that must have been what had happened, but still. You never expect something like that.'

The man is rambling, thought Peter. And he didn't have time for this. 'Jeff, if you can tell me anything that can help us, help the people that are still trapped down there with those... those things, you've got to tell me. Is there another way in? How can I get back down there without them seeing?'

'There's an older one. An older one who isn't like the others. Don't hurt him.'

'Okay, but I haven't seen any older one. Now, how can I get back down there?'

'They've been using her. They used her up.'

Peter had had enough, and was tempted to throw open the hatch, grab the cricket bat and get back in there the hard way. He called Dewey over, who had been sniffing the nearest pile of rubble. It looked like there'd been a demolition.

'What used to be here, Jeff?' Thing were falling into place, his subconscious was filling in blanks it didn't know it needed to. He remembered the lettering on the filthy jogging suits. It wasn't BIG, it wasn't a one size fits all clothing policy. 'What was this place? BIG?'

'Blackstoke Institute for Good.'

'And what was that?'

Jeff stopped sobbing, and deflated, the sadness of all the secrets he so obviously carried flushing out of him in one purge of posture.

'It was a hospital. For the people that worked there, like me, and the people who lived locally, we knew it as Blackstoke, the mental asylum.'

62

AS THE TUNNEL widened, the women slowed, and adopted a more cautious walk towards the room emerging at the end of the corridor. The shapes of the space were drawn in dim flickers. They clung tight to the left-hand wall, the middle offering nothing but exposure. Grace went first, adopting a position of leadership naturally and without thought. Now she'd found them, she was determined to get them out. She'd never baulked at a challenge in her life, and wasn't going to start now, especially when the consequences were just so severe.

As they moved, Grace peppered the women with questions, and it was Alice, who'd been there the longest, who seemed to be the one with both the most information and happiest to talk.

'There's four of them, that I've seen. I've kind of given them names, to keep track of them. Maroon, who's the one covered in blood tonight. He seems to be in charge, although it looks like Cue Ball wants that job for himself. He's the one with the really shiny pale head. The Giant is, well, the big one. And the little weirdo is Runt.'

Grace could have smiled. In the midst of mayhem, the human urge was always to make order of things as best as possible. As if creating sense and meaning might steady the ship. As they reached the tunnel mouth, she held out a hand to slow them, and in a receding line, they peered into the space.

Three of the men were visible.

The big one, Giant, was sitting on the edge of one of the beds, looking at his feet chittering to himself. The one with the perfect bald head was adding some sticks to the fire from a pile in the corner. And the little one was over by the back wall, almost beneath the stair well, preoccupied with something on the floor.

Grace was terrified that the object of his interest would be Peter or Dewey—but she was astonished to see that it was one of their own. The one covered in blood. Maroon. She could make out his body lying unnaturally, something fundamentally wrong in its rest. One of the arms was up, pointing to the ceiling, but the hand wasn't there - it was an elbow, and it was pointing the wrong way. The head was dented, a filthy misshapen egg.

Peter had killed one of them—and if Alice was right, it wasn't just anyone. It was their leader. Grace felt a rush of elation, but found it tinged with nausea. They'd had to sink to their level.

The little one didn't seem altogether bothered by what had happened, and what he was looking at. He just appeared a bit confused more than anything, his emotional machinery unable to make sense of things. Like he was trying to gene-sequence DNA on a Commodore 64.

Facts were facts, however. And the facts said there were only three left.

But Peter was gone. She scanned the room for him, but couldn't see any sign of him. Same with Dewey. She felt buoyed again.

Grace tried to weigh up probabilities and potential outcomes in her head. The most likely, given that they weren't here, and one of those disgusting brothers was dead, was that Peter and Dewey had fought and tried to escape, and had found some success in both.

Abruptly, Cue Ball got up from his place by the fire, barked at his brothers with a dismissive righteousness, and started walking—right towards the tunnel the women were hiding in. They huddled tighter in the shadows of the corner.

Giant jumped up, suddenly angry, and bellowed at Cue Ball with a shout far more animal than human. He caught up with his smaller brother in two strides, and whisked him around, shouting at him, thumping him on the chest, pointing at Runt, pointing at Maroon's body, and pointing down the tunnel.

Grace caught on at the same time as Alice whispered out loud: 'They're fighting over which one of them gets which one of us.'

'Oh Jesus,' said Pam.

'They were doing this before,' said Alice. 'They seem really interested in having women down here.'

Grace remembered the woman in the side room earlier. Dead. Died in childbirth. No use to them. No more babies if you don't have women. God in heaven, she thought. In capturing the younger women of Blackstoke, they were building a harem.

Runt hadn't really entered the disagreement, but had offered a few words before running to the tunnel entrance. The other two, not wanting him to get a head start, started after him.

'Did anyone see anywhere to hide?' Grace asked.

'No! The tunnel's a dead end behind us!' said Pam.

'Any doorways?'

'It was dark but I didn't see any.'

'Well we don't want to get trapped back down there with them,' Grace concluded out loud. 'Ladies, we have to take it to them. There's more of us than them.'

Four versus three. Back to maths.

Grace pointed. 'The tunnel to the right, over there, gets you out of here. You have to make a break for it, it's our only chance.'

'What about you?' whispered Pam.

'Call it the element of surprise. As soon as their backs are turned, go for it and don't look back. Follow the tunnel all the way down until you see a ladder. And take this.' She handed the torch to Alice, and didn't wait for any word of argument before moving.

Her plan was simple. If she went left, and drew their attention, she was getting closer to Christian. He hadn't come back out, so there had to be some degree of safety in there.

While she was occupying them, the rest of the women could go right.

Simple. Kind of.

'Hello,' she said, with as much confidence as she could muster as she walked into the space. As their eyes snapped to her in unison, and their glare of outraged surprise caught fire in each set of inky pupils, she realised just how likely it would be that this single word might get her killed.

But anything to stop brave young Alice West from becoming part of some underground clan's breeding programme.

She walked around the left-hand wall of the chamber, as confidently and as nonchalantly as she could. 'My name is Grace, it's nice to meet you.'

They looked at her like she was a foreign species, which in a lot of ways, she supposed she was to them. Then the Giant gurgled. It sounded a bit like approval. It turned Grace's stomach to stone.

But he was the real danger adversary, with his speed and size. 'Hi,' she said to him directly, maintaining eye contact, and by God, if his gaze didn't soften. She swallowed, her mouth suddenly full of sand. He took a step forward, his size overwhelming with every inch he closed between them.

Cue Ball chittered, and started to turn away, towards the tunnel.

'Hey! Hey!' she shouted. 'Here! Here look at me. I'm interesting aren't I? You've never really seen me before, have you?'

She caught his attention just in time, pulling his gaze back—as behind him, by the back wall, Alice, Pam and Joyce inched carefully away, eyes wide.

'Me, me here, I'm over here. That's it.'

Runt was transfixed, his jaw hanging slightly with Christmas morning wonder. She could see the acne on his cheeks. The Giant was also somewhat spellbound, his posture relaxed. He held no fear for this intruder, why should he? He outweighed her perhaps four times over.

She had to keep going, keep their attention fixed in this direction, and took one more step in the direction of the door Christian went through. God, that felt like hours ago to Grace now, but it could surely have been measured in minutes.

Cue Ball's interest changed. His eyes narrowed, that horrible reptilian coldness flickered through them, and Grace knew straight away that she'd been rumbled, that she should never have assumed, despite their base way of living and their lack of language skills, that they would be essentially dumb as cattle and easily led. Cue Ball, eyes slits, turned around fully, and saw Alice, Pam and Joyce. They froze in unison, caught out and scalded by Cue Ball's gaze.

'Run!' shouted Grace. The women, halfway to the exit tunnel, turned and sprinted for their lives. Somewhere above, a door opened—no two!—and if this place was already carrying the characteristics of Hell, they all broke loose once again.

63

PETER'S WORLD FELL to bits when, through the gap in the hatch frame, he saw his daughter appear, followed immediately by his wife. It felt like a sparkling magnesium trail across his scalp, and his breath caught. Watching Grace, and her brave act of heroism, had already settled that he was going in to help regardless.

But then his beautiful girl emerged.

She *had* been here. They *had* taken her.

In a flash, he wanted to know what had happened to her, if those monsters had hurt her, if they'd dared touch her—and his breath caught again when he saw Pam. Down here, in this pit?

Abruptly, all was forgotten. All ills gone. Any petty marital squabble, that they themselves had fertilised with ill-timed words and blinkered naval-gazing, were irrelevant. He loved the very bones of her, his darling wife, Pam.

Then those monsters in the room turned and saw them.

'Jeff, open the door,' he commanded, getting up. 'Dewey, come here fella.'

Jeff blinked back from his stupor and checked the gap for himself. Seeing the urgency, he unlocked the hatch, threw it open, and down the stairs Peter flew with a charge and a howl. All eyes in the space looked up at him, the mad bloke holding a cricket bat with the massive dog at his side—but as soon as their eyes hit him, another door opened. The one next to Grace.

Christian emerged, himself holding a metal pole that looked

a bit like a bed rail. He jumped between Grace and those boys, and held out the pointed end of his makeshift weapon. 'Back! Back, you fuckers!' he shouted.

The boys were not remotely perturbed or intimidated, but it did spark them into life. The big one started barrelling up the stairs, three at a time. The little one and the bald one ran after the women, Pam, Alice and Joyce, who started sprinting down the corridor. Christian remained in the doorway, blocking it from all comers, while Grace shouted for Dewey to 'get him boy!'.

Peter threw himself at the giant, catching him across the head and shoulders, hoping momentum would send him back down the stairs—but the huge man merely caught him, and tossed him over the side railing, sending him tumbling onto one of the filthy beds. He bounced off, his trajectory uncontrollable, and landed in a pained heap on the grimy floor. Something bounced cruelly off the point of his shoulder—his own cricket bat, which tumbled to one side, bouncing end over end.

Dewey and the giant were battling on the stairs, but the man was apparently overwhelming the animal, and had one hand on the dog's lower jaw, the other on its upper. He was trying to prise the dog's jaws apart, while Dewey was fighting for all he was worth. Grace was running up the stairs to get to him.

The cricket bat. He crawled over and grabbed it, then was struck by an idea. He carried it to the fire, and stuck the willow straight into the twigs and accelerant, whatever it was. He withdrew it, the bat fully aflame around its top half and launched it at the stairs.

'Grace!' he shouted, as the bat landed a third of the way up, just below Grace—who turned and saw it. Doubling back, she grabbed the flaming bat and, like demon, flew up the steps.

Peter could only watch in awe as the woman battered the giant with burning strikes to the head, and the big man whimpered and recoiled, letting Dewey go. Dewey bit the giant's calf, and yanked hard, and the man tripped, and crashed down the stairs in a tumble of smouldering limbs, landing at the bottom.

'Are you alright?' Peter shouted up to Grace, and she was about to say something, when the big man sat up. Peter felt his resolve waver, a reed in a hard breeze laced with brimstone. *We can never beat him.*

Grace obviously didn't think that, and as soon as she saw he was still moving, she was down the steps, and on him, clubbing him in the head repeatedly with the bat, the flames dancing and fanning with every strike.

He eventually stopped moving, and so did Grace. She turned, her eyes wild with fire dancing within. All Peter could do was nod to her.

He started after his wife and child, when a cry emerged from somewhere above them. It was a word, bellowed hard into the space. They both looked up, to see Jeff, the gatekeeper, carefully walking down the stairs. He was shouting a name. He was shouting the name 'Simon'.

64

WITH HOWLS AT their backs, spiking the purest terror, the women ran into the darkness of what Grace had called 'the exit tunnel'. Alice had the torch, and was at the front with her mother, Joyce behind. Alice was whippet fast, her young legs pumping, and Joyce lagged by just a few yards. In the darkness, that was all it took for her to trip, and, with a scream rising in her throat, fall flat on her face.

All she could think about was getting up, about moving, about escape, she'd become fully-realised prey animal and flight was all she had, but she'd botched it. Yet, as she pulled herself back up to her feet, she saw Cue Ball sprint past, completely ignoring her. Either that, or he'd just missed her. She knew what it was though. Cue Ball and the one that was dead, they'd both been arguing over Alice. And now he wasn't going to let his trophy get away. She edged backwards until her shoulders hit the wall, and she waited quietly. She wanted to help, she wanted to chase, but the prey animal in her, the one that had emerged from nowhere, just wouldn't let her. She was ashamed, but she was alive.

Then she heard a gurgle. Too close. She couldn't see what it was, but she knew too well that it could only be one of them. She waited, holding her breath, not daring to even shake with the mounting terror she felt.

She smelled him. That rank stench of sweet sweat and grime, of defecation, evil and bodies that hadn't been washed since they'd found their way into this appalling place.

It chittered and clicked. A number of times, and each time, in the tunnel's echo chamber, it sounded different. As if he was turning his head.

He was looking for her.

As silently as she could, Joyce lowered to the floor and lay there.

When, with a hollow clunk somewhere deep within the belly of the facility, like a rumble from an unseen gut, the tunnel was suddenly bright. The abruptness caused Joyce to shield her eyes, but there was no denying it, at the worst possible moment, the lights that were strung along the tunnel ceiling blinked on, exposing her in full, as power returned to Blackstoke.

And there, only a matter of yards from her, having seen her immediately, was the little one. Runt. He had come for her.

She knew it. She knew it from before.

She was his prize.

65

MOTHER AND DAUGHTER ran as if the hounds of hell were hot on their heels, when the tunnel suddenly burst into brightness and the torch Grace had given them was happily relegated to redundancy. The new contours of the tunnel showed more doorways, and recesses, all of which offered a boost to hope. But Cue Ball was right on them. They could smell him, his foul breath rasping against all surfaces, and seemed to come at them from every part of the tunnel, front and back, giving him the aura of the inescapable.

Pam abruptly pulled Alice into one of the side recesses, which the sudden light had shown to be a smaller tunnel branching off. It carried a slight incline. Pam's calves burned as she ran, the sudden rise plunging lactic acid into her muscles, but she wouldn't stop. Her daughter was just ahead of her, and if she was ahead, then Pam was the barrier between her and the beast. She knew what the monster wanted. Knew why he wanted her beautiful daughter. Women always knew, innately, when men looked at them a certain way. And even though this instance was so very different, it was still somehow just the same.

'Go, Alice, run!' she shouted, quietness be damned, as she knew Cue Ball was right behind them. He wasn't going to give up. He wasn't ever going to stop unless they killed him. She knew that.

She also knew that she was prepared to do it. She didn't know where this tunnel went, where it came out, or what lay ahead, but if there was a moment she had to stand and fight to the death to protect her daughter, she would. She would die to protect Alice—and do so with relish.

It's funny, what becomes important when the chips are down. The bonds that unite us, the familial chains both wanted and at times unwanted, all soar to the top of the list when the stakes are just so high. It reminded her just what they had to lose, if they didn't get out of here. And in finally understanding the importance of such things, what they had to *gain*. If she got out, the four of them safe, she would do whatever it took to make sure their family thrived in happiness, and prospered in the simple gift of togetherness. Forget material trappings. Survival would be a second chance, and she would fight dearly for it.

The strip lighting of the tunnel ended abruptly with a wide metal shutter, not unlike a garage door, only somewhat more industrial. All these trollies, Pam realised, would have to have been brought down here some way and a ramp was the best bet.

'We're at the end,' Alice shouted, panicked. 'How do we get it open?'

Pam slowed as she reached her. 'Try the panel. You'll think of something.'

'I think it needs a code!' she screeched back.

'Just think, darling.'

Pam turned round to face Cue Ball, who slowed himself when he saw there was nowhere for them to go. His mouth widened in the ugliest smile Pam had ever seen.

'Okay you, come on,' she said. 'You've got to go through me.'

Alice caught what her mum was saying. 'Mum, you can't,' she said with a quivering voice.

'Keep working on the door, sweetheart.'

Cue Ball looked at Alice, then at Pam, and snarled. God, up close and in the light, they were horrible. His head was indeed a near perfect moon, but underneath, everything was wrong. One eye was larger than the other, with the smaller one turned downwards at the corner, like the skin of the eyelid had melted. The other was shining and wide, rendering the dark pupil a vortex of hate and animalism. This thing in front of her knew no other way to be, operating only under the remit of the species basics. Eat, shit, fuck, repeat.

His arms were too long, and they fanned out in a vast, pale, featherless wingspan, as he bared teeth and stepped forward, twisting his features into pure anger.

Pam was terrified—but she was more terrified of harm coming to Alice. So against all the warnings sounding in her head, she charged. The thing scratched at her, but Pam fought back, punching and kicking as if she'd unlocked a hidden attribute in her, finding new depths of resolve and strength to protect her baby.

Cue Ball's arms held her tight all the way round, but she bit as hard as she could into his forearm, tugging a piece of flesh away from the sinew. It caused Cue Ball to scream and hit her on the top of the head as hard as he could, forcing her to release him. He pushed her to the ground. Pam's vision went funny, and somewhere in her head, it felt as if something had gone pop.

The garage door started to open with a loud whirr, and purple light crawled under the widening gap beneath the door. Fresh air followed it. Pam had never smelled anything so wonderful.

'Go Alice, sweetheart. Go!' she shouted from the floor, her voice quieter but still with a redolence of conviction.

Alice looked at her, pained with indecision.

'Go, baby,' said Pam, before making a last desperate lunge for Cue Ball, who was regrouped and primed for chase. She launched herself at him, grabbing him around the waist, and he rained blows on her back, while she shouted 'Go!' one last time.

'I love you,' said Alice through suddenly streaming tears, and Alice turned and ran, sobbing, for her life.

And Pam, for the first time in a long time, smiled—like she really meant it.

66

CHRISTIAN LOOKED UP to see the security guard, Jeff, coming down the steps, the sky a violet square behind him, painting him a silhouette. And he was shouting a name. Simon, it sounded like. There was nobody called Simon at Blackstoke.

Then behind him, he felt movement, and as he turned back into the dark space he'd found the children, he saw the man coming forward. The man he'd found in there. He was walking around the side of the pen, where the two toddlers sat looking at each other. He'd put Olivia back in when the chamber outside suddenly exploded into life again. He wasn't going to leave them, and would do whatever he could to prevent anyone from entering the room—but he just couldn't handle abandoning his neighbours again. When he heard Grace Milligan, alone, trying to reason with them, he had to do something.

Now two of them had run off, and two of them were still at the bottom of the stairway—and now the security guard was coming down into it, looking for a Simon.

The man behind him came to the door, a blank openness to his face, and Christian moved to let him pass. He walked into the large space, arms down at his side, mesmerised, and he looked up at the man coming down the steps.

On seeing him, Jeff's brow folded, and his eyes soaked. His cheeks reddened and puckered with a deep smile. He spoke in a voice thick with emotion.

'It's me, Simon, it's me. She wouldn't let me see you, but I'm here now, I've been looking for you everywhere, I'm here son.'

Both Christian and Grace stared at each other in bemused wonder, unsure if they'd really heard what they thought they'd heard—when a roar sang from behind them all.

The bottom of the stairs.

'Oh, Jesus,' said Christian, as he saw the giant, it's head unnaturally dented, claw himself to his feet. Blood sprayed as he stood and spat, his whole head a mess of bruises and cuts, and he charged at Grace. Christian could see that Grace was unarmed—she'd put her bat down. She immediately backed up, and tried to put distance between them. But the monster was too full of fire, and too far gone for reason. Anything human had been battered out of him moments earlier by Grace.

Dewey howled, but even he found the state of the behemoth just too terrifying, and hung back—only for a second, before he saw his master in danger, and bolted to her side.

Christian couldn't watch idly, and he knew that if he didn't intervene Grace would be dead and he'd be next. And once he was dead, that left…

He turned back into the room for just a second, and looked at his daughter, sat there, on the floor of the pen, her beautiful curls undampened by the horrors around her, her eyes wide with an innocence that told him if she could just survive this, she'd forget everything. This whole awful episode wouldn't even be a footnote to her story.

'Daddy loves you,' he said—and closed the door.

67

DAVID DROVE WITH the windows down, listening to the dog barks. The road had stopped, but he wouldn't, so he had to drive beneath overarching boughs to follow the sounds of ruckus—which soon incorporated human voices. Shouts, both male and female.

The car was powerful in a sporty way, which was just enough for pulling through the brush trails and deeper into the forest. Above the tree tops, the sky was conjuring shades brighter with every passing moment. He just hoped he could get there in time.

He went a little wrong, the voices suddenly seeming to come from his left, and as he corrected course, he saw, to his surprise, a space beyond the trees. An empty space. Except for...

Yes. A few large piles of rubble and dirt.

The sounds were agitated. Shouts, screaming, a dog barking. Some other sound. Animal howling. He was suddenly terrified.

He pulled out into the clearing, and looked around for the source of the commotion. *There*, in the far corner, a fat cone of light pointed to the sky. He drove towards it, and saw a hatch embedded in the ground. Jumping out, he stood on the ledge of the opening and looked down.

He hadn't been prepared for the sight. It pushed every boundary of logic he possessed.

A huge, clearly-injured hairless man was at the bottom of a stairwell, and it took a moment to realise that he, David, was at the top. The man was attacking, fighting ferociously, with Grace who lived across the street—and, in a realisation that squeezed his heart, his husband, Christian. Near them, somehow disconnected from the violence just yards away, a man in a security outfit appeared to be pleading with a guy who looked homeless and confused.

He was drawn to help and protect his husband, and started down the stairs.

But the giant turned and started running up them. It seemed as if Christian, Grace and her dog had managed to beat the massive foe back, but was sending him directly in David's direction. The man really was both monstrous and monstrously injured. And he had just seen David.

The monster stopped and looked at him with such dark, blood-drenched malevolence that David was in no doubt he was looking into evil, that this thing was going to kill and kill again until its own death. It turned and looked back at his husband, Christian. David's eyes met Christian's, and in that split second an unspoken message of adoration was passed between them, and David's decision was made.

He jumped back in the car, and drove to the hatch. It was just wide enough for his car to pass through, and he angled the car's nose over the top of the steps. He had to kill this thing to protect his husband—and Olivia, his darling baby girl, wherever she was.

David touched the accelerator, not wanting to floor it until Christian and Grace had caught his intention to fly down the steps and ram the beast. The car tipped forward, everyone in the room turned to look, the giant man included, and it started lurching down the stairs. David hit the brakes once, twice, but nothing was stopping it now, and he started to think he'd made a terrible error. The giant's eyes went wide with something close to fear, as David's car hurtled down the stairway, and, almost exactly halfway down, poleaxed the behemoth—but the nose of the car had bounced up on the steps, and the bonnet hit the giant in the chest, momentum sending the flying car right on top of him.

The car didn't slow, not even fractionally, but it did start to spin, and David started to tilt. The room went sideways, David saw his husband coming up too fast, and he pumped the brakes as hard as he could but nothing stop it and suddenly Christian, his wonderful husband, was right *there*.

For a second moment in quick succession, the men's eyes locked to pass a message of affection—but this time, the love shared was dosed heavily with regret.

68

JOYCE WAS ON her feet before she could think of her next move, her sole overriding thought being *I'm not dying here, curled up, in the foetal position, like a wretch.* Although she didn't really believe that killing her was Runt's aim.

The lights sparking to life had brought stark geography to the corridors of the boys' underground lair, and offered areas she simply hadn't seen. One of these was a recessed door some ten yards away, in the brickwork of the tunnel wall. She started to run to it, but Runt was moving to block her way—so she did what she'd been taught to do to any belligerent man—something she'd oddly forgotten when Fletcher had first pursued her—and kneed the youngest creature as hard in the bollocks as she possibly could.

The Runt crumpled like plastic by a hot flame, clutching his groin, rotten saliva roiling over yellow, pointed teeth.

She'd got him good, the throb in her knee telling her as much, and she ran for the door, tried it, it opened first time, and she flung herself inside.

She shut the door, and looked for a lock, but, finding there was none, instead looked for something to arm herself with. She also needed to see if this room actually offered a way out.

Power. She remembered there was power down here now, and she fumbled for a switch. Immediately the room lit via two bulbs, one of which popped instantly, raining glass and shards, and forced Joyce to cover her head. The other struggled to offer anything resembling a solid cast of light, but valiantly held firm enough to let her see.

Joyce opened her eyes fully.

Bodies. On a bed. Stacked like firewood. Limbs tangling over one another, heads in groins, fluid leaking from one onto the next. The most undignified scene she'd ever witnessed.

Through the revulsion, familiarity began to strike.

The top one was almost headless, just a poking tangle of flesh jutting from over a floral smock. Wendy Fenchurch. The one below, sandwiched in the middle. His face burned to a crisp, but the singed grey patches above could only belong to her husband, Quint. Pam said they'd been killed. They had. Then brought down here.

Then the last one.

The clothes. The shape.

The hair still possessing a lustre persuaded by hours of preening and expensive products.

She knew him.

Her husband—gobby MP for North Lancashire, and scourge of liberal mindsets everywhere.

Fletcher Adams.

Her first thought was: *you stupid, pig-headed bastard.*

The second was: *thank God.*

The third was*: I'm just glad the boys aren't here.*

The grief she imagined she was supposed to feel was nowhere near the shock at the viscera she was seeing first hand—shock which stopped her from fully-acknowledging the door swing open behind her. Looking at Fletcher there, she felt pity. Pity because he'd become nothing more than an addition to a pile of meat, and because she didn't think anyone deserved that.

A pile of meat.

The thought hit into her as the door behind crashed open.

This was a meat store.

They'd been kept as *food*.

But as she turned away, Runt was there, and baring down on her with careful calculating steps. His arms were outstretched, as if to beckon her into them.

She looked around the space. It was just a room, simple yet congested with stuff. There was an odd chair over to the right, surrounded by machinery. Looked like a dentist's chair, with a halo round the top.

It was such a strange time for it to happen, but she suddenly felt free. Suddenly felt emboldened and powerful. Whether it was the knowledge of her husband's death or an out of body experience prompted by acute fear, but she felt in control.

It was her own life now, and her own life to save.

And, as the stink of Runt became too much to bear without retching, she realised what that chair over there was. She looked at the lightbulb shards on the floor, plan forming.

'Alright,' she said calmly, with her hands up in front of her. 'You win.' As she spoke, she moved. 'I know what you want. And you're the little one, aren't you? You never get what you want.'

Runt looked at her with abject shock, like he'd never known civility, conversation. He'd certainly never experienced the hand on his cheek, which Joyce carefully placed there, trying so hard to mask the tremor of revulsion coursing through her arm.

'Come with me,' she said, her hand still on his cratered face, still moving across the room.

After all this time, she felt *powerful*. Her husband, that sad streak of piss lying there, had robbed her of agency, of power, of autonomy in a steady coup which had gone on for years. Everything she was, had been eroded by him. But he wasn't here anymore. And the chains were off.

'That's it. This will be more comfortable for us both,' she said, as she lay back in the chair.

The chair had restraints, but she paid no heed to them, and with as much confidence as she could, she spread her legs and pulled runt slowly between. He was shaking almost as much as her now. Eyes darting, his brow furrowed with incomprehension. Placing a hand on the back of his neck, she pulled him down to her.

'That's okay, I'm grateful you chose me.'

Runt was firmly under her spell, his eyes so wide and close that she could see that the irises weren't black, but the deepest purple.

And as she held him tight with clamped thighs, trying not to scream through fear and horror, she reached up and grabbed the pronged halo above her head—before bringing it down, jamming it onto Runt's head as hard as she could. She kicked him off and he fell back.

The halo was still stuck there because one of the prongs was stuck in his eyeball, she'd jammed it that fiercely. Kicking him clear, she dove off the chair, and hit the switch on the wall next to it. The big red one. Hard to miss.

Sparks exploded from Runt's head, and he screamed as his entire head fizzed and sizzled. The chair, she'd noticed, was an old electro-shock therapy unit. Zapping people back to full mental health.

Runt's knees buckled slightly as she found the dial, the halo still stuck in his eye, blood and smoke now rupturing from every orifice, as he clawed to get if off.

This free and all-new Joyce twisted the dial on the unit, sending raw voltage down the halo prong through Runt's eye socket and into his skull, cooking his brain.

Runt fell to his knees, his arms dropped to his side, his head fell forward, smoke ballooning from his pate, and finally, he dropped onto his face.

69

HE HEARD THE scuffling, as if it was being transmitted to him via megaphone, the ramped tunnel offering perfect conduction of the sounds, as Peter's wife and daughter battled with that bastard he'd sprinted after. He'd left the main chamber and moments later it seemed to have been filled with an impact of some kind he just couldn't place. He just had no idea at all what could have done that, but he couldn't stop. He felt bad leaving his neighbours to it—these friends that had been through so much with him—but his family's lives were in the balance.

As he ran up the corridor, and the incline reminded him just how tired he was, just how fraught and exhausting the night had been, he heard a loud whirring sound. Down at the bottom, in the distance, a rectangle of light emerged and started to get taller. And he could soon make out figures brawling in the light. One of them, the one on the floor was his wife. She had her arms around the man's waist, and was stopping him from getting to Alice, who sprinted out of the door.

Peter's legs pumped as he tried to convince them to go even faster, but it was no use, as the man unleashed a torrent of blows to his wife's head, his beautiful wife Pam, and she fell. The monster reared up, pulled his knee high, bracing to stamp on Pam's face as she lay there, when Peter screamed, 'No!'

The man turned and saw him, and, after a moment's indecision, ran after Alice, out of the door and into the dawn light.

He went to his wife's side, and put a hand on her shoulder, unsure of whether to touch her. She was clearly in a bad way. To what extent, he didn't know, and wouldn't risk it.

'Sweetheart,' was all he could say, all the words he should have said so any times jamming his throat tight.

'Alice. Save Alice,' she croaked.

The parental bond between them was so strong, their roles so starkly etched on their hearts, that Peter knew she was right. He kissed her lightly on the lips, whispered, 'I'll come back for you,' and ran.

Suddenly outside, wrapped in cool, fresh, clean air, he felt partly reinvigorated. He had no idea where he was, but he was surrounded by trees at the mouth of a tunnel entrance that merely pulled up and out of the ground, emerging like a vast, open-mouthed, brick earthworm. He shouted his daughter's name into the trees. 'Alice!'

'Dad!' came the near immediate response.

Not far away. Close enough to get a fix on a direction.

'I'm coming!' he shouted, as he took off in a sprint.

GRACE DIDN'T EVER think she'd forget the terror she felt when the car started to tumble, then spin like one of her little brother's toys, discarded and tossed down the stairs at their childhood home. The bottom front bumper took the Giant's head clean off, punting it deep into the room, but she didn't have any time for relief when the vehicle didn't stop. Sideways, like a twirling arrow, it flew down the stairs at them. Grace dove off the stairway, over the bannister, feeling the heat of the flying vehicle on her back as she fell, and landed hard on the filthy floor.

The scream of twisting metal split the air of the chamber, as a deafening impact shook the room, and even the tunnel system itself, to its foundations. She hoped, prayed, pleaded, that everyone that mattered to her had got out of the way. Dewey and Christian.

When she came to survey the wreckage, she saw immediately that one had survived, and one hadn't.

Christian was pinned bloodily to the wall, which in itself had caved in, leaving him held in place by a bent fender and dislodged bricks. Further along, the body of his husband, David, lay in a disjointed jumble, evidently thrown through the windshield. She hadn't even seen him. He wasn't moving.

And under the car, the back wheel resting on his belly, was the security guard who had so abruptly appeared. He too, was still.

The other man who had appeared, the one who looked so much like the brothers but didn't at the same time, was nowhere to be seen.

And over the bonnet, hopping right as rain with a click of claws, came Dewey.

'Oh Dew,' said Grace, the words falling out of her with such relief—although a good measure of grief came along for the ride.

She had no idea what injuries had befallen the men, aside from the obvious—but the fact that none were moving or conscious told her all she needed to know.

'I think it's time we got some help, Dew,' she said, as the giant dog lapped at her face, and she looked up at the stairway to freedom. There, at the top, was a soft blue square of promise— but any sense of elation was dashed when she saw that the top portion of the stairway had completely given way under the weight of the tumbling vehicle.

She was *still* stuck in the tunnels, and her only way out was to embrace them again. It was bright now however, the power back in full force, and they wouldn't hold the same fear. This time would be different. She just hoped she wouldn't run into Cue Ball and Runt.

She got up to go, when her eyes were drawn to the door that Christian was protecting. *What had kept him in there? And what was the other man, the other brother, doing in there too?*

With keen memories of the last time she opened a door in this place, she entered, and couldn't believe it. Olivia, the missing child, sat there, as if nothing in the world was amiss—next to another, who one simply couldn't apply the same assessment to. And there in the room's shadowed corner, lay a pile of fresh, clean baby clothes. Surely, she thought, the ones from Olivia's nursery.

An instinct kicked in, untried and clumsy in its infancy, and she felt moved to assist in a way that went beyond obligation. She went to the children and Olivia reached up with a playful smile, unknowing that her parents were dead on the other side of the wall, while the other merely hissed. This other child, clearly born with the same afflictions as the others, was a boy, and clearly happy in Olivia's company, but not Grace's. But she refused to leave him here. Refused to leave him to this. It wasn't his choice, this birthing into horror.

She scoured the main chamber, taking care to avoid faeces, blood and bodies, until she found something that could help. By the pile of sticks, was an overturned wheelbarrow. It would do. She put Olivia in, careful that she didn't see what had happened to her fathers, and managed to do the same with the other infant, who kicked and scrabbled before settling, albeit grumpily.

She started to walk down the tunnel to the exit, Dewey in the lead, keeping close watch on everything.

It wasn't long before, with elation, she found Joyce, who had been wondering which way to go. And together, they took another upward tunnel, firmly reasoning that up was always going to be better than down in this place. They soon found Pam. She had been badly beaten, but she was hanging on in there.

And so from a dank tunnel into the daylight of a frosty winter morning, their breath preceding them in ghostly flares of steam, emerged three bruised but defiant women, a wheelbarrow with two toddlers, both confused but safe, and one massive, proud, shaggy dog.

70

PETER WEST PUSHED through the brush and bushes, dodging trunks, listening for the sound of his daughter's cries. It hadn't even really occurred to him that they were outside, because, while escaping the tunnels had been their objective all night, the threat was still very much alive.

'Dad!' came the cry again, and Peter pushed harder. The trees parted and revealed a muddy track—and there, further down the track, in the morning fog, was his daughter, running for her life, from a bald, broad monster who had obviously taken the most appalling of shines to her.

He gave chase, and within seconds another shape emerged from the haze, high above, over the trees. A frame. Tall and boxy, on ever revealing stilts.

A watchtower.

And on the track below, preceded by frosted tyre tracks, was a car. It had the word *security* emblazoned on the side in navy lettering.

In the distance he saw Alice turn after the car, evidently having noticed something, and run towards the base of the tower. Peter heard her footsteps taking the metal as she ran, staccato clangs echoing through the forest. And that creep was following her. Peter soon made it to the bottom of the tower too, which was now fully formed, standing proud in the haze, and he climbed too. A handful of tight, calf-burning moments later, he was at the top.

The air was cool and fresh, the sky now white in all directions, as the day had just broken like a giant egg. And on the platform, a hand around his daughter's throat, was this fucking creature.

In daylight, he could finally get a good look at it, and he was immediately glad it had taken this long—because if he'd known what he'd been chasing, his fears might have stopped him. Its skin was a mass of pustuled lesions, all except for the smooth crown. His eyes were gross flaps in his face like two leeches had made their homes by burrowing into the skin below his forehead. His nose was a hooked crook, tapered to a sharp point off to one side. And his mouth was black, filled with rotten brown teeth. All sharp.

His daughter looked at the thing, and he took immense pride in the knowledge that she was nowhere near as scared as he.

'Give her to me,' Peter said.

The thing looked at him, and bellowed. It echoed throughout the forest, a Tarzan call of outrage and belligerent evil.

It was an impasse, and before Peter could think what to do next, the monster's call was answered. Somewhere else in the forest beneath the treetops below, rang sirens.

Peter could have cried, such was the relief he felt. But still, this thing had his Alice.

The sirens caught the monster off guard, and he reacted exactly as an animal would when its cry had been unexpectedly answered. It looked out at its territory for answers.

Alice, who had never been a slouch, always quick off the mark ever since she'd been a bright tumble of a toddler, took the initiative, and hit the monster as hard as she could with Grace's torch, right in the temple, which caused it to howl.

Peter took his cue, saw how close the monster was to the railing, and charged it, driving his shoulder into the monster's midriff, pushing him back into the barrier—which, to Peter's horror, gave way. It had looked old—and now, as he met fresh air, he knew just how old. Monster and man fell freely into the morning, sirens growing in stature all around them, and Peter saw, over the tree tops, way in the distance, a familiar handful of rooftops. It was the Broadoak cul-de-sac, of the Blackstoke Estate. The place that started this whole thing. He'd always felt this place would be the death of him. He could have smiled with the irony, but saw the roof of the security car come up fast.

Everything stopped with noisy abruptness, and mercifully went very dark.

71

THE WARMTH OF the tunnels, his home for almost five decades, dissipated. He knew it wasn't a real warmth—those dark corridors were freezing and always had been—but their smells and dimensions breathed an unshakeable fundamental resonance within him. A fondness. A sanctuary. It was womb-like. It was *warmth*.

His home, with Mother, was gone, infiltrated. And while the events of the night were the final chapters to the story of him and Mother, the infiltration had taken place years before. When she had promised him so much. When she had tricked him, when he was young enough to be tricked. When the boys came.

He found it. He'd never been up it before, but he'd often looked up the ladder, at the circle of stars formed by the shape of the vent's mouth.

There were no stars today. The sky was a soft pink. Clouds rolled like great ships. It was dawn.

He knew his time here was over, that it was time for a rebirth. He put a foot on the bottom step and, shakily, began to climb. One foot, after the other.

Up.

That man confused him. With his words. With his voice. The man in blue, who he felt like he knew, but he couldn't ever have seen him before.

Up he went.

It was cooler up here. The air growing crisper, the higher he ascended. It felt strange.

Every step higher removed him from Mother, leaving the smell and warmth he knew so well. He'd had visited her one last time, before coming here. Before leaving.

Seeing her like that compounded it. Made it somehow real. There was nothing for him here anymore.

So he climbed.

And suddenly, for the first time in his life, he felt sunlight.

Epilogue

GRACE MILLIGAN DIPPED her hand in the cold jug of water next to her bed, and enjoyed the cool kiss of the water on her fingertips. It was clean. Pure. Her gown was also spotless. The sheets were neat. The sunshine itself was crisp and faultless. She revelled in it. Cleanliness, and light. Two things she had grown very fond of in the days since that awful night. Two things she would never take for granted again.

As was life. She was here and others weren't, the result of a demonic turn of events that few would care to believe. And as it happened, few did.

The table in front of her was stacked with files, the bedspread serving as an extension of her workspace. When the bodies were pulled up, and statements were taken, COMUDEV refuted everything and absolved themselves of all responsibility. They believed that what had happened was nothing to do with them, and to an extent, they were right. Nobody had made those people live down there in squalor. The truth was, they merely hadn't checked. They hadn't bothered to clear the tunnels before building, let alone demolish them. The budget had been deemed too high, so they simply saw an abandoned tunnel system and built on top of it.

What was living in the tunnel system was another issue entirely, and the authorities were trying to make sense of it. And what was making by far and away the most sense, was the science. Data. Irrefutable facts, in this case given by biological information.

The woman had been DNA tested, and, along with known records of the Blackstoke facility, archival material from the NHS and long buried court documents, her identity had been proven. Her name was Madeline Morgan. A serial killer, who had been a resident of Blackstoke Institute for Good. Killing four women in their beds had got her there—along with whoever happened to be in the beds with them. Sentenced to life imprisonment, she had ended up in the asylum thanks to heavy pressure on an insanity diagnosis on the part of her legal team, and a soft-as-butter judge who was a sucker for the pretty dame in the hot seat, who couldn't possibly have done these things without external factors playing a part. She was certified insane in the late sixties, and went into round-the-clock care at Blackstoke.

Thing was, the records also stated that she was missing, presumed dead, after a monstrous fire destroyed the asylum in June 1970. Also missing and presumed dead? Her baby son, just a couple of days old. She'd had the baby inside. Father unknown.

The mystery then expanded, the more Grace had dug. And dug she had. COMUDEV had indeed taken over dealings of the Blackstoke Estate, but the legal entity of the estate was still there. And she was gunning for both of them, in an epic legal battle, to bring them to account for the sheer negligence that resulted in many deaths of the people they had sold houses to. The people they promised new lives to.

The bodies brought up of The Boys, as they had become known, had all had their individual genetic makeups examined. And it pointed to all the more unsettling revelations. Madeline Morgan was each one's mother—including the toddler, in a direct DNA maternal lineage. The issue of fatherhood for each boy, was much more varied and unsettling. The two who killed Fletcher Adams, their DNA revealed a paternal link to another body pulled out, the gatekeeper, Jeff, although it had been diluted. Another generation had gone between.

Jeff was their grandfather.

Traces of Jeff's genetic lineage were also present in the two younger 'boys', namely the runt and the one with the perfect white head. But again, another generation along. He was their great grandfather, and they in turn were the sons of the other boys, one each.

It took a long time for her to work it out, and even longer to actually want to get it down, but Grace got there in the end, and had to commit one of the most disturbed family trees in history to paper.

At the top? Madeline and Jeff. He was an old employee, who, while working at the asylum, had fallen for a mass murderer, and they'd had a child. And he'd got a job at Blackstoke Estate presumably to reconnect with the son he thought he'd lost.

And under them? A question mark. And next to that had to be an arrow bringing Madeline down again. Mother, procreating with son.

Under that entirely unnatural union, the two Alice had described in her statements as Maroon and Cue Ball, which were as good a set of names as any. And another arrow, for Madeline again. Grandmother and grandsons having children now. Joyce found it hard to get the titles for the familial roles right at this point, it was so muddled and confusing.

Under that, was The Runt, and the Toddler.

Madeline Morgan was the mother of every single boy in there, while some of the boys were also brothers and parents to each other as well.

It made Grace's head hurt, and stomach lurch.

That wasn't the whole tale. There had been others. In the firepit, the authorities had found a number of older bones of other newborns.

There were many others that hadn't made it.

And the question mark?

The one they saw with the gatekeeper. The one Jeff was pleading to.

She heard him call him Simon.

It had to be him.

Simon was the only one born of unrelated parents, and it was thanks to an entire life lived underground that his appearance had been shaped. The feral nature and appearance of his sons was all down to the inbreeding, and their environment concocting a crude evolutionary strand, buffeted and moulded by intermingled familial genetics.

Their behaviour had spiralled. But what could one expect for them?

Grace had been entrusted, she felt, to condemn the boys and their actions in the harshest terms, but what are we if we are not a product of our environment and our direct influences? Their matriarch was a serial killer, certified insane, and she went down in the tunnels with a newborn baby, desperate to survive. She'd remained hidden for years, and then she took, God knew how or when, the decision to procreate with her own son.

That sad sack of grey meat on that bed they'd found all those weeks ago, was the architect of all of this, and then it had all turned on her. She had gone about life in a lawless state, and that lawlessness had run away with itself. Base instincts were important. And with a woman present, the small issue of being their mother was not going to stop the boys from acting on their developing urges. Maybe it got out of hand? Maybe she wouldn't play ball anymore. She was restrained in childbirth—was she manacled full time? Or was that some primitive mode of labour control the boys had devised?

How much had Madeline Morgan wanted, and how much had happened simply because of the start she had given them?

They would never know until studies were made, and investigations enacted. But, as always, money spoke quicker than science, the need for recompense greater than the search for answers—and the legal matters were all running ahead, muddying the waters, while the research would have to wait until all that had happened. COMUDEV and the rest, they were all only interested in the *whose fault*, as opposed to the *why*.

All Grace knew, was that she and her neighbours had set about their new lives in good faith, and neglect from others had meant that the bumps in the night had become real. And they'd all lost a fortune finding that out. Nobody would buy on the estate, or the estate itself now. Whatever happened, COMUDEV was out of pocket already, without the threat of lawsuits from disgruntled ex-customers. And Grace, in a plight familiar to all the Broadoak survivors, had a house that nobody would ever dream of buying—unless she allowed COMUDEV to lie again, and cover it up.

She took her fingers from the water, and brought them to her lips—paused, then pressed the button for more. A button for help. She admired it. How simple it was. How they could have done with them in the tunnels that night.

The nurse arrived soon after, and Grace asked for some more water.

The cases would start soon. And she wanted to represent them all. She had to get going, and stop ruminating.

'How's your story going?' the nurse said.

'It's going fine, but it's not a story,' replied Grace with a small amount of tetchiness. They were always getting it wrong, the hospital staff, despite how well meaning they obviously were.

'Oh yes, of course,' said the nurse. 'The big case coming up?'

'Yes, that's the one.'

'And you got all those papers you asked for?'

'I did. Thank you for helping arrange it.'

'A pleasure, Grace. Good to keep the mind active in a place like this.'

Grace didn't reply, as she hated the condescension. Couldn't understand why her legal work wasn't taken more seriously in here. But she would get there. She'd get the truth out. And she'd save the survivors again.

'This is about the hospital isn't it? Spooky underground place?' the nurse asked.

'Yes, with the men, as I've told you.'

'Good, I remember. Have you had your medicine?'

'Yes.'

'You're being good?'

'Yes.'

'Good. I'll be back shortly to bob my head in. I'll let you get back to your project.'

Grace shook her head as she left—and as she did, reached up behind her molars with a finger. After a quick nudge, she pulled out two pink tablets, and put them on the table. She hated the way these one's made her feel, but the staff were insistent. Said it would keep her calm after her ordeal.

The case was only weeks away, and if she wanted to be there, she had to show them she was capable. That she could manage it. Because if she didn't, she might be in this place for a very long time indeed.

ACKNOWLEDGEMENTS

THANK YOU:

To everyone at Red Dog Press, especially Sean Coleman (thank you for taking a chance on this mad story and making it so much better!) and Meggy Roussel (for absolutely everything!). It's a privilege to be part of the kennel.

To the Northern Crime Syndicate – Trevor Wood, Judith O'Reilly, Fiona Erskine, Chris McGeorge, Adam Peacock, Robert Scragg and Dan Stubbings – and my Blood Brothers – Sean Coleman (you again!) and Chris McDonald. Your support and encouragement means the world.

To my family and friends. Simply, I love you all. Always grateful (just please still talk to me after this one!)

To the writing community – bloggers, readers, authors, everybody. Thank you for everything you do. It's a fabulous place to be, and I feel so lucky and grateful to be a part of it

ABOUT THE AUTHOR

Rob Parker is a married father of three, who lives in a village near Warrington, UK. The author of the Ben Bracken thrillers and the standalone post-Brexit country-noir *Crook's Hollow*, he enjoys a rural life on an old pig farm (now minus pigs), writing horrible things between school runs.

Rob writes full time, as well as organising and attending various author events across the UK – while boxing regularly for charity. Passionate about inspiring a love of the written word in young people, he spends a lot of time in schools across the North West, encouraging literacy, story-telling and creative-writing.

He is also a co-host of the For Your Reconsideration film podcast, and a regular voice on the Blood Brothers crime book podcast.

Also by Rob Parker

<u>The Ben Bracken Thrillers</u>

A Wanted Man
Morte Point
The Penny Black
Till Morning Is Nigh

<u>Standalone</u>

Crook's Hollow

<u>Thirty Miles Trilogy</u>

Far From the Tree

Follow Rob on social media at:

@robparkerauthor

@robparkerauthor

@robparkerauthor

www.robparkerauthor.com

info@robparkerauthor.com